The Great American Boogaloo

The Great American Boogaloo

Paul Flower

This edition published in 2022 by Farrago,
an imprint of Duckworth Books Ltd
1 Golden Court, Richmond, TW9 1EU, United Kingdom

www.farragobooks.com

Print ISBN: 978-1-78842-386-1
Ebook ISBN: 978-1-78842-387-8

For Lori.
Always and forever.

PART ONE

The Time That Woman Tried to Outlaw Beef

Chapter One

Tuesday morning

Big Bruddah woke up and wanted a burger. But no.

That Woman took his taxes. That Woman made him pay for welfare for lazy mothers who had babies by seven different fathers. That Woman coddled the lowlife drug dealers and gang bangers who came to America from the Third World. That Woman was doing everything in her power to get his guns.

Now That Woman was taking away his right to eat what he wanted to eat.

That Woman was President of the United States.

She was going to pay.

For the guns, first and foremost. But for the burgers, too.

Big Bruddah glowered out a window at the low-slung sky, which glowered back. Rain riffed like a metal band drummer on the roof. It had been storming like this off and on for days, which didn't help his mood. The idiot weather geeks were giving dire warning of "unprecedented events"—major floods on the rivers and streams and significant erosion on Lake Michigan. Above the din, Big Bruddah heard the ominous, steady rumble

3

of the tormented lake, which was just a quarter mile away as a wet crow flew. Freakish amounts of water gushed off the roof. Big Bruddah turned away, shuffled across the dirty carpet of his bedroom-office, his footwear doing more of a whisk-flap than the promised flip-flop, and lowered himself into a chair made of sweat and cracked leather. It was unusually warm and humid for an early Michigan May. He leaned over, fumbled for the switch of a battered fan, set it to medium and wiped his forehead with a meaty hand as he swung the chair to face his preferred window into the world; a flat, black Dell computer monitor. He skootched the chair forward, and bellied up to a desk cluttered with the residue of his online life. Bruddah backhanded a beer can to the floor, flicked a half-empty bag of Doritos out of his way and tapped his computer keyboard with a pudgy finger. The screen flared to life. His desktop image, a Photoshopped photo of Hillary Clinton in a prison jumpsuit and riding an elephant led by Barack Obama, stared back at him. He opened his Internet browser and clicked through to the Red Sky Brigade militia chapter's website. He found the blog post he'd added the day before and scrolled to the end, where he'd signed off with yesterday's date, May 13, 2024, and "BRUDDAH" in all caps.

Sweet. Below the signoff there were 1,572 comments.

Sid Breen, a reporter from one of the many left-leaning Michigan news sites, had arranged an interview, via Zoom, to discuss the blog post. To prep, Big Bruddah skimmed the comments, a smile blooming on his usually sullen face and a long-dormant surge of optimism warming his gut.

The tide of support was rising. The militia nation was with him.

The interview was going to be fun. And important.

Big Bruddah knew a lot about Sid Breen, thanks to the Red Sky Brigade's hand-in-iron-glove working relationship with the private military company, Silver Eagle Security. Silver Eagle's kick-ass intelligence team said Breen was a twenty-two-year-old Black guy who'd recently graduated from the Michigan State University School of Journalism and was probably intimidated by the thought of talking to Michigan's most highly visible militiaman. Sid, the intelligence said, dreamed of being a bare-knuckled reporter in the mold of his late paternal grandmother, the barrier-breaking African-American journalist Angela "G-Momma" Breen, who'd worn pants and drank whiskey with communists and hippies and hippie-communists as a freelance investigative reporter in the 1960s. She'd given birth to Sid's father in a London hospital, fourteen hours of mind-splitting labor after hitting the runway at Heathrow on the hot scent of a corrupt member of the Los Angeles district attorney's office and three months after Sid's grandpop jilted her for a pretty but soulless backup singer/waitress/actress from L.A. Sid had always wanted to be tough and bold like G-Momma, but he favored his father's side of the family tree; the branch of sensitivity and caution. Sid Breen worried that Big Bruddah knew more about him than he wanted Big Bruddah to know. Big Bruddah knew Sid Breen worried that he knew, which was why he was looking forward to the interview.

Chapter Two

"First off, some ground rules," Big Bruddah told Sid Breen, before the reporter's Zoomed mouth could say "hello." "Let me tell you how this is going to go."

"Actually, Mr. Watts, uh. First thing, hello. Thanks for taking this call," Sid Breen said, leaning forward, his expression earnest. "Actually, I would like to keep this sort of, like, free-wheeling. No holds barred. If that's okay."

Big Bruddah rummaged through the clutter on his desk, found a Ziploc bag of homemade beef jerky. He opened it as he spoke, intentionally avoiding eye contact, talking to the jerky. "Oh, holds will be barred, my friend," he said, selecting a sliver of the dried meat about three inches long. He bit off a chunk and chewed it contemplatively as he turned to meet Breen's gaze. "The wheeling will not be free; you feel me, my brother?"

Sid Breen blinked. "Could you start by sharing your thoughts on the climate crisis. That's really what brought us here, to the situation with beef and…"

Big Bruddah rocked back and twisted to his left; competing groans stuttered from his chair and belly. He flipped open a strategically placed mini fridge, grabbed a half-liter bottle of Mountain Dew from the top shelf, flipped the door shut, and rocked back to an upright position. A twist. A *pshht* from the bottle. A long pull. A belch. He wiped his mouth with the back of his hand. Wiped the back of his hand on his jeans. Took his time finding a place for the bottle on his desk. Finally, Big Bruddah looked at Breen. The reporter stared back at him through the type of oh-so-ironic-Malcom-X-throwback-style-black-rimmed glasses Big Bruddah hated. "Here's a couple of things we're gonna remember during this conversation. By 'we're', I mean you," he said, his voice lowered an octave. "First, you don't dictate the rules. And number two, you already know that I can barely stomach the mainstream fake news bullshit about the climate. We agreed you could record this. So there's no need to ask me to clarify myself. I say things once, very clearly, and we're not going to waste a lot of time going over every comment. Is that understood?"

Breen thought about it, then said, "I just want to get some background first."

"Listen, kid. I need your readers' eyeballs, but I don't need your attitude. I'm willing to give you ten minutes, as long as we play by my rules."

"Fine. Yes. Yes."

"Okay then."

"Okay then," Breen said. "You and your group oppose any restrictions on meat because you deny the climate science."

"Nope, we deny the government's right to tell us what to eat." Big Bruddah took a bite of jerky. "And the climate science."

"Yes, but one study showed if cows were a country, they would be the third-largest greenhouse gas emitter in the world. And the vast trove of statistical evidence has pointed to man's dramatic negative impact—both through industrial and vehicle emissions and the global farming of animals for meat—on the climate."

Big Bruddah laughed. He hated the kid's hipster superiority, but the intellectual debate? He welcomed it. It energized him. His ex-wife had hated his campfired nights of beer-fueled debates with other militia men. When their marriage was beginning to unspool, when the traitor in his house had begun to reveal herself, she'd come home one night, had too much wine, and let him have it. She was, she said, exhausted with the debates, the endless chasing of outrages and conspiracies, the dancing to death over theories that were based on nothing more than what she called "White male grievance." Big Bruddah had scoffed at her smug self-righteousness. This Breen with his glasses and tone was no better.

"You think you have the market cornered on your trove of statistical evidence," Big Bruddah said. Without shifting his gaze, he fumbled with the Ziploc, his fingers finding jerky. He leveled his gaze not at Breen's image but at the green pinprick of light that was his computer's eye, glancing at the tiny inset image on his screen to ensure he was giving the reporter a stern stare. "I mean, I get it. You're one of those guys who studied all night and got Phi Beta Asshole in college, but not everyone does that. Most don't. I mean, back in the day, I majored in weed at CMU, but even I got a degree. Know what I'm saying? Doesn't make me an expert on anything except how to pull all-nighters and do enough to get by with a 2.5 GPA. I mean, I don't have a liberal arts degree in Lesbian Studies and Poetry Reading like you, but I've got a mind of my own still—unlike ninety percent of who they churn out of those places these days."

Breen opened his mouth, but Big Bruddah swiftly blocked the banter path. "Point is, there are doctors who finished last in their classes. There are scientists—a whole lot of them—who partied away their undergrad degrees, just like yours truly, but they're out there now getting federal grants to study what cows do to the atmosphere and the reproductive rates of teste flies or whatever."

"I think you mean Tsetse flies."

"Whatever. Point is, there are many very smart people with not just the education but the thinking skills to look at the big picture. For years and years, they've been trying to explain that these big shifts in rains and winds and storms and so on are just part of nature being nature and climate being climate. So, it's warmer in some places, colder in some others. Big whoopdeedo. That's why we call it 'earth.' There are lots of perfectly sane, perfectly normal reasons for it. You guys are always focused on the liberal slant on everything. You think you know more than the rest of us, but you're just out there letting these liberal professors think for you. You fall for their whole agenda."

Big Bruddah smiled. He let the moment fester. Another bite. A twist off of the cap and a swallow from the bottle of Dew. A re-capping. "By falling for the agenda, you fall into the trap they've set," he said.

"Trap?"

"Yes. Trap. They've trapped you into thinking they know more about this than the regular Joe with half a brain ever could."

"But they do. Right?"

"Who do?"

"The scientists. They're, like, *scientists*. They know."

Big Bruddah grinned. "Exactly where you guys get tripped up. Studying things doesn't make people smarter. Half the scientists out there are no smarter than a stray dog peeing on a tree. They're all looking for money to do their…" Big Bruddah bracketed the words in air quotes. "'…research.' And they got you guys out there drinking up their climate craziness, reporting on it like it's the gospel handed down from the mountain by Moses, which gives these eggheads in their labs

9

street cred to ask for more government grants. And the deep swamp in Washington DC, all of those thousands of so-called civil servants, they just process the paperwork and write the checks. Checks that come straight out of the bank accounts of who?"

Again Breen, mouth open, failed to launch a word.

"I'll tell you who. Me. And you. That's who," Big Bruddah was on a roll now. It felt good. It had been a while. "And the bureaucrats, most of who are involved in all kinds of immoral shit—QAnon dudes say half of them are in an international pedophilia ring. Me, I've honest-to-g-o-d heard there's some weird monkey worship deal at the Department of Labor or maybe Housing and Urban Development." He took a breath. "Point is, they got government jobs so they can keep our money flowing to these so-called scientists because they know that what the scientists study, you guys will lap up and feed to the masses like mamma birds and it will freak everyone out. And that will allow the government to exert control so the dudes in government can do what they do. Which is the point, Mr. Breen. Con-trol."

"Hold up. You're... The pedophilia and monkey worship—can we go back?"

Big Bruddah didn't hear him. "Point is, we got thousands and thousands of people in this country employed by dear old Uncle Samuel; which is, not coincidentally, a Hebrew name, and they're taking our own money and using it to control everything we do, everything we say, so they can do their agenda or whatever. You guys are all so neurotic and feminized and paranoid you don't see the forest for the trees you're all hugging." Big Bruddah smiled; he'd have to remember that line.

"Sir, listen. I hear you. But could we—"

"Bullshit, Breen. You don't hear me. If you heard me, you'd be asking me about the root of all this. The root runs clear back to the beginning of this country—back to the people that behind the government, guys like Doral Hutchison. You know about him, right?" Bruddah belched earnestly.

"I..."

"Of course you don't. You're over there listening to your hip and hop and getting dreads in your hair over whatever. You're not reading, Breen. If you were, you'd know the common, everyday American people who landed on Plymouth Rock or wherever..."

"The original White settlers? This goes back to..."

Big Bruddah nodded. "Absolutely. The people the good Lord built this country for. They never got a chance because, see, by the time we revolted against old King George and all, the deep state was already setting itself up. Doral Hutchison and his cronies pretty much controlled the Washington administration from the get-go."

"The George...?"

"The George Washington administration. Yes. Hutchison, he was from old old money in Louisiana. Got himself named to a low-level job in that first government. Used his connections and money to gather intelligence about George and the guys in his cabinet, to use as leverage against them, all so they could exert control over the government and, therefore, over who?"

Breen's mouth didn't even open. His eyes narrowed.

"Over the people. The pee-pul. And it was easy. Way I heard it, it was a good thing the Father of Our Country was shooting blanks or else at least one daughter of the revolution might've had roots on the dark continent, if you know what I'm saying."

Breen's mouth was open. His words were stuck.

Big Bruddah pounded the table. "Oh, you're perfect, Breen, my man, you come on all confident and superior, but I throw some facts your way that challenge the shit you're used to eating and, boom, you're all confused."

"It's not that. I'm not confused. It's just…"

From somewhere in the pile of junk on his desk, Big Bruddah's right hand found a compact Ruger. Before he thought about it, the gun was pointed at Breen's image and Breen's video-face was contracting in horror.

"Bang," Big Bruddah said. The kid flinched.

Big Bruddah turned the pistol to look at it. He looked back at the now obviously rattled reporter. "I'm not gonna shoot you. I mean, I just bought this monitor." He pointed the gun at his own head and pulled the trigger. The empty gun clicked. Breen's eyes were dinner plates of horror. Big Bruddah laughed and tossed the Ruger back into the debris on his desk. "You never leave a weapon loaded unless you intend to use it, my man."

"I… you… what?" Breen said.

"Look," Big Bruddah said sharply, suddenly serious. I'll send you some links to some sites that will open your eyes. For now, suffice it to say that you don't know what you don't know." He coughed once more, took a deep breath. Shook his head. He looked at the keyboard of his computer—white keys stained black—and was struck sober by the weight of what he knew, of what drove him. He looked up. "I've been researching this stuff since I was a kid, dude. And it's always been this tug of war. I mean, we're s'posedly a free country. They wrote all that freedom shit in there. The constitution. The Bill of Rights. All that. And the government—the secret part of it, the bureaucracy or whatever that no one really sees—has been working to take the freedom away. Bit by bit. And it's people like us, militia people, who've stood in your breach or whatever." Big Bruddah paused, his mind suddenly a jumble, his heart a rumbling truck. "It's been one big cluster…" Big Bruddah's voice grew thick. He looked away for a moment, sniffed. "Sorry, man," he said to Breen's high-def face. "This is what's always been in my heart, you know. I care about this." As he said it, Big Bruddah knew it was true. He did care. He cared too much. Always had. People—his ex—couldn't understand. "Back in the day, they had this perfect concept for a nation, but there were all these dark forces that kept holding it back."

"Like slavery," Breen said, his anxiety over the gun suddenly forgotten.

Big Bruddah felt the slap.

"It's a logical example. America's original sin. Right?" Breen said. "I mean, all due respect. We were going to talk about beef, I know, but you took us down a bit of a rabbit hole here."

Irritated, Big Bruddah thought for a moment, put down the Mountain Dew. Stared at Breen's earnest face. Thought harder. "What I took us down was a reality check of how this government has never been for the people. Not like it's supposed to be. There's always been powers working against real Americans, taking away our liberties and rights. We come here for a better way of life. Worked hard to get it. You look at most of the Africans who came here, they got a pretty square deal. They were cared for. A roof over their heads and three meals and so on. A good job. Hard work, but they loved working outdoors, your ancestors did. They'd be ashamed of this current generation of African-Americans and what not, I tell you that."

Breen was just staring now, his face stone.

"It's the regular White folks that got the bad deal here. Starting back then and going to today, the only thing that stood between us and total absolute tyranny was the right to bear arms and our right to assemble and our right to have a private militia. This administration with this woman in charge, she's trying to get at all our freedoms through this climate nonsense that's coming from inside the government, just like always."

Breen had taken off those glasses of his and was scowling. "You wanna rewind that a bit? Back to the part about Africans getting a square deal? You are aware I will quote you on that, right?"

But Big Bruddah was lost in his passion. "Pretty soon, we're going to wake up and see that an armed militia won't be able to carry out its constitutionally given right to arm itself against a government running amok—and everyone, your people, the Mexicans, and Americans and even Arabs and all will be sunk."

"Because of beef regulations," Breen said quietly.

"Beef elimination, my friend. It's the tip of the ice-whatever." Big Bruddah leaned toward the monitor, knowing Breen didn't know—couldn't know—what he knew. "They're disappearing cattle over the border as we speak."

He smiled at the awe he saw on Breen's face.

"You bet your ass, Son. Put that on your record: The whole process of beef elimination is under-fucking-way." Big Bruddah's voice was rising the way it always had when he was sharing his heart to his militia bros and ladies. The sound of it, the heat in his chest from it, took him back to a night scented with the smoke of burning maple wood and cheap but effective weed—a night when the soon-to-be-ex love of his life sat across the drifting smoke and banked coals, smiling while plotting to cut that heart from his chest with a knife he didn't know she had. This fed the fire of course. And Big Bruddah soon realized he was gnawing on the mouth of the Mountain Dew bottle. He caught himself. Looked at Breen. What had he been talking about? The thought eluded him. He took a slug of Dew and swallowed. Felt a piece of plastic ride down his throat with the fizz. Coughed. "Anyways, this whole thing's as clear as a wart on your pecker, man." Big Bruddah said, gesturing with the now heavily scarred bottle.

"Oh sure. Deep state. Happy Africans. Washington. Climate and cows." Breen was looking down at something, reading.

"You've pretty much covered it all, I guess." He looked up at Bruddah. "Except boogaloo."

Big Bruddah gulped. He tried to smile. Mountain Dew burned in his nose.

"C'mon, you have to know I'd ask about this. I mean, a group of men and women who show up at militia rallies and protests armed, a lot of them wearing ironic Hawaiian shirts just to throw off the evil media from their intent to replace or, what the heck, just eliminate the government. I got that right?

Big Bruddah tried to swallow his anger, but it was getting difficult, what with all the acid boiling up from his gut.

"I particularly love the fact that they've taken their name from an eighties flick. What was the name of it?"

"*Breakin' 2: Electric Boogaloo*," Big Bruddah said with a belch.

"Yeah, that's it. All because they want to ignite a second civil war, which they call—staying with the theme—the boogaloo."

Big Bruddah swallowed a hiccup. It hurt.

"Are you and your followers, your fellow militia members, embracing the boogaloo movement now?" Breen said.

"Put it this way, some real strong people inside the government want me eating grapes or some shit instead of red meat. And it's a slippery slope from there. Like Boston and the tea. The party, you know? This is like that."

"The Boston Tea Party?" Breen drew it out slowly.

"Exactly."

"I'm sorry, um, sir. You've lost me."

Big Bruddah smiled. "Of course I have. Because you're too busy with all your precious elite bullshit to see the forest for the horses you rode in on. The original militia, the Minutemen of, like, our revolution, they dumped tea in that harbor, but it wasn't because of tea. The King, George, he didn't even drink tea on account of his gout. Look it up."

15

Breen seemed to make a note, which gave Big Bruddah a rush of satisfaction.

"He was using the tea tax to assert control," Big Bruddah said. "Same here. Meat is the first step. But only the first one."

Breen looked bewildered and a little angry.

Big Bruddah liked the look. So he hit Leave Meeting.

Several minutes passed. Big Bruddah stood and paced, his thoughts churning. The rain drummed overhead. He opened a window slightly and watched the water coursing down a muddy gully in the gravel driveway, the wet breeze cooling an exposed inch of his hairy belly.

His cell rang. It was a video call. Big Bruddah crossed to his chair, sat, and then answered.

"Sir," Breen said, his voice quivering ever so slightly. "Please don't hang up."

Big Bruddah sighed. "What?"

"I really—well, my editor wants background for the story. She asked me to ask you... She said I should make sure we covered, you know, the thing with Wisconsin. I mean, you haven't given many interviews since then—"

"I've given exactly none."

"And you talking to me—I'm absolutely grateful. But, I hope you would, for my editor, just share your thoughts of how that went and how that impacts the militia movement now."

Big Bruddah thought about the intel he'd gotten on Breen. He'd need to question Silver Eagle's researchers, and question them hard, before he used their data again. This kid was persistent. Big Bruddah hated persistent.

And the kid just kept talking.

"I mean, I know you weren't actually part of, you know, Operation Cheesus," Breen said. "And we've all read the stories. I've read the book, too. The one by Todd Lindquist, the guy who was sucked into the whole plot to, you know, invade Wisconsin. We know how Governor Hoeksma was impeached as a result—everyone knows that—and that he's now running, you know, Silver Eagle Security in South Carolina. And I, we—my editor—know… knows that your wife—"

"My ex-wife," Big Bruddah said.

"Right. Your ex… Sorry. Yes. Sorry."

"If you're sorry, you wouldn't be bringing this up."

'Well, um. Yeah. I know. It's my editor…"

"Oh, it's someone else's fault. You people…"

"Look, just… If you could give me some perspective. I mean, I know the back story about how Will Hoeksma, Sr. was this Michigan gazillionaire who started Silver Eagle Security after September 11th. He had this weird, like, wingman, Wilbur Tuttle, the colonel, whatever they called him."

"Call him, you mean."

"Yes. Right. Right."

"I mean, the man basically runs Silver Eagle now. Tuttle does. Billy Hoeksma doesn't do shit."

"Exactly. So, everyone knows Will Hoeksma got his son, Bill Jr., elected governor. Then Bill Jr. names Tuttle state police commander blah blah blah. One day, Governor Bill's buddy, the state senate majority leader…"

"Ham DenBraber, as in the guy who is now governor."

"Yes. DenBraber tells the then-governor, Billy Hoeksma, that Michigan has been attacked by Wisconsin as some sort of conspiracy over stolen cheese recipes."

Big Bruddah closed his eyes. "I do not want to talk about this."

"Just bear with me. Please. Wisconsin supposedly used monkeypox-carrying prairie dogs to, like, sicken Michigan political leaders, including Mr. DenBraber. All of that has been talked about in the media extensively. We know now that it was just a crazy conspiracy theory concocted by Mr. Tuttle and Will Hoeksma."

"We don't know shit. You don't, anyway."

"So, you believe it was true?"

"No friggin' comment."

"Okay. Okay. Okay." Breen looked down, read from his notes, then continued: "So, Governor Bill was supposed to hire his father's company, Silver Eagle, to launch a counterattack against Wisconsin, which would have ignited some wider conflict and given Silver Eagle international visibility, which was what old man Hoeksma wanted, but Governor Bill threw the whole thing upside down by asking his buddies in the militia to do the counterattack." Breen stopped. "Have I got that right?"

Big Bruddah's chest heaved. He reached for his bag of jerky, realized the bag was empty, and threw it at the cluttered floor.

Breen continued. "The problem was, you and most of the other militia members were out of state at some secret convention when all this went down."

"It wasn't secret."

"But you were blacked out, right? What I heard is no one could contact you."

The kid was good. "No. No one could call me. Or email. Or test. Or fucking smoke signal me."

"So, then what happened?"

"You know what happened."

"No one knows your version of it."

Big Bruddah felt steam rising in his gut. He'd spent hours online reading trial testimony, watching news accounts, and festering over the events of that day.

He would not speak of it. Ever.

Breen would, though, apparently. He just went on, slashing at his ego and his pride and his memory. "So, your wife and the only two other militia members who were still in Michigan went to Wisconsin, to launch some kind of invasion on their own. The two guys ended up getting shot by Wisconsin cops at…" He looked at his notes.

"A Cracker Barrel restaurant."

"Yes, yes. The infamous Cracker Barrel. Then things got really weird, right? Tuttle and Will Hoeksma tried to swoop in and get Silver Eagle involved with some kind of military drone strike on a bus they called 'a bioweapons lab' only your wife and some other guy—"

"They stopped it. Yes. Yes. Yes." Big Bruddah spit the words at his phone's screen. "She and some half-drunk, rich Indian asshole and a lesbo congresswoman put an end to it. She turned her back on her people, her upbringing—on our chance to make a statement, on our opportunity to be part something that would show the country what we stand for. She did that. She did it. No one else. Her. She could have made the right choice. But no. No. She destroyed everything we were working for. Then Will Hoeksma dropped dead of a stroke. And I wish she…"

Breen waited. Big Bruddah glared at him.

Breen looked at him through those damn glasses, all wide-eyed and encouraging. "So they threw Governor Bill Hoeksma out of office for his part in it and Tuttle admitted to killing an FBI agent who was on to the plot? He did serious time, right?"

Big Bruddah didn't respond.

The kid wouldn't take the hint. "Rumor was, Governor Bill actually shot the agent by accident. Tuttle took the fall. That's what I heard. They all knew Ham DenBraber would win the election to replace Hoeksma and pardon Tuttle, which he did."

Before Breen could say another word, Big Bruddah ended the call. Resisting the renewed urge to throw the phone across the room, he instead slid the device into the kangaroo pocket of his hoody.

The phone rang. Big Bruddah fumbled furiously in the pocket for the thing. He grimaced and swore silently, extracted another small handgun—a Beretta Pico given to him by Miky on their first wedding anniversary; his wife had betrayed him, but she knew a good firearm—and dropped it on the desk in front of him. The phone rang again. He pulled it free of the pocket, glanced at the screen, and stopped. It wasn't Breen. He answered the call, held the device to his ear, and waited for the caller to speak.

Seconds passed, the conversation unborn. Bruddah could hear, faintly, a song from long ago, playing in the caller's background. Classic rock. He smiled.

"What's that song, Tuttle?" Bruddah said.

"Boston. 'Don't Look Back.' From 1978. Album kicks ass." Tuttle's voice was soft but rough, tires slowly moving through gravel.

"You and your oldies."

From Tuttle's side of the conversation, a woman giggled softly. It was a sexy giggle. "You check your inbox this morning?" Tuttle said.

Bruddah's eyes turned back to his computer screen. He shifted his considerable weight in the chair and tapped the keyboard. The monitor reawakened… "I was just about to do that."

"Don't bother," Tuttle said. A small dog barked bigly, in a distant room. "Quiet," Tuttle said loudly. To the dog. The dog paid no heed. The woman giggled.

Bruddah really liked the giggle and, for a moment, lost his mental path.

"Honey, you need to get dressed," Tuttle said, breaking Bruddah's reverie. There was a rustling—Bruddah imagined sheets moving—then Tuttle's voice louder, into the phone: "My friend, we need to do the thing. The video, the YouTube. Or whatever."

Bruddah's brain caught up. He looked at Hillary on the elephant. "Shit. We're ready? She's doing this thing—the complete ban?"

"That's what we've heard."

"Sheesh. Your guys ready?"

"Ready as we'll ever be," Tuttle said. "All my research numbers, the chatter we've been monitoring—and you with that post. My gut says go."

"We're talking," Bruddah paused, a grin spread across his face, "Seriously?"

From Tuttle, silence. No dog. No rustle. No giggle. Then, suddenly, a new song. The music grew louder. Ringo Starr. "Back Off Boogaloo."

Bruddah chuckled.

"Get some rest today. Tomorrow we boogie," Tuttle said.

Chapter Three

Bo Watts had been a hero of the Michigan militia movement from the moment he was old enough to pick up a gun—sixteen months or two years old, depending on who told the story. His mom and dad, Shirley and Willy Watts, were among the first members of the Red Sky Brigade.

He grew up in the womb of the militia movement, on a fruit and vegetable farm near the small southwest Michigan town of Berrien Springs. He came of age at militia events and weekend bivouacs in the woods. Along with the other children of Red Sky, Bo mastered numerous weapons and learned to fend for himself in the event of natural disaster, civil unrest, or government attack—all by early adolescence.

By age seven, he had earned his militia Rifleman Junior Grade Badge. At nine, Bo became a Red Sky voting member by meeting the militia's Basic Readiness standard. To do so, he put together a backpack defense kit that included a rifle, one hundred rounds of ammunition, a canteen of water, a first-aid kit, water purification tablets, bayonet, flashlight, multi-tool knife, camo waterproof poncho, tarp, fire stick, toilet paper, compass, and laminated copies of the Declaration of Independence and the U.S. constitution. He then dressed in a camouflage uniform (enthusiastically made by Shirley on her Singer sewing machine), camouflaged his exposed skin, recited the militia's top rules and alert levels to the Red Sky leadership team, and lugged that backpack on a two-mile hike, during which he stripped and cleaned the rifle, buried eight out of ten shots in a nine-inch target at 125 yards and, "just for yucks," started a small campfire before shooting, dressing, cooking, and eating a squirrel.

The only child who could rival young Bo's precociousness was Miky Spike, the daughter of Red Sky's founders, "Rub" and Colette Spike.

Like Bo, Miky—rhymes with "Mickey," the name chosen by her father before she presented herself in a raucous birth on the kitchen table of the family farmhouse—was destined to be a militia prodigy, particularly after Colette's fatal decision, three years later, to board a carnival ride during a thunderstorm.

Miky attended her first militia bivouac with her dad at age eight and won her militia Rifleman Junior Grade Badge at nine. By adolescence, she was a level three rifleman, capable of handling a full military-style operation and leading a team.

By sixteen, Miky and Bo were in love. With the militia life. And each other.

In high school, hardened by a childhood of paramilitary training, they became dominant distance runners. Central Michigan University awarded both of them cross-country/track scholarships. At CMU, they managed to juggle the demands of eighty-mile training weeks, classes and part-time jobs until Rub choked to death on a piece of bratwurst during a militia event in a secluded forest. The grief was brutal. Miky and Bo quit their teams. They became heavy partiers, and Bo developed a keen taste for recreational drugs. Even so, they earned their four-year degrees in four years.

Bo and Miky graduated, married, and bought a Victorian farmhouse in a mostly rural area near Kalamazoo. Miky became a high school teacher and cross-country coach. Bo, armed with a degree in Agricultural Engineering and a jones for weed, translated a referral from a guy he knew in the militia into an assistant product manager gig for the Frosted Flakes brand at Kellogg's, in Battle Creek. Bo was overqualified, but he was not highly motivated to work in the corporate world. It was a good career fit.

By the early 2000s, Bo was a rock star in the militia world. His blog and podcast, "Diary of the Mitten Maniac," attracted a maniacally devoted audience of several hundred thousand. He and Miky attended national militia events, where Bo was often asked to speak. Backed by a much-used PowerPoint presentation on the "The Bastardization of the American Dream," he was adored because he was hardcore.

Bo hated government. He worshipped the Second Amendment and had no tolerance for people, especially woke liberals and loudmouthed Black guys and illegal immigrants who accused other people of being racist.

The nation, Bo proclaimed, was losing touch with what made it great: values that put men at the head of families, that expected a woman who made a baby to keep the baby, and that, above all, emphasized the personal liberty of all true Americans.

He believed America was sliding into laziness and a lax, permissive liberal order.

When shit got real, he intended to be ready.

His wife was a different story. As fate would show, Miky never could match her parents or husband zeal for zeal. To her, the militia was family. But she felt like the odd woman out at the militia banquet of gun rights, paranoia, coy racism, casual misogyny, and apocalyptic anti-government blather.

Self-sufficiency, personal freedom, shooting guns she embraced. The rest of it—the extreme of it—she found, well, silly and stupid.

Miky tried to talk with Bo about it. She tried to make him laugh about being what she called "a militia fire-breather." But, as you might expect from a fire-breather, he wasn't interested in the cold water of his wife's wisdom.

So, one now infamous sunny day at a Cracker Barrel in Wisconsin, Miky, in the words of Springsteen, took a wrong turn and just kept going.

That day, Bo Watts lost the one person who mattered most to him. But he kept the thing that meant more.

After a quick but painful divorce, Bo cracked open his nest egg—money earned through speaking fees and the sales of his books and other writings. He bought fourteen acres of woods near the Lake Michigan beach town of South Haven. Twelve acres into it, he cleared the trees for his personal militia retreat. First, with the help of four militia friends and a sympathetic heavy equipment contractor, he built an underground bunker. The walls and ceiling were eighteen inches of reinforced concrete. A duct, for ventilation, extended one hundred yards beneath the surrounding woods before rising into the hollow trunk of a very authentic fake Douglas fir. The air-filtration system was certified by the seller (a militia contact named Killshot) to offer military-grade protection against nuclear, biological, and chemical attack. Propane stored in a buried tank fired the bunker's furnace, which would be vented through the home's furnace vent. A gasoline generator would provide backup electricity. The toilet was composting. Bo lowered in a personal safe for money and other valuables: two gun safes, fully stocked; as well as carefully packaged and protected bomb-making materials and an assortment of pre-built small explosive devices. He then added a couch, two chairs, a laptop and all critical Internet infrastructure, as well as pallets of bottled water, toilet paper, canned goods, meals-ready-to-eat (MREs), and an autographed poster of Kid Rock. Clothes, blankets, reading material, and medical supplies would come later.

Once the bunker was ready, the militia-sympathetic contractor delivered the factory-built house in halves. A trap door in a bedroom provided access to the underground room.

When the work was done, Bo settled into life after Miky. The zealot became wholly, utterly committed to his cause. He set up the second bedroom, the one with the trap door, as his office. When he wasn't writing, recording his podcast, or away on militia business, Bo taught himself to repair personal computers and small engines.

At the entrance to his long gravel driveway, Bo posted a crude homemade sign that read "PC (but not politically correct) and Small Engine Repair." The sign was one of the few things that made Bo smile, which he did nearly every time he turned from two-lane Blue Star Highway onto his property.

Bo took in enough repair work through the militia network and his posts on social media and Craigslist to eke out an existence and still have extra money to stash in the safe in the bunker. He did not spend much time there; to him, it was a sacred space, reserved for the godawful-but-inevitable moment when right-thinking men and women would need to defend themselves against government tyranny, marauding mobs, or any number of threats to personal liberty.

During a local flareup of the coronavirus, Bo and his pony-tailed, ex-con buddy Jerry Plannenberg grabbed their guns and led a group of militia members into the Michigan State Capitol to remind the then-governor not to shut down the state's businesses. A day later, Bo and Jerry were on CNN talking about the right to bear arms and to not wear masks and that it was China who'd released the virus, but, even so, it was blown out of proportion and in no way as big a deal as the mainstream media were saying it was, and then a week after that Bo was almost dying from it.

He spent weeks on a ventilator. The docs sedated him and put tubes in him so he could poop and pee and eat. Jerry Plannenberg and some of his other buds lied to the press, saying he'd had a serious accident on his four-wheeler. Miky worried over him, she said, but had to worry by text and email from her ranch out in Timbukwherever, Colorado because of the quarantine.

Bo went through a long convalescence that ate up the better part of the next year. He was weak. He was skinny. The breathing difficulties and the chest pain came and went with horrible unpredictability. He couldn't work. He couldn't work out.

Jerry and Bo's other militia friends got him through the worst of it. They took him to doctor's appointments, killed hours watching gun and paramilitary videos with him, and kept him stocked with food and beer. Money flooded in through a GoFundMe campaign, which claimed Bo had rolled his quad while being followed by Antifa agents. They even hired him a visiting nurse; a cousin of Jerry's who was a militia groupie and who, it turned out, was willing to handle all intimate matters of a medical and personal nature.

His energy level eventually improved and the horrible waxing and waning of symptoms faded a bit, but he was no longer the energized, athletic, politically savvy leader of the militia movement. In addition to being out of shape, his brain felt cloudy and he was often depressed. He was also angry. The medical community had saved him. But not one doc or nurse, Jerry's cousin aside, had done a damn thing to clear the fog in his head, extinguish the flame of pain in his lungs, or completely eliminate the exhaustion that plagued him. He'd sent messages and made phone calls. He'd plowed through dozens of websites. He'd tried hydroxychloroquine, extract of oleander, and even toyed with the idea of gargling bleach. Nothing had given him relief. His passion for fitness and running disappeared; it was replaced by bitterness toward the nameless, shadowy Chinese cabal he was sure had created the monster and the healthcare system that had conspired to let him suffer. Also, the media for making him think the bug would only last two weeks.

He'd missed Miky during the illness and recovery. But he hadn't texted her—not once. She gave up trying to reach him, a fact he could see on his phone. He'd kept the hundreds of unanswered emails and messages from her. They ended with one that began, "FU then."

One night, in a stroke of weed-fueled inspiration as he prowled his woods in search of edible mushrooms and poison ones he could maybe send to a congressman he loathed, Bo Watts found himself scrolling through those messages. He couldn't shake an image of Miky in their kitchen in Kalamazoo, dancing like a goofball to some stupid damn song whose words and title escaped him. As it often did, that fantasy shifted to her in court, sitting in the hot seat, looking so cool and drop-dead gorgeous as she threw his life and everything they'd ever shared outside of running and love, along with two dead militiamen, under a big old school bus.

That's when he decided not just to let her go. But also to let his old self go. He decided to change his name. To what? To "Zealot Watts?" That was funny. Because she'd called him that. A "zealot."

What else had she called him? Fire. Fire something.

Then for some stupid reason he later attributed to the weed, he thought of a football player who died at a party while they were at CMU. The guy tried to blow a mouthful of kerosene out of his mouth and light it—like Gene Simmons from

KISS—but he started to giggle and inhaled. The guy's name was Big Bruddah Baker.

For $29.95 and a few minutes filling out online forms, Bo, the fire-breather, became Big Bruddah Watts. And his previous life with his wife was no more.

The militia's 300-plus members were now organized into twelve units they called "brigades." These were scattered across the state. Each local organization was independently run, but a governing board consisting of the division commanders met monthly at a bar in Saginaw to coordinate training and policy, to get tanked on beer, and to talk for hours about the horrible direction their country was taking. The most recent meetings had taken on an edgier air. Big Bruddah, whose gut-level reactions to current events were infectious and gospel, had for the first time begun suggesting civil insurrection was inevitable. And imminent.

Big Bruddah and the rest of the board despised the President of the United States. They would not utter her name. She'd pushed through new taxes to fund universal healthcare, restrictions on gasoline-powered vehicles, and what Big Bruddah's blog post called "a shitload of unconstitutional, liberty-gutting policies meant to destroy God-given rights." But the straw that broke Big Bruddah's broad back was the President's proposed executive order on "all types of cattle," part of an admittedly drastic attempt "to reduce methane in the atmosphere and stem the growing impact of climate change." Although the order didn't ban beef and dairy consumption, social media and militia chat rooms were red hot with reports that the President had sent a secret executive order telling retailers to start getting rid of their beef and milk products.

For months, the militia community—fiercely united in outrage across multiple social media platforms—had been ablaze with talk of a plot to completely eliminate the American beef and dairy industries by cutting them off at the moment of conception. Rumors, mostly verified on militia chat sites, said federal agents were already confiscating and destroying bull semen in covert raids that were made to look like standard bull semen thefts. Unborn calves were being ripped from cow wombs. Grown cattle were disappearing—a head here, a head there—particularly in the West. There was already a disinformation campaign underway, designed by the federal government to scare people away from cows. One frequent poster on the Red Sky Facebook page, a woman from Manistee who called herself Manic Mona, shared what looked like a pretty genuine copy of a CDC memo that said bull semen and bovines carried a mutant remnant of old Covid-19 virus, and were therefore dangerous to "anyone in contact with them." The way Manic Mona told it, the memo was written in "both English and Mexican" and was "being distributed across the West mostly, but soon would be online in all its glory." According to Mona, the government was "even having it translated into Muslim and the Jewish language."

In recent weeks, things had gone from Mona's musings to worse. Militia members from Arizona and Texas reported U.S. Border Patrol agents were paying Mexicans to smuggle American cattle across the southern border. A totally American but bilingual militia guy from Brownsville, Texas who called himself Conquistador posted on a popular militia site that he'd stowed away on a cow smuggler's unventilated tractor-trailer rig and stayed onboard until "the smuggler amigos" arrived at their destination, a slaughterhouse in Reynosa, Mexico. Half-conscious from the long drive with the obviously digestively panicked animals, Conquistador managed to revive himself with two cans of Red Bull and a shot of whiskey at a nearby bar. In the bar's gravel parking lot, Conquistador said, he'd met a "Mexican guy—let's call him Pedro." Conquistador used his mastery of the local language and a Glock to coerce the truth out of "Pedro." The stolen American cattle were being slaughtered for what? Not food. No. For fat. The Mexicans melted down the fat and stored it in empty Tequila barrels. This fat, slightly tequila scented, was used to make candles for Muslim religious rituals in Mexico and elsewhere, even in the Holy Land, Conquistador said.

Conquistador, verified by responses to his post, was a straight shooter. Dude wouldn't lie.

That the President and her friends were supposedly vegetarians only made his story and all the others more believable.

And that wasn't the worst of it.

One militia member on Reddit had shared real evidence that the President of the United States, who everyone knew looked a little Oriental, was a direct descendant of a nineteenth-century Chinese gangster named Mo Lin, had aborted at least two babies and sold the fetal tissue on the Chinese black market to be used as ingredients in an Asian version of Gummi Bears prized as aphrodisiacs.

And that, *that,* wasn't the worst of it, either.

The President Whose Name Could Not Be Uttered was going to use the cattle crisis to ban cow hugging, a tradition called "koe knuffelen" in the land where it began, the Netherlands. Fueling rumors of the ban was a widely circulated but unverified report that proved relaxed cattle burped more and, therefore, produced more methane. (What kind of cow was more relaxed than a hugged one?) It wasn't clear how the President was going to enforce a ban. But she most definitely was going to do it. It was "as obvious as spoiled pot roast in a bath of milk-based gravy," one Reddit poster with a flair for creativity had said. Hugging cows had become a thing since the coronavirus pandemic, particularly in West Michigan, which was home to dairy farms and a large population of Dutch Americans. Farmers charged up to $50 an hour for stressed families to hug bovine during the pandemic and many of those agri-businessmen and agri-businesswomen now saw koe knuffelen as a permanent revenue stream. One, Jon Moksma of Allegan, had begun recruiting a network of distributors to franchise his branded version of koe knuffelen, KowWow, nationwide. Moksma's business model included a worst-case-scenario plan that advised local franchisees to hold night-time "coffees/hug-ins" in barns to recruit new distributors "out of the sight of regulators." Most of the members of the Red Sky militia, Big Bruddah included, were descendants of Dutch settlers. They saw the koe knuffelen ban as a direct attack aimed at them. The kerfuffle over koe knuffelen had electrified social media almost as powerfully as the beef ban had.

Since his dance with Covid, the guy previously known as Bo Watts had transformed from a college running star and weightlifting, organic-food-eating militia sex symbol into an overweight, shaggy-haired, stretched-tee-shirt-wearing avatar for the liberal Michigan-native filmmaker Michael Moore—a comparison Big Bruddah had mildly shot a friend over—in large part by smoking a lot of dope and eating fast-food hamburgers and all-you-can-eat-restaurant steaks. He loved cheap red meat.

To demonstrate the tyrannical impact of both rumored and real beef regulations and the various related conspiracies, Big Bruddah had driven his pickup, a gleaming back monster of a Ford Super Duty 350 XLT, through three different drive-thru lanes of three different fast-food restaurants. He took pictures of the restaurants' drive-thru menus and put a bullet through the electronic brain of the last menu, nailing it right between "Caesar Salad Meal" and "Incredi-Veggie Burger." This "Bruddah Survey," which he'd cited in the now widely shared blog post on the militia website, demonstrated that the government's heavy hand was already having a serious effect on the free market. Each of the fast-food franchises had eliminated at least two hamburger options and increased the prices on the remaining ones. The menus were filled with new salads and chicken options—that only made Big Bruddah angrier. Michelle Obama had wanted everyone to eat more salads. He hated the Obamas and salads.

Chapter Four

Carpville, South Carolina

Tuesday morning

For Wilbur Tuttle, four years in the state penitentiary system had been well spent. He used the time away to reinforce his reputation as a volatile, brilliant, dangerous purveyor of dirty tricks and strategically sound violence and to harden his network of proven thugs and anarchists-in-training—human and near-human assets he would need as he returned to his discomforting place in society.

His relationship with Will Hoeksma Sr. had helped him carve his dark niche in the subterranean rooms of global security and paramilitary organizations. And while he didn't miss his former accomplice, he was grateful for what they'd done together.

Tuttle had met Will at the University of Michigan in the late 1960s. On the surface, they were an odd match: Tuttle the Vietnam vet and former CIA spook with a penchant for extravagant disguises and a startling but useful array of eccentricities, Will, the no-nonsense rising capitalist, born with a golden opportunity in one hand and a laundry list of grievances against the antiwar, free-love, and civil rights movements in the other. Will's wealthy uncle, Jake, the founder of the global appliance manufacturer, Amerispin, had pulled strings to keep him out of the mess in Vietnam. That didn't keep Will from hating the war protesters and "hippie scum" who held "hash bashes" and burned draft cards and bras at bonfire rallies on campus. Will backed the people who backed the war; if that meant some young men of lesser means fought, so be it; natural selection sucked.

Tuttle gladly served two tours in 'Nam as a military policeman and smuggler of stolen goods before wandering to Singapore, where he fell in love with a local girl. Turned out the girl was CIA; she recruited Tuttle, who'd gone on to a handful of special ops for the agency before getting homesick, quitting the spy business cold, and returning to Michigan.

Tuttle and Will Hoeksma first met in a dingy dorm laundry room, drawn together over Tuttle's need for fabric softener. The always-buttoned-down Will, with his crewcut and khakis, tried to ignore the shaggy-haired, army-fatigue-wearing Tuttle. But Tuttle, who smelled of old baloney and Brut aftershave, played to Will's sense of superiority by asking if his family's company had made the washing machines into which Tuttle had just dumped an overload of his dirty clothes. Amerispin had, in fact made the machines, under its industrial brand "Liberty."

Will thought he was meeting another ignorant peacenik, but he soon found himself deep in a rapturous discussion of the orange red chemical lava that flowed across a jungle on a napalm morning. Will loved having not been in the war but savored stories of American military might. Tuttle shared his war memories as a highlight reel of his young life. He'd dropped a lot of LSD. Expanded his mind. Made a lot of money on the side. His skills in intelligence-gathering and knack for disguises, he figured, had eventually led the CIA to his beaded Singapore door. After the post-war stint with the Agency, he'd enrolled at U of M, planning for a career in "law enforcement or something."

His one regret from his long, strange trip through southeast Asia, he explained, was a love affair with a Saigon teenager who'd broken his heart at the war's end; he'd wished he'd had the chance to kill her. He'd said this last part without smiling.

Tuttle and Will recognized each other that day they met. Each fully appreciated the other's warped moral code and the competitive advantages it gave them over adversaries. They were two peas from the same dark pod.

In the 1970s, Will Hoeksma rose to the presidency of Amerispin. Under his leadership, from its headquarters in Ada, Michigan, Amerispin grew into a global leader and earned the Hoeksma family what even their conservative, Calvinistic friends, neighbors, and relatives called a ridiculous level of wealth and power. Will Hoeksma used that wealth and power to fuel right-wing political causes, particularly his own.

As Will became known for his ruthless business tactics, right-wing Christian worldview, and knack for being in position for the next million at the right time, Wilbur Tuttle, known to most who loved or feared him (there was plenty of overlap) as "the colonel," was less Will's righthand man than he was his black claw, his dark alter ego.

That moment in the laundry room launched an unlikely relationship that left its sometimes-bloody footprints across six subsequent decades, a relationship that culminated in Operation Cheesus, the contrived near-war between Michigan and Wisconsin that ended Bo Watts's marriage to Miky Spike, put Tuttle in prison, and sent Will Hoeksma to a relatively early grave.

Now, as second in command at Silver Eagle, Tuttle was using his connections with the militia and with Will's namesake to rekindle his career. Rekindle, in a napalm kind of way.

Tuttle stepped off the treadmill in the Silver Eagle Security gym with a soft "whoo" of self-congratulation. He'd needed the workout. There was much to be done.

Since his release from prison, Tuttle had helped build Silver Eagle into a lethal army of mercenaries and killers-for-hire that was now the most-sought-after paramilitary organization in the world. But what drove him, what made him eager to leave his often-shared bed to work each day at the rumored-but-never-verified age of eighty-one, was Project Black Dog, an off-the-books, blacker-than-black, dark-web-lurking division of Silver Eagle that handled clients and "situations" Tuttle didn't share with most of the rest of the security firm's command structure. Tuttle had used Project Black Dog's specially trained resources to carry out voter intimidation and ballot fraud to ensure Ham DenBraber succeeded Governor Bill as Michigan's governor. Since then, Project Black Dog had grown to be the home for money laundering, civil insurrection, assassination and other messy security-related interdictions for state and foreign governments, drug kingpins, international conglomerates, and far-right media organizations. The operation was in many ways a reflection of its commander: morally flexible, rabidly ruthless, and damn good at doing bad shit. Commander Bill and a small circle of the management team knew about the Project Black Dog but never spoke about it. It was mayhem as a service, and it generated a positive revenue stream. Enough said.

The hands-off approach allowed Tuttle to not only operate with impunity but also gave him an open gate through which to push pet projects. His personal favorite, his obsession, was the pursuit of the girl who'd broken his heart at the end of his last tour in Vietnam. The older he'd become, the more frantic that search had become. And lately, his bottomless energy and relentless goading of Southeast Asian contacts had miraculously borne fruit. He was, he believed, on the verge of reuniting with his long-lost love. He chuckled at the thought of that reunion.

Of course, the attempt to find the girl-now-woman was a sideshow compared to the operation he'd just set in motion with his strange-bedfellow militia ally, Big Bruddah Watts. Operation Boogaloo was the culmination of years of festering frustration with the country's leftward political drift.

It had started with a favorite tactic: the fake conspiracy, this one about the destruction of America's cattle herd and smuggled animals being destroyed in Mexico, their fat sold to make candles for Muslims. Tuttle had used his network of online trolls to spread the story. He'd thrown in the part about cow hugging, a real custom in the Netherlands, as a crisis enhancer. The internet had done the rest.

Tuttle smiled. He took a deep breath. He heard what sounded like thunder. Smelled sweat and hope and danger.

His four-mile run complete, he shotgunned his mid-morning power drink of steroids and vitamins while studying himself in the gym's mirrored wall. He was wearing running tights, red Asics running shoes and nothing more; the wall reflected the tanned, wrinkled-yet-muscled hairless torso of an old runner who embraced the dangers and benefits of performance enhancing drugs. Tuttle liked the look. Finished with the drink, he recapped the bottle and walked toward the locker room. There were six other Silver Eagle associates—four men and two women—working out at the fully equipped gym. The women were running on adjacent treadmills. Two of the men were lifting weights. A third was riding a stationary bike. The fourth was using a large knife to dry shave in the mirrored wall. As Tuttle walked, he held his back ramrod straight and his bald head high. The guy shaving, a trickle of blood running from near his right ear to his chin, nodded at Tuttle in his reflected image. Tuttle nodded back.

In the locker room, Zen breathing techniques and a marijuana-infused protein bar restored Tuttle's heart to its usual resting rate. He showered and dressed.

He was ready to boogie.

The Kidnapping of Donovan Reed by a Guy who Looked Like John Lennon

PART TWO

The Kidnapping of
Donovan Reed
by a Guy who Looked
Like John Lennon

Chapter Five

Boulder, Colorado

Tuesday afternoon

Jackson Nguyen was starting to think Brent Stevens was God.

Not so much God the father of Jesus or Yahweh God or Allah God. God, blight-and-besot-the-world-with-weather-calamity, that God.

Computer science was Jackson's bread and butter, but weather was his crack cocaine. Stevens was the heroic meteorologist on The Weather Channel who'd pioneered the grab-a-palm-tree-and-hold-on coverage of calamity that all other weather geeks now imitated. Earlier in the day, at the airport in Seattle, Jackson had streamed on his iPhone Stevens's take on a freak late-season blizzard. Adding to the adrenalin rush of the massive storm was that the blizzard was hammering the Boulder, Colorado brewpub in which Jackson was now sitting as another meteorological disaster-to-be—an early-season hurricane—was also approaching the southeastern U.S., in an area that was currently besieged by wildfires. There were early-season fires in other states as well. Also, the upper Midwest, including his home state, was getting hammered by torrential rain. The weather events were performing exactly as Stevens predicted. They threatened to distract Jackson from the career crisis at hand. He welcomed that.

"So geeked I chose to come here during this. Exactly what I was hoping for. This is awesome," he said. "If it keeps coming down at this rate we're going to have a shitload. And, oh, we won't be getting back to Denver tomorrow." He felt giddy.

Donovan Reed laughed. "You've always enjoyed your weather. And since you're the Michigan native who thought it would be fun to have a drinking lunch in the godforsaken Rockies during a snowstorm, you can be the one who drives, whenever we decide to give it a try."

Jackson looked at his old friend. They'd been on the outs since their catastrophic financial fuckup twelve months before. It was Donovan who'd suggested this reunion. Jackson had borrowed a mutual friend's mountain retreat for the weekend hoping the predictions of a crazy late-May storm would be accurate. "Oh, you know I miss this. Haven't lived in the snow belt in twenty years. Haven't seen weather like this since my youth. This is perfect."

"Well, this London boy has not driven a motor vehicle in twenty years." Donovan took a sip of scotch. "I barely know how to open a car door without a driver."

"Sure sucks to be poor now, doesn't it?"

"Ow," Donovan said, feigning pain. "Tad too soon to joke about poverty, mate."

Jackson sighed and stared into his beer choice, a wheat ale with a cowboy-themed label that identified it as a High Plains Drifter. "Which brings us right around to the point, doesn't it? Our mutually shared financial distress." Jackson watched as the gale played with a metal sign hanging over the doorway of the restaurant across the street. The weather did remind him of his childhood in Traverse City. "We used to get these lake effect storms. The cold air comes across the big lake, Lake Michigan, see, and the lake is just warm enough that it generates a ton of snow. We got snow days all the time when those lake effect bands set up. No school."

"But you fled to sunny California and never looked back."

"Opportunity knocked."

"The refugee lad rides the Internet to wealth and fame—sans his special Lake Michigan snow."

"Lake effect snow."

"Yes. That."

"It was worth it. But I do miss it sometimes."

"You miss what? Snow? Or money?"

Jackson laughed but he felt another pang. The meal with Donovan Reed was taking his emotions for a dance. He tried to swallow the feelings with another sip.

Jackson's mom and dad, An and Duc, departed their birth country with their sixteen-year-old daughter, Lalani, on the second to last day of April 1975 via an American helicopter that ever so briefly alighted on the U.S. embassy roof in Saigon. The chopper pilot, Sgt. Wilbur Tuttle of Ann Arbor, Michigan, thought he was in love with Lalani, whom Tuttle had met in a Saigon restaurant just two months before. With America abandoning its Vietnam adventure, twenty-year-old Tuttle had made his intentions obvious: he wanted to take home a pretty local girl or at the very least make love to her one final time before the first domino in the global communist conspiracy fell. Lalani didn't love Tuttle, but the war bored her. She loved the liberating danger of their clandestine interludes, and the certainty that her mother was furious about them. The elder Nguyens had married when they were teenagers to avoid the disgrace of Lalani being born out of wedlock. During the war, they were terrified to have more children, but they dreamed of raising a bigger family in a safer country. Lalani figured the love-drunk Tuttle might be the family's ticket out of hell. She was right on all counts. So it was that, as the remaining Americans were preparing to leave and the communists slowly choked the city, Sgt. Tuttle landed his testosterone-fueled chopper and the Nguyens jumped aboard.

The rest was family lore. Somehow, Lalani broke up with Tuttle as soon as the chopper cleared Vietnamese airspace, yet the family landed on its feet in a state shaped like a mitten. There, with the support of the smiling if not entirely comfortable members of the Cherry Hill Reformed Church, the Nguyens quietly built a life as line workers in a plant that made pies. Her first year in college, Lalani fell in love with a grad student from Nova Scotia who turned out to be wanted by the Royal Canadian Mounted Police. Legal trouble ensued, from which she extracted herself through the help of an understanding local magistrate. Fearing she'd brought shame to her family, Lalani fled to a convent in Vermont, and a year later was in Bangladesh serving the poor when the first of her three American siblings was born; bereft and bewildered by the turn of events, An and Doc named him after Lalani's favorite singer, Jackson Browne.

Jackson became a spectacularly important kid in his household. He was, in his parents' minds, the anchor Nguyen—the one who would fill the hole in their hearts and establish a long line in their adopted country.

Jackson felt his parents' high expectations. And he embraced those expectations. He never felt particularly close to either of them, but he had a distinctively Old World deference to his elders. Jackson became the obedient, hard-working, brilliant overachiever other American parents and their offspring instinctively resented. He wrecked test-grading curves. He turned in extra extra-credit projects. He quietly charmed pretty girls without noticing or caring. He said "thanks" and "no thank you" in a soft voice faintly scented with his parents' Vietnamese accent. He sang in the church choir—a tenor who was the first "foreigner" to solo in his church's annual presentation of Handel's "Messiah." And he memorized Bible verses with the dedication and accuracy of a death row convert.

In teenaged Jackson's mind, Traverse City was peopled by righteous White Christians with big hearts and only slightly opened minds. He suspected the idea of sponsoring foreign refugees was far more warmly embraced than were the actual refugees and their offspring. He wasn't wrong. Raised Catholic, An and Duc made the arduous transition to the Christian Reformed Church out of respect for their sponsors. Both took English classes through a community college. They learned to appreciate rural Americans' love for pickup trucks and country music. They watched TV. Ate frozen pizza. They bought guns and talked about shooting them in all the right places, which meant gun ranges and local woods and fields during deer hunting season, as well as the mental spaces occupied by visions of young African-American and Latino men who, they were told through TV, meant them gruesome harm.

Despite their attempts to fit in, An and Duc never did. They missed their native country as much as they missed their first-born daughter. Both had grown up in Saigon, a thriving, sprawling city. Traverse City was a small farming and tourist town that was warm just three months out of the year. Both longed for Saigon's scents and chaos—its noise. Both secretly dreamed of chatting again with Lalani.

Jackson was blessed with a laser focus and a thick skin. He liked school. He loved learning. He devoured information. While his peers hung out and hooked up after school and activities, his idea of screwing around involved a soldering iron, motherboards, and other hardware he could scrounge.

Jackson took the first rusty Toyota Corolla he could find out of town. His grades, test scores, and his family's (lack of) income got him a near-full ride to the University of Michigan. He worked nights at the computer lab to fill in the gaps of his funding and knowledge base. He was Phi Beta Everything at U of M. From there, it was a natural leap to Silicon Valley; Jackson arrived just as the Internet bubble was reaching full elasticity. His initial gig, as lead engineer for an online company that was going to parlay ultra-cheap Third World shipping resources to sell cut-rate South American produce online under the name Asparagrapes fell through when the guys funding it were charged in a somewhat-related cocaine smuggling venture. Jackson was exactly two weeks into his California career when the FBI and ATF agents padlocked the door to the startup. He hadn't been paid. The deposit on his tiny apartment had swallowed what little post-college savings he had.

Jackson, determined not to fall back on his parents, didn't have to. Three days after the mess with the startup, the down-on-his-luck Vietnamese immigrants' son from Michigan wandered into a Palo Alto coffee shop and into a conversation with a British expat who was looking for a non-fat chai latte and a partner in his new software gamble. Jackson and the Brit, Donovan Reed, started talking while standing in line and within two hours were boarding Donovan's private jet, bound for Comic Con in Cairo. The robust debate between the two tech nerds covered X's and O's, superheroes and Jobs v Gates. And it continued from that day through their first multi-million-dollar software firm to their rise on the "Richest Thirty-Somethings" lists until the bubble burst and both took a one hundred-million-dollar punch in the gut on ill-advised investments in two failed Canadian robotics companies.

They hadn't spoken to each other in more than a year. But theirs was a marriage rooted in the powerful magnetics of cyberspace. Despite online debate to the contrary, both remained ridiculously wealthy. Both were just forty-five years old. And they had an intellectual connection neither could understand nor fully sever.

It was Donovan who sent the first text, which quickly reignited the conversation that brought them to the snow-hammered brewpub in Boulder.

A black SUV had parked, illegally, just up the street from the brewpub. As Jackson watched, three men in black overcoats struggled to get out of it; they were fighting to keep the doors open and could barely stand against the wind.

"Well that's interesting," Jackson said, eyes frozen on the wintry tableau. "Apparently not everyone worries about parking tickets in Boulder during a massive snow dump."

"You always have played by the rules," Donovan said.

"I'm a boy from that heartland, that's for sure. Raised to praise Jesus, dot my i's and cross my t's and never ever park in front of a fire hydrant. Then again, the fire hydrants won't be visible in an hour."

"True that," Donovan said with a grin. He turned from the scene, put his beer down and surveyed the restaurant. Small, intimate, with a homey-rustic decor and a menu of locally sourced foods, it was perfectly Colorado. They'd tossed their coats on one of their table's empty chairs, both men remarking approvingly at the laid-back, hipster vibe. A twenty-something guy with a man bun and a full beard greeted the three black-overcoated men as they entered, stomping the snow from their feet, brushing it off their coats.

Donovan looked at Jackson. "Let's drill down into the robotics thing."

"Ugh. You want to start there? Really?"

"Give me your take."

"An abysmal failure. Horrible. And that's why I've spent so much time trying to understand why it blew up and distracting myself so I wouldn't understand."

"How'd that work out?"

"Not well. The distractions included tracing the ol' family tree back to the old country, which started a whole unrelated crisis. Also, I figured out that the robotics deal was a really really dumb idea from the start."

"Right. Acknowledged." Donovan said. "I mean, I'm not arguing with you. I know."

"You brought it up."

"Yes, yes I did. Because it's on me." Donovan's hand trembled as he took a drink. "I did bring the supposed investment potential to your attention."

Jackson held a hand up, palm out. "Water under the whatever."

"You mean that?"

"Yep. I paid a therapist a lot of money to help me work through that whole thing."

"And how did she or he do it?"

"She didn't. I drank a lot for about six weeks and then figured a few things out for myself. Such as the fact that we're both filthy rich."

Donovan allowed himself a laugh. "That's accurate. Yes. From where we both sit, a hundred-million-dollar fail was not mortal." He thought for a moment. "Cost me a marriage, too, as I recall."

"One you weren't all that keen on, as I recall."

"Ow," Donovan closed his eyes and clutched his chest as though he'd been shot. "You are nothing if not brutally honest this evening."

"If the shoe…"

"It most definitely does. Fit." Donovan allowed himself a faint smile. His marriage, to Mary Ashford Townsend, had been a paparazzi's' dream. Mary was the daughter of London theater royalty. Her mother, Maria Ashford, had been the toast of the West End in the late 1970s, appearing in a string of hits directed by Mary's father, Milford Townsend. Mary, an only child, was as beautiful as she was impossible; she'd left a wreckage of rock stars and at least one prince in her wake before hooking up with the equally spoiled offspring of the uber-wealthy Pip Reed and the source of that wealth, Edna Pollyworth Reed, she the heiress to the Pollyworth Fish fortune. Donovan Reed and Mary Townsend met at a rave in a London basement and woke up three days later in a Kensington Holiday Inn Express. At first, neither remembered the other's name but, eventually, as reality crept into view, both knew they'd had a good time, judging by the empty champagne bottles and traces of coke on the countertop next to the in-room coffee maker. Long story short, they had the kind of courtship that beautiful, wealthy, miserable young people have—short, lots of sex, lots of fights, alcohol, drugs, wrecked hotel rooms, court-mandated counseling—and were married in a seaside ceremony attended by a who's who of London's business and theater communities. Mary and Donovan fled their homeland for America (a Malibu mansion that had been in the Reed family since Pip's Great-Uncle Damian had won it from Charlie Chaplin in a ridiculously high stakes poker game) for the honeymoon and stayed. Mary used her family connections to land an agent and cameos in a string of low-budget romcoms before hitting it big in a Netflix dramedy, *Jody's Song*, about an anorexic British girl searching for her identity in an inner-city Los Angeles high school. Donovan parlayed his MBA from Oxford and unexpected knack for tech to fund a remarkably successful series of startups. They spent a lot of time apart, but it was Donovan's commitment to infidelity that killed the thing.

"Might I add that the marriage was not ended on the cheap."

"Double whammy for you, my friend. First, robots. Then, the ex."

Donovan sighed. "Look, we need to change the subject."

"Subtle segue," Jackson said. "But if you want to go down old robot road again, take a detour. That's over and done." He held up a hand. "All is forgiven. Actually, nothing to forgive. I'm a big boy. I make my own choices."

Donovan sighed. "Bravo. That's a relief." He leaned slightly to one side, reached into a pants pocket, pulled something out, and slid it across the table toward Jackson. A flash drive. "Because, actually, I have a new opportunity to discuss."

Jackson stared at the drive for several seconds, then at Donovan. "How about we go back to talking about your thing with women?"

"Oh this is better than women."

"But I thought you would never…"

"This is a first-rate idea, my friend." Donovan's face seemed to glow, his cheeks were flushed. Jackson had seen this happen before. It was the look Donovan Reed got when he was ready to jump into what Jackson had described to a business reporter once as "the big burning lake called 'risk.'"

Jackson stared at the drive. "Let me guess, it's a can't-miss…"

"…business opportunity," Donovan said.

Jackson groaned. Without thinking about it, without telling himself this was too much too soon, he picked up the device, reached for his coat, stuffed it in a pocket and shook his head. "I'm going to need another beer," he said.

Chapter Six

The three men from the black SUV had been standing at the host's desk, one of them talking intently to the bearded restaurant employee. The employee and the man scanned the dining room as his companions thumbed their phones. The guy in the overcoat made eye contact with Jackson. He smiled tersely, nodded a word of thanks to the bearded guy, and then muttered something to his companions. The two thumbers slipped their phones into pockets and looked toward Donovan and Jackson.

"Expecting company?" Donovan said.

Jackson followed his gaze. "Not that I'm aware of." He studied the three men. Two of them had the anonymous good looks of movie-actor FBI agents. The third, the one that seemed to be the leader, looked, like "John Lennon," Donovan said aloud.

Jackson laughed. "You got that right. Weird look for a dude in a suit." He pulled his phone out of his pocket and, when the three weren't looking his way, snapped the guy's picture. He looked at the result on his screen and shook his head, showed it to Donovan. "Uncanny."

The guy who looked like Lennon said something to the other two and nodded over the top of his wire-rimmed glasses in the direction of Jackson and Donovan. He turned, pushed open the door, and stepped outside, his longish hair going wild in the wind.

The FBI types wound their way to Jackson and Donovan's table and stood for a moment, melted snow glistening on their crewcuts. They attempted to ooze some level of gravitas, neither pulling it off.

"I love your friend's White album," Donovan said. Jackson snorted a laugh. Neither of the other men laughed. One guy said, "I am Inspector Clive Bunker and this is Inspector Owen; we're with the special crimes division of the Treasury Department's western district. I need you to come with us."

"Who?" Jackson said.

"Me?" Donovan said.

"Him?" Jackson said.

"Or both?" they said in unison and smiled at each other.

The men frowned nearly identical frowns.

Other diners had stopped dining. Heads had turned. A phone or two popped up. One flashed—a viral opportunity not missed. Bunker and Owen were nervous.

"I'm going to have to see some ID here, my good sir," Donovan said, flashing an apologetic smile. "Just like in the movies."

From the pocket of his overcoat, the one calling himself Bunker retrieved a wallet, flipped it open, gave a glimpse of a badge, flipped the wallet shut, fumbled it, dropped it on the floor, picked it up, and—red-faced—shoved it back into his pocket.

"Let's go," Owen said, glancing nervously over his shoulder toward the door. "We need to move out."

"C'mon," Bunker said, grabbing Donovan by an arm and nodding toward the door. To Jackson he said, "You sit tight. We just want to ask your boyfriend here a couple of questions."

"Having to do with what?" Donovan said as he stood. The other guy, Owen, grabbed Jackson's coat off the chair.

"You might want to put this on. It's chilly," Owen said with a laugh.

"That's not my coat," Donovan said.

Owen threw down the coat, grabbed the right one, and handed it to Donovan, Jackson watching it all, mouth agape.

"What is this about?" Donovan said. He looked at Owen and then at Bunker. Nothing.

Donovan paused, thought for a moment, his face suddenly paler. "Oh shit," he said. "Are you sure you want, like, me?" He glanced at Jackson.

Owen looked at Bunker. Bunker looked out the window. The guy who looked like John Lennon was getting out of the SUV, closing his coat against the wind, coming toward the restaurant.

"Shut up," Bunker said. He forced Donovan into his coat, grabbed him by the arm and started leading him toward the door. Owen followed, the three of them snaking through the tables and the murmuring, nudging customers. People rose and aimed their phones.

"Cover his face," Bunker said.

Owen unwound a long black scarf from his own neck and wrapped it around Donovan's head. They reached the door. Donovan Reed, his voice now muffled by the scarf, said something about "bitches."

The guy who looked like John Lennon yanked open the door from the outside.

The men headed out into the storm.

Jackson knew Donovan was no choirboy. It was one of the things that drew Jackson to him. While Jackson was known as the one guy in Silicon Valley who kept his nose to the desktop, working hard at building a tech empire on a foundation of sometimes risky but never shady deals, Donovan loved riding the razor edge between doing things the right way and the murky abyss that is corporate law breaking.

The disaster of their investment in the Canadian companies had been thoroughly vetted by the appropriate agencies in both countries. Federal agencies stuck a flashlight into the dark maw of Donovan's and Jackson's partnership. Stones were turned. A forest's worth of paper was inked, read, analyzed, reviewed, and exchanged. The deposable were deposed. Accountants were held to account. And, in the end, their combined empire was declared, miraculously, sound. The only things broken were the pride and reputation of two of tech's golden boys and, temporarily it appeared, the relationship between the two of them.

All of this, together, made the incident at the brewpub more distressing than driving a rented Tesla up a two-lane mountain road in a snowstorm. And it occupied a much-needed portion of Jackson's thoughts as he careened along, visibility near zero, the edge of the mountain road a guardrail somewhere inches to his right.

By the time he guided the car up the treacherous driveway and safely into his borrowed home's pleasantly heated garage, he had reached some conclusions: Donovan's captors obviously weren't law enforcement; he needed to figure out who they were without rousing a lot of public attention (they'd had enough public attention). He needed discreet, powerful help now.

Also, Teslas sucked in snow.

Chapter Seven

Donovan Reed sat in a crooked kitchen chair at a weary table in a wheezy old house that smelled like incontinent cats, faced the obviously-not-federal-agents who had taken him into fake custody, and figured he was in a certain—perhaps a relatively high—level of danger. Two of the men, Bunker and Owen, sat across the table from him. They seemed, to Donovan, lost and a little embarrassed. Bunker fondled a plastic saltshaker that looked like a miniature, time-bitten golden retriever and shot furtive glances past Donovan, avoiding eye contact; he seemed preoccupied with whatever the shadows hid in the house beyond the kitchen. Owen, meanwhile, was in serious contemplation of a bowl of surprisingly fresh-looking fruit.

The storm pounded the house despite the windows' screams for it to stop. The trip from the restaurant, during which Donovan's head had been wrapped in a knit scarf, had taken hours. The men had spent the trip in silence. When they'd arrived, one of the "agents" had immediately turned up the thermostat, but the furnace wasn't keeping up with the need. Each of the kidnappers had started to take off his black overcoat but had decided, with nearly identical grimaces, to leave it on.

Donovan still wore his coat. His head was sweaty but cooling rapidly.

"Mr. Not Lennon" as Donovan had come to think of him, had not spoken. He had the air of a serious man, a sophisticated one. The guy had just finished eating a peach. He tossed the pit into the kitchen sink; it clinked against the porcelain. He turned on a faucet. The plumbing coughed, belched, and whined before discharging a trickle of brown liquid. Mr. Not Lennon's nose wrinkled. He twisted the faucet off, turned— hands in the air, disdain staining his face—and wiped his hands carefully on the black overcoat.

Mr. Not Lennon pulled something from his pocket. "Put your hands behind your back," he said, "then turn so I can get at them." Despite the gravity of the situation, Donovan smiled in disappointment. The guy spoke without a hint of Brit in his voice; he was disappointingly American.

"I said, hands behind your back," the guy repeated, his vowels more Illinois than London.

Donovan, hesitant but realistic, complied. The guy cinched his wrists; thin plastic dug into his skin. Donovan swallowed a complaint. Mr. Not Lennon grabbed him by the shoulders and twisted Donovan back into a normal sitting position, pulled out his phone, and snapped a photo of Donovan's face.

"Why do that?" It was Bunker, talking to the saltshaker. "Seems dumb."

Mr. Not-Lennon said, "We have our protocols to adhere to here. And I am hired to follow them." He spoke in the measured tones of a man trying vainly to use his superior status and breeding to cover the fact that he was about to lose his shit at the imbeciles with whom he worked.

Bunker frowned and shrugged. "I was just saying there's no need to tie him up. We're in the middle of nowhere. And there's a blizzard. Plus," he patted his coat, gave the saltshaker a half-assed smile, and said, "guns."

Donovan mentally urged himself to proceed with caution, but his mouth had a way of operating independently of the control center of his brain, particularly when he was anxious and/or off his meds for being anxious, which—yes.

"Who the hell are you?" He aimed the question at Owen, then repeated it to Bunker.

When no answer came, his anxiety escalated. "WHAT IS THIS ABOUT? I DID WHAT WAS ASKED OF ME."

The house whined. The room held its breath.

"Okay fine. Whatever. Play your game," Donovan said. He looked at Mr. Not Lennon. "You look like the hippie John Lennon, by the way, not the mop top one. One might even assume you're attempting to look more like him than you naturally do. It's as though you're wearing a disguise, which is odd because you're not. You already look like the man you're trying to look like. The effect, I must say, is stunning and completely disorienting."

"Hey, listen, bruh." It was Bunker. "Look at me." Donovan looked. Bunker was wearing sunglasses. Donovan hadn't recalled him putting them on. "You want to maybe back off here? Lennon was all 'peace-y and love-y.' My friend here," he nodded at the leader fake agent, "he's not coming in the name of peace. None of us are. We mean business." Bunker glanced at his boss and then leaned toward Donovan. "You understand what I'm telling you?"

"No. I have no idea what you're telling me." He shifted his gaze to the other guy, Owen, who was now nervously eating a plum. Purple juice spoiled the clean perfection of his cleft chin. Both of these men would be on his short list for any number of good-looking dumb guys in a supporting role. "I understand nothing. If you're working for who I think you're working for, then you hoped to be talking to my friend Jackson. Otherwise, I am completely at a loss. I…" He stopped himself. Thought for a moment and felt a familiar dread. "Unless you're not working for who I think you're working for." He swallowed. "In which case, you could be any number of wretched people."

Bunker said, "If we're going to be stuck here in the middle of God's country in the middle of a blizzard, I'm gonna find a sock for that mouth." He started to rise from his chair.

"Sit." Mr. Not Lennon said.

Bunker sat.

"You mentioned this 'Jackson.' I'm curious about that," Mr. Not Lennon said.

"Yeah, Jackson Nguyen. The guy who was with me."

"He's of Vietnamese origin, I believe," Mr. Not Lennon said.

Owen, who'd apparently eaten his last piece of fruit for now, let out a sigh and studied nothing intently on the dirty linoleum. Mr. Not Lennon looked at him. He waited.

"Bunker grabbed this guy," Owen said, raising his head, avoiding Bunker's mirrored gaze. "This dude doesn't even look Oriental or whatever. And he sounds fucking British."

Bunker made a noise that had nowhere to go.

Mr. Not-Lennon cleared his throat. "Yes, he probably sounds fucking British because he is. Fucking British." He stared over his glasses at Bunker then Owen. Both men avoided his gaze.

Heads up, chins jutted, Owen and Bunker appeared to nod but neither one seemed to mean it.

The guy who looked like John Lennon pulled from an inside pocket of his coat some kind of handgun. He began screwing into the barrel what Donovan recognized from movies and television as a silencing device. Donovan's heart tripped and tumbled down the stairs in his chest.

The guy finished with the silencer and looked at Donovan. "I have a proposition for you," Mr. Not-Lennon said, gesturing with the now stupidly long weapon. "I will tell you my name— it's Jasper Joyce—and you will tell me yours."

Donovan Reed thought about this. "That doesn't sound like much of a proposition. I mean, in general, a proposition is a situation in which one party makes a proffer and then…"

"Let me guess, you're that asshole billionaire friend of Jackson Nguyen's, Donovan Reed," Jasper Joyce said through gritted teeth. He clicked something on the gun. "Am I right?"

Donovan nodded.

The first shot was a scalding sonic slap. By the time it registered as gunfire, the second shot had come, both of Jasper Joyce's accomplices were dead, and Donovan couldn't stop screaming.

Several miles from his business partner's hell, Jackson hurried through the expansive mountain home he'd borrowed for the night, snapping on lights and getting a feel for the layout. He found the thermostat and kicked it up to seventy-two, dropped his luggage in the master bedroom, relieved himself in the ensuite bathroom, washed his hands and face, and dried them on a thick towel that smelled faintly of lilacs and mountain air. Then he trotted downstairs, MacBook Pro under an arm. In the kitchen, he chose a bottle of Stranahan's and a glass tumbler from the liquor cabinet, scooped ice from the freezer, two cubes, dropped them in the tumbler, poured three fingers of the Stranny's over the ice, pounded the stopper home, and took the computer, drink, and bottle into the cavernous, open-concept living-dining area. He carefully placed the whiskey bottle and glass on a gleaming wood coffee table that squatted in front of a black leather couch, dropped the MacBook Pro on the couch, then pulled his iPhone from a pocket of his jeans and tossed it next to the MacBook.

Jackson found a box of long matches on the oak mantle over the stone fireplace and used it to ignite the kindling and logs already awaiting their fate on the inner hearth. He allowed himself a tiny smile as he remembered to open the damper, a vital step impressed on him by smoky memories from his Michigan childhood.

Finally, whiskey in hand, the cubes clinking softly, with his socked feet resting on the coffee table, the laptop on his lap, and the tumbler of Stranny's teetering precariously on the couch next to him, he signed onto his VPN.

He was confident his search would bear fruit. He'd invested heavily in the startup that developed FacePlant, the platform that now dominated the face-recognition software industry. "Faceplanting" was so reliable, it had become shorthand for any face-facilitated image search.

Jackson clicked on the FacePlant dashboard and opened his browser. He began with the Treasury Department's website. As expected, there was no one who looked anything like John Lennon. There was no Clive Bunker. No Inspector Owen.

No surprise.

He uploaded to FacePlant the photo he'd taken of the Lennon lookalike, On a whim, he ran a broad scan of the Internet, casting a wide net in case he got lucky. He half expected the software to return photos of John Lennon; he was mildly excited when it didn't—a win for the updated FacePlant algorithm. That the search returned no other matches was surprising; it meant the men who'd taken Donovan were off the grid—not part of law enforcement, not on social media. They were cyber ghosts.

The evening lurched forward, the storm intensifying, Jackson oblivious as he cyber-walked across the dark web. He'd been there before, on similar searches, nerding out by testing the practicality of FacePlant and its various iterations. He skirted the slums—the sites where people and drugs and the most shocking of human behavior were for sale. He zeroed in on the espionage marketplace, the paramilitary and weapons chat rooms—the places where you could hire someone to manage your civil insurrection and/or get rid of problems, enemies, and loser guys who were beating your sister. His gut told him the men who took Donovan Reed would be lurking here. Or in the swampy vicinity.

He got some possibilities; they were men who the app indicated had Plausible Parallel Facial Characteristics (PPFCs). Through his own logic—eliminating the men who, evidence suggested, were dead, imprisoned or no longer in the mood to commit anarchy—Jackson narrowed the search, and then ran a second, deeper analysis of the database that contained the photos of the remaining men with PPFCs.

He got a hit. And then another. And another. All the same guy: a navy SEAL who'd taken a hard turn after leaving the service and was now a mercenary. Scotland Yard, Interpol, the Mossad, the FBI, and the county sheriff in Peru, Indiana all had unkind words about him. He was suspected in the murder of a politician in London, the kidnapping of a French aristocrat, the organization of an uprising on the West Bank, and a cyberattack at a New York investment firm. The Indiana thing involved the theft of two fighter jets from an air force base. Jackson could find no links to any of the legitimate military companies. Nor could he find a name. The guy lived in the lone wolf world—solo ops.

Jackson ended his search. He poured another finger of whiskey. The storm was still a low-groaning monster heaving against the lodge. He was stymied, trapped between what he knew and not knowing what he didn't know. If Donovan had done something illegal or quasi-illegal; if he'd, say, cheated some wealthy guy in Mozambique out of a few hundred thousand meticais and now the Mozambique guy was seeking revenge; contacting law enforcement seemed risky. As did not contacting law enforcement. And what of the people in the restaurant or the man-bunned maître d'? Would one of them post a pic of the confrontation in the restaurant? Had they been recognized?

To allay some of his fears, Jackson Google-searched his name and Donovan's. There were no new stories or images. Just the same old same old.

The decision to jump to the Silver Eagle website was almost involuntary. For someone in Jackson's world, someone in his income bracket and status, Silver Eagle was the go-to source for bodyguards, event security, and discreet, world-class help in times of indelicate trouble. The company had grown up where he'd grown up—West Michigan. The owners, the Hoeksma family, had a long and colorful resume, to put it mildly. Years of shady shenanigans in business had led to the mess with Wisconsin, when crazy old William Hoeksma Sr. died and his son, the governor, was run out of office. Even so, Silver Eagle was now a global brand name with a reputation for getting a lot of dirty work done. If you needed a war wrapped up, you called Silver Eagle. If you wanted a political movement crushed, you called Silver Eagle. If your famous friend with a dicey reputation was missing or murdered or worse—Silver Eagle. Jackson knew this. Everyone knew this.

It was the perfect place to start.

He wrote a short, encrypted email via the Silver Eagle site, and felt a surge of relief and worry in his gut when he hit "send."

Finally, he closed the Mac. He listened for several minutes to the wind and felt the rush and crushing disappointment that came with a colossal snow—he couldn't go anywhere. He finished the last of his pour, pulled an afghan from the back of the couch and stretched out, facing the fire.

Jackson drifted to sleep. Deep in the storm, he thought he heard the voice of Brent Stevens, which became the voice of John Lennon.

PART THREE

Commander Bill
and The Little Pink Gun

Chapter Eight

Carpville, South Carolina

Tuesday afternoon

Commander Bill Hoeksma walked in with a smile he didn't mean, and the meeting went downhill from there.

He stood, sauntered to the bulletproof-glassed windows of the conference room he'd named Freedom's Blood, and tried not to think about how he'd come to be stuck in yet another late-afternoon meeting.

His dad was five years dead. The events that led to his death and cost Bill the governorship of Michigan had, just as the late Will Hoeksma hoped, launched Silver Eagle into the private military and security stratosphere. The company provided enhanced (heavily armed) corporate security and bodyguarded the dangerous and important. It tracked down runaway drug lords, killers, illegal immigrant hordes, and the kidnapped wealthy. Silver Eagle was also in demand for minor and major military operations across the globe: a civil insurrection here, a targeted drone strike there, weapons manufacturing and distribution to a half dozen small wars there and there. And there. Silver Eagle personnel trained and equipped soldiers, snipers, rebel groups, cyber warriors, and homegrown militia members. Silver Eagle-branded weapons and ammunition were in the sweating hands of desert commandos and in the kitchen drawers of soccer moms. Silver Eagle contact information swirled in the data river flowing through the smartphones of CEOs, Directors of National Intelligence, Third World insurrectionists, and thousands of bunker-building doomsday preppers.

Beyond Commander Bill's window, the Silver Eagle compound bristled across 4,500 acres of rural South Carolina, near Carpville, encompassing military training ranges and facilities that rivaled those of most small countries. There were three airstrips and a helipad, four nondescript barracks with capacity for 500 personnel, a rustic but comfortable lodge that housed up to 200 guests, a dining hall that was a small-scale replica of the Pentagon, and enough still-forested space to train small armies for every sort of combat or clandestine op. Five hangars housed a fleet of planes, drones, choppers, armored personnel carriers, and Humvees. Three one-story classroom buildings, sided in battleship-grade steel and painted blood red, marked the compound's perimeter, which was wrapped in a security blanket of cyclone fencing topped with razor wire.

At the beating heart of the base were the five stories (three above ground, two below) of the windowless William Hoeksma Memorial headquarters building. The meeting in which Commander Bill now stewed was on the first floor. Known as The Will, the company's headquarters had blast-proof walls "that rise like an obsidian apparition out of what was once a rolling meadow," according to Silver Eagle recruiting materials. The conference rooms—there were six—were decorated in standard American corporate dull, a nod to the frugality of the Hoeksma family and the great deals Bill's siblings cut with an old family friend in the office furniture industry.

When Silver Eagle first began stripping away old-growth forest and fertile farmland for its Carpville hub, locals, skeptical by nature were, naturally, skeptical. But when word got out about the company's purpose and leadership, things changed. Bill Hoeksma, the former "Gunvernor" of Michigan, was a conservative-folk hero, and his company—with its support-staff job opportunities, commitment to second amendment ideals, and role in "kicking the asses of the world's scumlords," a phrase in the first draft of the employee guidebook that was deleted in the final version in the favor of "battling for freedom's reign"—quickly became an object of local pride.

Of the locals who worked there, the majority handled maintenance, dining hall, and lodging duties. Two dozen of them worked in clerical and support inside The Will's walls; these "A-CIVs" (Authorized Civilians) were bound by ominously worded non-disclosure agreements that prohibited them from revealing almost everything they did during the day. This gave them tremendous street cred in the local community; there was a Silver Eagle A-CIV dating site. Not being able to tell what you did inside the Will, it turned out, made you "a little hot."

Commander Bill had little to do with the company's success, which was exactly what was expected of him. In the wake of Operation Cheesus, his hard-driving siblings, Mel and Bev—the financial managers who'd helped build both of their father's companies—made Bill the public face of Silver Eagle because he had a nice face. And because his role in the scandal gave him marketing cachet.

From childhood, Bill made up for being lazy by being apathetic about his life's direction. His assets; good looks, weird charisma, and uncanny knack for avoiding uncomfortable truths; served him well in his role as Silver Eagle CEO. It also helped that he loved guns.

In speeches and interviews, all written and carefully orchestrated by Silver Eagle's communications team, he talked in vague but heartfelt terms about how he'd been the victim in the Cheesus scandal. He painted a stained-glass picture of his new life in South Carolina, focusing on the church he wasn't active in; the wonderful relationship he had with his wife, Marcia, who barely spoke to him; the admiration he shared with his two lovable kids, twelve-year-old Amelia and ten-year-old William III, who were fighting a legal battle to emancipate themselves; and his amazing weapons collection. The speechwriters made him an evangelist of hyper-Christian-military gospel in which central governments and nation-state armies were so last millennium. Silver Eagle, he proclaimed, was not of this world; it was of "an exciting new world where justice and security were available to all decent, God-fearing people at a reasonable price." Commander Bill believed everything he said even though he hadn't listened to himself in at least two years.

The meeting droned on at the table behind him. Commander Bill tried to ignore it; it wasn't easy. This job, his job, was hard. A reporter from the BBC named Peg something had called him on his way to work that morning to ask a few questions about Silver Eagle's involvement in the overthrow of the government in Burundi, and Commander Bill had said "no comment," partly because he didn't know anything about Burundi but mostly because he just didn't want to be in charge of whatever was happening there. Also, he didn't understand Peg something because of her accent.

Commander Bill yearned to be in politics again. In politics, granted, you couldn't trust anybody and there were people ready to stab you in the back every day. But in Silver Eagle's business, the knives were real. As a politician with the right base of support, if you made a few speeches, raised money, and did what your (trusted) advisors said, well, you could skate along for years, comfortable, apparently successful, and really good at golf. He knew he'd never be a governor again. And that was fine. A U.S. congressman or senator—those seemed like easier gigs, truth be told. As the meeting continued—blah blah blah—Commander Bill imagined himself in Washington DC, leading the fight to preserve the Second Amendment. Eating a good steak. Going on conservative news shows and talk shows. Golfing.

Politics did get complicated at times, such as when you shot a woman in your office. After Commander Bill shot FBI agent Babsy Witt, he testified that his state police commander, his dead dad's good old buddy Wilbur Tuttle, had done it. Tuttle agreed to take the fall for the crime in exchange for "a piece of the action" at Silver Eagle. Now Tuttle was Commander Bill's second in command, which meant he was pretty much in charge of Silver Eagle. In fact, he sat right next to Commander Bill in every godforsaken meeting. This was fine but it wasn't easy working with a crazy old guy who'd done hard time for something he, Bill Hoeksma Jr., had done.

He sighed, turned from the window, and returned to the chair next to Tuttle just as his phone buzz-walked across the conference room table. He stopped it with a hand.

A text: "There's something very important we need to talk about. Tuttle. Also, that bitch, Miky. WTF. She's been talking about us. Tuttle."

Tuttle was constantly talking about getting revenge on the militia woman who'd stopped Operation Cheesus. Commander Bill had heard she was in Colorado. She was drop-dead pretty. Nice body, too, as he recalled.

The phone buzzed again. Another text.

"I've got an op started. Dealing with Spike. Also, don't forget. Something even bigger to discuss. Tuttle."

Commander Bill thought about skiing in Colorado. It was snowing there—strange for May. He turned to say something to Tuttle, who was just inches away, texting like a fiend. But Commander Bill's gaze was again drawn to the window. A row of palm trees that bordered the Silver Eagle parking lot were bending dramatically like tormented brooms whisking the grayed-out sky. Debris—Styrofoam cups, fast-food wrappers, plastic water bottles—skittered, lunged, tumbled, and chased one another, set free from an overturned trash can. Commander Bill thought he saw a chicken fly by, but quickly decided it was some kind of children's toy. Or something. A woman he didn't know leaned into the zephyr. She was trying gamely to carry a briefcase and hold the flap of her skirt closed.

His phone buzzed. Another Tuttle text: "Don't worry about weather. Least of your concerns right now. Tuttle."

Wildfires were burning uncontrollably in the low country and a very-early season hurricane boiled off the coast. The national media were calling the situation in his adopted state "Stormageddon." Commander Bill smiled and shook his head. He'd done a ten-minute appearance on a radio show the day before in which he called the media coverage "overhyped garbage." This description, his communications team reported, had generated thousands of clicks on social media and had been featured heavily in the chyron crawls of at least two twenty-four-hour news channels. What made it even better was, in this case, Commander Bill believed his words. They'd had a record-setting hot period in April after a record dry spell in the winter. Then lightning had come along, like lightning does, and lit up the dried-out forests. Now the fires had killed a few people dumb enough to build their zillion dollar homes in places that were at risk. It was a tragedy, yes. But it also was an act of God, not of man. As far as the incoming storm was concerned, he rationalized, with sweating palms, that they were in for a pretty good blow, but nothing like the Cat Five craziness the talking heads were describing.

His greatest concern was that, before the meeting ended, one of his goody-two-shoes administrators—likely Skip Donaldson, Vice President/Gun Outreach and Children's Ambassador, who was in charge of Silver Eagle's community program that supplied resources and protection programs for elementary schools—would bring up again that The Will was built to withstand a category five hurricane and that it would be good public relations to offer the building to local families in advance of the storm.

The local government had already sent emissaries: the town's emergency preparedness director/fire chief, two city councilpersons and the mayor. Commander Bill had met with them and politely assured them that there was no need for alarm, that local residents would be safer to shelter in place and that, besides, Silver Eagle's headquarters really didn't have the space necessary for housing large numbers of frightened South Carolinians.

Of course they had the space. He just couldn't allow everyday people to wander around The Will. The place was a reinforced box of secrets. Some mullet-wearing tobacco farmer wasn't going to stumble into a PowerPoint presentation on waterboarding. His dad would call that a major fuckup. Commander Bill hated hearing him say that, even in his head.

Besides, he figured the storm would blow down a few leaves and set a few skirts flapping. Probably douse the fires. Managing an evacuation sounded like one big headache.

Chapter Nine

Commander Bill picked up a small pink pistol from the conference room table and held it in a two-fisted grip.

That got them to stop talking.

"This bad boy does not do much for my macho image now, does it?" he said. The men around the table laughed. All of them, except Tuttle, were White, barrel-chested thirty-somethings with tree-trunk-sized biceps and the glint of football and military glory in their close-set eyes. They wore the standard Silver Eagle office uniform: khakis and company-issued blood-red polo shirts with the Silver Eagle Security logo—a silver eagle clutching the bible (KJV for "King James Version" on the tiny spine in tiny gold print) in its left talons and an AR15 rifle in its right—over the left breast.

"Hey, Larrrrrry, don't flinch." Commander Bill squinted, aimed, and pulled the pink gun's pink trigger. The gun made a "plink" sound.

Marty Fichter, Chief Product Officer/New Markets, flinched and doubled over, both hands over his logo. A bright-yellow pellet caromed off him and then off the table. "It's Marty, sir," Fichter said.

Skip Donaldson rolled his chair across the floor, retrieved the pellet, and rolled back. He studied the pellet in his palm. Fichter, still holding his hands over the spot where the projectile had hit him, softly banged his forehead on the table. "Shit, shit, shit," he said.

"Watch the language, my man," Commander Bill said, "or someone's going to be putting a little somethin' in the swear jar."

Donaldson held the pellet aloft between a forefinger and thumb. "No blood, no foul," Donaldson said. The room exploded in laughter. Even Tuttle smiled.

Fichter managed a half grimace. He straightened and sat back in his chair with a groan. Donaldson dropped the pellet on the table and flicked it toward Fichter. Fichter picked it up. He managed a smile. "Little bastard," he said. Everyone on the team except Tuttle applauded.

When the men had quieted, Commander Bill asked Fichter to stand and raise his shirt. The big man complied, revealing a muscular, hairless torso with an angry red welt on his left breast. Fichter tucked in his chin and looked down to consider the damage. He raised his eyes to look at Commander Bill. "You gave me a new nipple, sir." More laughter. Commander Bill blushed.

Fichter lowered his shirt and sat down. There was an uncomfortable pause as the men waited for Commander Bill to say something, but Commander Bill had nothing to say.

"You caught us a bit off guard there, sir. But it's all good," Donaldson finally said with a forced laugh. He stood, glanced, picked up a remote-control device from the table and pressed a button. The lights dimmed. Donaldson pressed another button, and the video monitor that covered one wall came to life.

"I can never get that gosh-darned remote to work," Commander Bill said, "I was in here last week, trying to get the Golf Channel, and got nothing."

Donaldson smiled. He walked to a position to the right of the screen. "That remote takes hours of highly classified training, sir." An obligatory chuckle rippled through the room. "Now then…"

"Threat check," Commander Bill said. He leaped to his feet and pulled his weapon, a 9mm Sig Sauer, from a shoulder holster; Commander Bill held it in the air, flipped the safety, and chambered a round. In a heartbeat, every man at the table responded in kind. Donaldson, his 9mm, a Glock, in his right hand, pointed at the ceiling, stood next to the video screen, the gosh-darned remote now on the floor.

Nobody moved.

"Nobody move," Commander Bill said solemnly, only his eyes and heaving chest disobeying the order.

They held their positions. The Silver Eagle men counted the seconds in their heads. At twenty-one, in unison, they relaxed, unchambered rounds, flipped safeties on, and secured weapons in shoulder holsters. Still sternly surveying the room, Commander Bill lowered his own weapon. Eyes swiveling from one man to the next, he tried to unchamber the round without looking at the weapon, and nearly dropped it. Two of the men, Dustin "One Eye" Bellows and Travis "Hopalong" Andrews, both of whom had been wounded during murky training incidents involving Commander Bill, flinched.

"Oh, the devil with it," Commander Bill said. He looked down at the Sig Sauer and, with shaking hands, unchambered, struggled to grasp the flap of the holster, tried to insert the weapon, missed, almost dropped it again, and then—his face now Silver Eagle red—jammed the weapon in place. He snapped the holster, straightened it and quickly tried to portray the air of someone in supreme control. "Well done. Good response, then. Yes. Definitely good. Good good." He sniffed, hitched his belt, and looked at Donaldson. "Don?"

"Donaldson, sir."

"Yes, yes. Of course." Commander Bill retrieved his chair, sat, gripped the edge of the table and pulled himself closer. Chin up, eyes on the yellow Post-It note pad in front of him, he paused as though thinking of something, uncapped a pen, looked at the note sternly, thought of nothing, and so scribbled "Benghazi" on the top Post-It, then savagely underlined it twice. "Carry on," he said, his glare shifting from the Post-It to Donaldson. "But tell you what, let's skip the video entertainment for now. Let's just…" Commander Bill looked at the Post-It with pursed lips, then back at Donaldson. With a dismissive gesture, he said, "Let's, you know, move on. Forward. To the other."

Donaldson released a barely perceptible sigh. He used the remote to turn off the screen and raise the room lights, picked up a blood-red marker, and wrote across the top of a whiteboard, "Yellow Dotz." He capped the pen, turned to the other men and shot an is-this-what-you-want glance at Commander Bill. Commander Bill nodded.

"Well then," Donaldson said, "it would appear that our Yellow Dotz are plenty effective at halting a shooter's forward progress." There were nods of agreement around the room. He turned, uncapped, squiggled "Halt forward progress" as a bullet point, and then looked over his shoulder at Fichter. "Wouldn't you agree, Fichter? Was your forward progress stopped just now?"

Fichter managed a grim smile. He couldn't move his left arm; the pain radiated from the throbbing point of contact, through his shoulder and down his arm. He could barely breathe and would later tell his wife, Jen, who was an ex-Marine turned urgent care nurse, "that sucker hurt like a sonofabitch." Jen, an expert, would agree that it likely warranted sonofabitch status. But now Fichter simply said, with considerable effort at sounding fine, "I would say forward progress stopped." The other men chuckled.

"We also know this particular iteration of Yellow Dotz checks off the rest of our boxes," Donaldson called out the remaining bullet points as he wrote them: "Delivers max pain, check. Non-fatal. Check. Visually positive for max appeal to elementary demo, check."

"What are those little dots there on the board, bullets?" Commander Bill said. "Are you writing red bullets about Yellow Dotz, which are a kind of bullet. Is that it?"

Donaldson stood, expressionless as Commander Bill pounded the table and the men joined him in another round of unfelt laughter.

"Sorry, just trying to keep things light," Commander Bill said.

Donaldson looked at the men around the table. With a taut smile, he said, "Any thoughts at this point?"

Rex VanTuren raised a meaty hand. He was Silver Eagle's Public Affairs Liaison for Children's Media. He had crewcut strawberry-blond hair, black-rimmed glasses, and a tiny, wrinkled voice that seemed to come from someone else. In Afghanistan, VanTuren had killed three men with a fork when they'd ambushed him at a café. Back in the U.S., recruited by Silver Eagle, he'd earned a Master's in Marketing from Cornell to supplement his skills as a field-level paramilitary technician. His voice, the result of a childhood run-in with a hockey puck, always made Commander Bill smile. He smiled now.

"Rex?" Donaldson said.

"This could be a huge win, marketing wise," VanTuren said. "I mean a yellow bullet in a pink or blue gun; it shouts 'kids eight to ten years.' I just think we've hit the sweet spot here. Am I right? I mean, I'd love to see them in a back-to-school two-pack."

"Anyone got something to say to that?" Commander Bill said, trying his best to imitate VanTuren. VanTuren's face went crimson.

"J-K, my man," Commander Bill said in his normal voice. He held up a palm, face out. "I kid because I love." To Donaldson he said, "What do you say, Skip? We got two-pack potential, here?"

Donaldson closed his eyes, took a deep breath, and tried to calm himself. "Let's put a pin in that situation now. We'll circle back to our various marketing channels and the competitive issues tomorrow." He paused, looked at VanTuren. "I will say this about the gun and this particular projectile. They are a great combo. As you know, we focus-grouped it and kids, teachers, moms and dads, they're all netting out very positive. We had a little pushback from the teachers. But to be expected. A lot of liberal handwringing about "weaponizing students" and such. As I said, though, we're overall good. Good good."

"Good," Commander Bill said. "But why don't we cover that in tomorrow's meeting? Let's not waste our time on it today."

Despite Commander Bill's attempt to hurry things along, the meeting dragged along for another ninety minutes, Donaldson explaining to the rest of Silver Eagles brain-and-muscle trust in painfully tedious detail the steps taken by Silver Eagle's manufacturing subsidiary, AmericoWeapons, to develop and produce first the pistol and then Yellow Dotz. It had taken two years and nearly two million dollars, Donaldson said. As if Commander Bill needed to be reminded.

It was Tuttle who'd gotten him to spend all that money. He'd come to him, fresh from prison, and presented Commander Bill with the idea of arming grade school kids. It had been at a dinner meeting. Tuttle had brought in Donaldson, an Army Ranger turned bail bondsman turned weapons consultant. Tuttle and Donaldson painted a pretty rosy picture, sitting there in a small private dining room at one of Charleston's better steakhouses. Commander Bill had thought Tuttle and his guest were going to talk cyber security. But as it turned out, Tuttle and the tough-looking, then-bearded Donaldson had other plans. One minute they were sipping a nice California Zin after polishing off perfectly aged thirty-two-ounce Porterhouses, the next they were pitching him on selling Silver Eagle-brand weapons to children.

"Hey, with all the school shootings, someone's going to think of arming kids. This is a market ripe for investment, and that investment might as well come from us." Tuttle had used that word, "ripe" which made Commander Bill think of a naked woman every time he heard it, which he thought was sinful, which made him avoid using "ripe" in most of his conversations but, truth was, that word was exactly why he returned to the mental image of this particular conversation so often.

"Other companies are out there with kiddie armored vests and so on—a lot of passive shit," Donaldson said, that big beard of his making him look dangerously earnest, those dark eyes getting small, his voice rising. "The way we see it, these are our most-precious citizens. Shouldn't we give our most-precious citizens the means to save their own lives?"

Commander Bill squinted at Tuttle. "You mean, like, shoot people? The kids themselves, like, have them confront the bad guy and kill him?"

Tuttle and Donaldson exchanged glances. "We prefer the term 'actively subdue,'" Tuttle said.

Donaldson smiled. "Yes, exactly. This doesn't have to involve termination of the attacker."

"It doesn't have to. No," Tuttle said.

"If it happens…" Donaldson said, his hands in the air, palms up.

"So be it," Tuttle and Donaldson said in unison.

They paused. Commander Bill frowned. He imagined kids in school with big guns in their hands, the guns too heavy and going all wobbly as the kids tried to aim them at some guy in a black hoodie coming at them with an AR-15.

"Sir, we think it's high time someone gave these kids the chance to do something every man, woman and, yes, child is entitled to do when faced with a mortal threat," Tuttle said.

"Something a little more substantive than, say, hiding in a closet," Donaldson said. He and Tuttle laughed.

"Right," Tuttle said. "We want all the kids out of the closet." The two men laughed again. "I mean, rather than hiding behind some lame-ass teacher's skirt like a bunch of babies, what if we gave these kids a shot at doing some damage; maybe pop some lowlife's eyes out?"

Commander Bill frowned. "Could they pop an eye out?"

"Perhaps," Donaldson said, clearing relishing the possibility.

Commander Bill took a serious sip of wine. "I've got a lot of questions here," he said.

"Shoot," Tuttle said. He and Donaldson grinned.

"First off, there's got to be some liability. I mean, we arm kids, and things go south, someone's going to sue us, right?"

"Actually, no," Donaldson said. "Any liability, we've been assured, is the purchaser's. Worst case, we sell some parents a gun for little Susie and whatever happens, all the responsibility is on those parents."

"We'll put it into the sales agreement," Tuttle said. "Fine print."

"Very fine print," Donaldson said.

"The finest," Tuttle said.

Governor Bill lifted his wine glass again, started to take a sip, stopped, the glass inches from his lips. "Not sure I buy that. My dad always warned about liability stuff."

"He also knew the value of taking a risk," Tuttle said, his face suddenly solemn. "God rest his soul. The man was brilliant at balancing risk and reward."

"Great man, your dad—may he rest," said Donaldson.

"You knew my dad?"

"No, I know the legend." Donaldson said. "I think we all know it. In this business, who doesn't? Quite a man, sir."

They sat in silence for a moment, Commander Bill deep in thought. Finally, he said, "So, if we do this, arm kids, you say we won't have any blood on our hands, whatever happens…"

"Not a drop," Donaldson said.

"With the up-side being we get credit when things go well," Tuttle said. "That up-side is huge. Very huge."

"Huge to the extreme," said Donaldson. "I mean, if Little Elementary School Susie pops some bastard and stops an attack, Silver Eagle's going to merchandise the hell out of Susie. Advertising. Public Relations. Paid appearances."

"'Second amendment meets the second grade,'" Tuttle said with a smile. "That's your headline right there."

"Boom," Donaldson said, his meaty, tattooed hands rising upward, imitating an explosion. He and Tuttle bumped fists.

Donaldson pulled a pink pistol prototype from the briefcase and handed it to Commander Bill.

Commander Bill had always loved guns. All of them. As he held the pink pistol, a rumor of a smile spread across his face. This thing, the simple beauty of the design—hefty enough to feel like a gun but small enough for little Susie or whoever to shoot—was genius.

Commander Bill asked about the firing power. About the as-yet-to-be-designed projectile. About the materials they'd used to make the weapon itself. All the answers pleased him. Soon, he was running out of the wiggle room he needed to not approve the project while not appearing to not approve of it.

"Look, he said. "I mean, it's not that arming kids bothers me. It's that, you know, this is on me. This whole decision."

"You're worried about the money," Tuttle said. "That it?"

Ow. That hurt. Commander Bill took a sip of wine. Commander Bill had a lot of money, thanks to his inheritance from his dead parents' estate and the success of Silver Eagle Security. But Commander Bill was a thrifty man and also fairly greedy.

He didn't know what to say.

Donaldson said, "We've crunched some numbers, Commander. Conservative estimate has us earning back our initial investment in what one, maybe two ye—"

"Two years," Tuttle said, nodding.

"Two, yes, exactly two," said Donaldson. "Three at the outset."

"Three. At the very very outset." Tuttle looked at Donaldson, frowned, and then looked at Commander Bill. "Commander, we can run numbers until our eyes pop out and we're bleeding from our empty sockets, like the Viet Cong commie snipers did back during Tet when I was just a buck private trying to learn how to use an M16, but it's not going to change the reality. The reality is kids and teachers are dying for something to hit back with. Fear is a huge purchase motivator. Our estimates on sales are good, but we really have no idea how fast these products could take off. We get rolling, get retailers inventoried up, and let's say another elementary school gets shot up."

"Or, say, a high school," Donaldson said.

"Whatever," Tuttle said. "Irregardless."

"Yes, moot point," Donaldson said. "The likelihood of serious, emotionally motivated mass killings that impact sales in a positive way is very high."

"Very. High," Tuttle said.

"We crunched the numbers."

"Crushed them."

"Absolutely."

"They look good."

"Very, very good."

"This is one hot market."

"We're talking red hot."

"It's damn hot, Commander, and you know what? It's going to stay that way," Tuttle said, leaning forward, elbows on the table, his voice going low. "See, there's no way," Tuttle glanced to the left, then to the right. "There's no *fucking* way the sickos are gonna stop shooting shit up. They're gonna sit in their rooms and play their violent games and watch their bloody movies and their sick porn and get all worked up when their mommies don't bring their Cheetos to the basement and then what?" He slammed his palm on the table. Commander Bill jumped, nearly dropping his wine. Tuttle looked at Donaldson.

The two men smiled. Both turned to Commander Bill. In unison, they said, "They're gonna shoot someone."

"Shoot. Someone."

They let that sink in for a moment.

Donaldson continued, his tone conciliatory. "Listen, Commander. You have nothing to worry about here. Your upfront costs, yes, they're significant. But you got to pay to play, am I right?" He looked at Tuttle for affirmation.

'Got to pay. To. Play," Tuttle said.

"Damn. Right," Donaldson said, slapping the table.

"Right as a fully loaded Glock in my pants," Tuttle said. "We get this rolling; we'll be swimming in orders. All the research says so."

"All of it," Donaldson said.

Tuttle took a slow, deliberate sip of wine and then slowly placed his glass on the white tablecloth. He let the moment simmer, his eyes on the empty bottle of Zinfandel. "Look, sir," Tuttle said, "this is a big opportunity here, as I see it. Hell, it's a moral obligation. I mean, wouldn't all of us feel better if kids could be the first line of their own defense? With just a little capital to start the ol' ball rolling a company like Silver Eagle could own this market. Your father would be proud of us and, especially, you."

Donaldson came onboard, hired a marketing firm and a research and development team, and launched the schoolkid gun program under the name Project Baby Boom. Other names— Good Kids With Guns, Bullets4Babies, and Pistols4Pipsqueeks among them—fared better in focus group testing, but Commander Bill giggled at Project Baby Boom.

Project Baby Boom it was.

The first million or so of the budget went to lobbying efforts supporting federal legislation that allowed kids age eight and under to carry guns in schools. The debate over the bill was intense. Liberals demonstrated against it. Conservatives demonstrated for it. Parents and mental health experts weighed in. Security experts yelled at each other about it on cable news. Eventually, the legislation passed. It permitted schoolchildren to use for self-defense a gun or gun-like weapon that would "cause significant, non-lethal injury to an assailant deemed a physical threat in the school environment (excluding teachers, administration personnel and designated others—those tasked with meal preparation, for example—whose jobs, by nature may be misconstrued by children as threatening)."

Developing the weapon, which Donaldson designated a Child Level Threat Response Tool (CLTRT), and what he called the Non Bullet Projectile (NBP) proved equally difficult and costly. The R&D team quickly blew through most of the original budget on designs and prototypes. Even as they zeroed in on the gun design, which was made from a proprietary blend of lightweight polymers and produced by a 3D printer, they had a lot of swings and misses on the NBP. Eventually, Donaldson and his team resorted to shooting projectile options into dead salmon purchased in bulk from a local seafood provider. The mathematical equation to determine lethality was based on whether or not the projectile penetrated a salmon's skin and exposed the meat.

The final iteration of the weapon delivered its payload of Yellow Dotz via a blast of compressed air. Parents were encouraged to load three rounds in the weapon's tiny clip and then fill the air bladder inside the gun before each school day; filling the bladder required five presses of a bright orange button shaped like a cupcake, on the weapon's grip.

The weapon would definitely slow down an assailant. It might even poke out the occasional bad-guy eye.

Chapter Ten

As he listened to Donaldson and the others drone on, sleep clawed at Commander Bill's eyes. It had been another stupidly long day at the office. To make matters worse, the sky was darkening. What was left of a palm frond whistled by the window.

He tried to think of something other than the men talking business and mayhem. He wrote "politics?" below "Benghazi" on his Post-It.

His phone buzzed again. It was his long-time assistant, Kelli Alexander calling. Commander Bill jumped to his feet, excused himself and stepped into the hallway outside the conference room.

"Thanks for saving me. What's up, Kell?"

"No problem. Ops got an incoming from someone you might know," Kelli said. "Colonel Tuttle has been so busy; he's not responding to Simmons, so I thought I would call you directly."

Commander Bill leaned his non-phone shoulder against the wall and stared down the empty hallway toward the steel security door at the far end. "Man, these hallways are white. We ever give any thought to maybe adding some of our red to them? Maybe make one wall Silver Eagle red? That would look sweet, Kell. Don't you think? Maybe talk to the facilities team about it."

Kelli let out a sigh. "Sure. Sure, sir." She paused and Commander Bill imagined her writing a note, "RED PAINT" on the pad of Post-Its he'd asked her to keep on her desk for moments such as these.

Commander Bill appreciated Kelli and made a point to tell her whenever he thought of it, which wasn't often. Kelli's ex-husband, whose name escaped him, had been their militia contact during the mess with Wisconsin. Commander Bill often thought about the day Kelli's then-husband had left her. It was shortly after the guy's not-very-memorable name became public—"unindicted co-conspirator" they'd called him. Kelli had called to tell Governor Bill about it and had spent a lot of time just sobbing. Then-Governor Bill, on his way to see a dermatologist about a stress-ignited rash in his right armpit, had told her to go ahead and take a day or two off.

"So, as I said, Simmons took in this request via encrypted email…" Kelli was saying.

"Simmons?"

"Jack Simmons; he's the new guy on incoming ops opportunities. Anyways, there's this guy named Jackson Nguyen, he's from back home—Michigan; Traverse City, to be precise. He—"

"Oh, right. I know him. Kinda muscular guy."

"Sir, I don't really know what he looks like. I mean, I've heard of him, you know. He's like some big tech wiz."

"Simmons? If he's such a wiz, why are we paying him to read emails?" Commander Bill said, genuinely frustrated. "We could hire some woman, some temp to do that."

Kelli snorted. "Sir, no. Jackson Nguyen. He's the tech guy. Simmons is an ex-cop on ops intake as part of the standard rotation for new hires."

Commander Bill nodded to no one. "Yes, right. I think I authorized that. A training thing—getting everyone a taste of how we generate business. Good. Good good for Simmons."

"This Jackson Nguyen says he knows Silver Eagle and knows that you're from the Grand Rapids area."

"Winn?"

"Nguyen, sir. N-g-u-y-e-n."

"And he pronounces it Winn?"

"No, Commander, more like When."

Commander Bill laughed. "Sounds foreign. Oriental."

"Yes, I believe his family was, is, Asian. I've seen pictures. He's one of the guys behind that face-recognition company, I think," Kelli said. "FacePlant. And some other things. He's originally from Traverse City. The call came from Colorado."

Commander Bill frowned. This kind of phone call was exactly why his job was so hard. Far too many complications. As governor, he'd let people read the briefing materials then topline them. He'd stayed at 30,000 feet. "Let's get out of the weeds here, Kell. What's this guy want?"

The lights flickered. "Holy shit. What was that?" Commander Bill stood up straight. "Our guys shooting mortars near the power station again, Kelli? Should I be bunkered?"

"No, no, sir. It's the wind. It's really cranking up out there," Kelli said. "But no worries, I understand the PowPack team is prepping the generators."

Commander Bill, tentative, leaned back against the wall. "PowPack?"

"Our electrical infrastructure team? You named them that?"

"Right, yes."

"Anywho, as I was saying, this Jackson Nguyen reached out. It seems Donovan Reed—that name rings a bell, right? The British zillionaire? Jackson and him are buds."

"Could this hurricane be as bad as…it's not really a big deal, right? I mean, I've been right about that, right?" Commander Bill imagined having to evacuate. He pictured his family frantically shoving things in their SUV, his son being stupid about bringing the ugly little shelter dog he'd conned them into adopting, his daughter trying to take all her clothes, some of them ripping from her arms in the wind as she carried them defiantly from the house and the dog running down the street of their gated community, his son chasing it, rain suddenly coming in sheets and whipping them like punishment from God for his arrogance about the forecasts and his lusting after women and various other sins he wouldn't speak of to himself, Commander Bill yelling for his wife not to chase after the damn kid while also frantically sitting in the driver's seat of the SUV, eyeing his watch and calculating the minutes he'd give all of them before he honked the horn and started rolling down the driveway, the reverie cut short by Kelli's voice.

"…all of the forecast data," Kelli was saying, "so while I know you don't want to believe the hype, I am thinking this could be, well, a pretty dangerous storm." Kelly's voice was firm but calm in his ear. "That said, right now, let's focus on the situation with Mr. Nguyen. Donovan Reed is a high-profile Brit—that's a critical market for us. Both he and Nguyen are actually pretty well known in the right circles. Worth a great deal of money."

Commander Bill stared down the ridiculously white hallway. "Yes, yes. Donovan Reed. I know of him. I can't say I know the Asian guy."

"Well, Donovan Reed was kidnapped. In Colorado. Three men disguised as federal agents snatched him. Jackson Nguyen believes something horrible may be happening, but with Mr. Reed's rather…" Kelli fumbled for a word, "…challenging personal history he does not want to call the authorities. I just figured I'd run it by you since Colonel Tuttle is so slammed."

Commander Bill smiled. Kelli usually went to Tuttle with such requests. But, this time, she'd come to him. Tuttle had just mentioned Colorado. Now this, from Colorado. Commander Bill tried to picture God's hand, reaching down the long white hall, taking his hand. He imagined winging his way to the mountains, away from this wretched weather. Who knew? Maybe he'd get a little media attention out of it. Might help his political career.

"Tell him we're on our way," he said, wondering where his skis were.

The lights flickered.

PART FOUR

The Mohawked Lady and the Singing Fish

Chapter Eleven

Gunnison, Colorado

Tuesday evening

Wind and snow were attacking the plate-glass windows and rocking the light posts in the near-empty parking lot of the Safeway. An obviously bored twenty-something woman with a pink mohawk slouched at the only open checkout lane, thumbing through whatever on her iPhone.

Miky Spike rushed her cart down the packaged drink aisle, picked up a six-pack of Diet Coke, glanced over her shoulder and immediately imagined Rub, her father, mumbling, "You can't fix dumb." Two ambitiously bearded guys, each in the local winter uniform of greasy knit caps and camo coats over Carhartt overalls, were earnestly pondering a case of bottled water while shooting her the occasional side eye. They had followed her to Gunnison from Crested Butte in a battered Jeep Cherokee with half-hearted headlights—the only other morons (other than Miky and a snowplow driver or two) on CO-135 on a day like this. They'd parked well away from her Subaru in the otherwise deserted parking lot and had waited until she was inside to enter the store.

Now they were acting like they weren't watching her while they were watching her.

It was hard not to laugh. The dudes were the only other customers in the store. It crossed her mind to just confront them right there between the craft brews and the Gatorade, but she knew when to pick her battles. Besides, the storm was ratcheting up. She moved quickly to finish the rest of her shopping.

Miky had left the high school in Crested Butte long after the rest of the staff and student body. The superintendent had closed the district early—sent everyone home before "no one could get home," but Miky had had shit to do. Track season was underway and the distance runners she coached were deep into a training schedule she needed to rethink—tough to run trails at 9,000 feet when you couldn't find them under six-foot drifts. She'd spent two hours in her classroom revising the running plan, adjusting the mileage and intensity for treadmills and a couple of hoped-for team runs through the streets of town. Then she'd emailed it to the kids. Afterwards, she'd done four easy on the ancient treadmill in the high school gym, cursing climate change and the ignorant politicians who never did anything about it for messing with the kids' training and for forcing her to run on the damn treadmill as a May blizzard buzzed the Rockies.

Miky took off her ski cap, jammed it in a pocket as she unzipped her down coat and loosened the scarf around her neck. She stuck out her lower lip and then looked at her phone for the next item on her list. She thought again about her dad, how he'd laugh at her for being in a grocery store thirty miles from home during a snowstorm, two half-rotten kiwis, a molding leftover eggplant parm, and a near-empty bag of dog food away from literally nothing to eat in the house. She'd let life control her rather than the other way around. Not normal. Not good. So, focus, she thought. "Work the plan and plan the…" Yada yada yada, Rub's long-dead voice whispered one of its many mantras to her subconscious.

As she rushed her cart through the empty aisles of the grocery story, Miky felt the hum of endorphins and smiled. She had needed the run. It had brought clarity. Get food. Get ready. For whatever was coming.

The years had flown by since Miky and two other Michigan militia members had been sucked into Operation Cheesus, the now globally infamous plot to invade Wisconsin. She'd built a life in Colorado thanks in no small part to the school superintendent who believed in second chances and who desperately needed a high-school English teacher and cross-country coach. Locals had initially regarded her with a mix of anxious suspicion, bold-faced curiosity, and groupie-like admiration. But it hadn't taken long for her to make a smooth transition from notorious outsider celebrity to cool teacher-coach. Crested Butte's cowboy-hippie ski town vibe suited Miky. Hers was just another badass backstory in a place filled with them. Plus, hers had the added weight of being true.

Divorced and defiantly single—men courageous enough to ask, and there were several, got a soft smile and a hard "no"—she lived on a small ranch with a horse she called Horse and a black lab named Nothing. There, she'd endured a fire that ate 400 acres of surrounding forest, killed her first dog and first horse, and crawled to within twenty feet of her back door before she'd put a stop to it. She'd coached two state champion cross-country teams, one each for boys and girls; won a half marathon and finished third in the Bolder Boulder 10k; and had become a quiet but regular visitor to "The Rock," a church that met in the basement of a pizza joint. Miky had a small circle of friends and a usual table at a coffee shop where the owner knew her name but never bothered with it. She graded papers, grew organic vegetables for a couple of farm-to-table restaurants, rode Horse, trained her teams, ran alone on mountain trails, and read long novels about unimportant things. "Capable of shooting the nose off a fly at 100 yards" (her father's words), she hadn't touched a gun since she'd left Michigan.

Operation Cheesus was never far from her mind. She'd watched two militia men die violently. She'd saved a school bus full of kids threatened by a missile-carrying drone. In the heat of battle, she'd made lifesaving and life-altering choices. But she had been with the two now-dead militia men when they kidnapped two people and then attacked the Wisconsin restaurant. At trial, Miky was credited for helping to stop the attack, saving the kids on the bus and, as one breathless cable news host told her audience, "preventing violence from spreading like melted pepper jack across the prairie." The judge gave her a brief probation and an order to never again fraternize with members of the militia movement—an unnecessary admonishment since Miky, in court, had declared militia members "a bunch of lost asshole-bros with Chuck Norris complexes and bad beer."

Many nights now she sat with Nothing on her front porch, staring into the gloaming, the soul-comforting scent of earth, sage and pine embracing her, the yips and howls of coyotes melding with the comforting, looming presence of the Elk mountains to fill her heart with peace but leaving her mind restless and roving. The surviving men involved in the plot, especially the former Michigan governor, Bill Hoeksma, his political bud Ham DenBraber, and Wilbur Tuttle, the aging weirdo who'd masterminded the thing as a marketing operation for the billionaire William Hoeksma and his paramilitary company, had paid so little for their parts in the stupid scheme. And now Hoeksma and Tuttle were making millions running Hoeksma

Sr.'s army of legal mercenaries while DenBraber was sitting in the Michigan governor's chair.

The previous week, she'd called Benjamin Nighthorse, one of the Operation Cheesus kidnap victims. Miky had freed him during the Cracker Barrel attack, and Benjamin had helped her save the kids on the bus. They'd become close in the years since, a relationship forged over cell, text, email, and FaceTime and cemented in PTSD.

Benjamin answered the phone in his usual way, "Operation Cheesus survivor network. How may I help you?"

She smiled. "Exactly what I needed to hear today. Seriously."

"Struggling a bit, are we?"

"Yeah. So, I called my favorite accomplice."

"Or victim."

"Yeah. Take your pick."

"So, what's happening?" Benjamin said.

"You tell me."

"That's a loaded response."

"You still in wherever doing whatever?"

Benjamin's deep rumble of laughter was a tonic.

"Well?" she said.

He groaned; she imagined him in a lounge chair by a pool.

"Well, if you must know, I'm in a lounge chair by a pool."

Bingo.

"It's part of my rehab, babe," he said, sarcastically.

"You haven't had a drink in more than two years, as far as I know."

"752 days, to be exact," he said. "And to be sober here for a second, I'm damn proud."

"As you should be," she said. "I'm proud of you."

"Thanks."

"But you know, just because you inherited millions doesn't mean you don't have to work like the rest of us."

"Well actually, it does."

Miky's laugh felt good. "Yeah, I guess you're right." Benjamin's family had owned Blue Indian Baking Soda Co. since its founding in the late 1800s in Back Prairie, Wisconsin. But, at an early age, he'd drunk-fumbled his chance at a cushy job in the firm's posh headquarters. During a stint at Northwestern University in Evanston, Illinois he'd established his high capacities for alcohol and women as well as a reputation for ardent, articulate, historically accurate debate on American Indian issues. After leaving the school well short of his degree and hurting from the end of an affair with a professor who'd lost interest, Benjamin wandered in the valley of the shadow of all the dangerous things a trust fund could buy. The day a reluctant Miky and her two militia brethren launched the attack on Wisconsin, Benjamin was on a bender with stripper and flask in tow. His bright-green Hummer grabbed the attention of the militia men in part due to the fact that Benjamin was drunk enough to be weaving between lanes of northbound I-94 in rural Wisconsin.

The events of that day nearly killed him and saved his life. He'd told Miky that repeatedly. Her support and encouragement drove him into counseling and rehab and then back to school. He'd finished his degree in poli-sci and now traveled the country lobbying and speaking for indigenous people. The former pudgy rich Wisconsin kid with the casino tan was now a fit health nut with a home base in the Florida Keys. His talk about not working was a standing joke but the part about the pool was not. He helped people in need, but that hadn't stopped him from buying a lavish home "with all the assholy amenities a rich Indian could want," as he described them.

"Want to come down for a visit?" he said. "I mean, I'll be here all week. You can try the Mahi Mahi."

"Ha. Right." This was all a familiar conversational tangent, Benjamin flirting with her, asking her to come for a visit. She wasn't entirely against it.

"You could get out of the snowstorm," he said, pressing the issue.

"What about the hurricane? They say one's forming in the Caribbean."

"That's sticking to the Carolinas, according to the storm track," Benjamin said. He paused. "I do have a spare bedroom or six. Rooms. With beds."

Miky sighed. Something about his discussion didn't seem like joking. Both of them knew it. She thought both of them did. Maybe. Her phone dinged. She held it away from her ear and tapped the incoming message. From Benjamin. It was a selfie of him in a lounge chair, a palm tree and part of the Spanish-tiled roof of his house in the background. He was smiling that beautiful smile of his. He was wearing a gold Speedo. She swiped the message away. And put the phone to her ear. "Put some clothes on. That's disgusting."

He laughed. "Yeah, sorry, when I'm home alone, it's the Speedo or nothing at all."

"There's no need to apologize."

'So, you like the look."

"I didn't say that." She closed her eyes. Saw the image again. Gross. Benjamin could be such an idiot.

"You didn't not say it."

There was a long pause. Finally, Benjamin said, "Listen. Sorry. I don't always… What I mean is, you've been through hell and back, especially where menfolk are concerned. Just trying, you know, keeping it light. Okay? Just know you're welcome down here, even when I'm not here. Feel free. I can leave a key."

"I know. I know. Don't apologize." Miky thought for a moment. "Listen. About why I called. I think I have to speak up."

"You mean about the thing?"

"Yeah. The thing."

Neither spoke for several seconds. Finally, Benjamin said. "You've said that before."

"Yeah, I know."

"So, what's different now? And why are you calling—for my approval?"

Ow. He really did know her well. "I don't know. I think…" Miky thought for a moment. "I think it's just time. I mean, Hoeksma Junior is suddenly this huge success with his dad's company. Like the whole thing worked out perfectly for him—for all of them. And I'm seeing talk that he wants to run for office again—someone said somewhere that he'd be a good president."

Benjamin snorted. "President? Little Billy Hoeksma? You're kidding me."

"I am not. I mean, can you imagine?"

"I'm trying not to."

"I know. That's my point. They, he, got away with murder. Literally. And the whole goal of the thing was to make his dad's war company a big success, and now it is. I'm thinking little Billy is going to use it all to catapult back into politics. And Tuttle? He's up to bad shit; you just know he is."

"Tuttle. What motivates that guy? I mean, he's like 400 years old. He's as wealthy as," Benjamin thought about it and laughed, "as I am."

"He's just evil and greedy and soulless. My dad explained guys like him as having dead hearts. He's always been this way."

"Dead heart."

"Uh-huh. I'm sure he has something to do with all of this conspiracy talk about beef. You've heard the latest, right? The government's stealing cattle and throwing out semen and melting down…"

"…fat for candles…"

"For Muslims?"

"Yeah. These conspiracies keep getting weirder if that's possible."

"It's so like Bo to chase this," Miky said with a sigh.

"You mean 'Big Bruddah.'"

"Yeah," she said. It was hard to refer to Bo with his new identity. "I just wish I never had to read or hear about him and his insane theories."

"And you read too much. On too many sites you shouldn't be reading."

"I just feel like I need to know. Like somehow I can stop them."

"Stop who?"

"You know, them. Bo… Bruddah. And the rest of—all of them."

"From what? Boogaloo? You don't think that could happen, do you?"

"It could. Yes. And if Silver Eagle and Tuttle and whoever out there, they might just jump into it. Or help it happen."

"Now who's the conspiracy theorist?"

"Dude. Ow."

"Yeah, but I have a point, right? There's been talk of boogaloo for years and it's never…"

"Yeah, and there was talk about starting a war over cheese. And then it nearly happened."

Benjamin took a deep breath. "I know."

"I really have this vibe from reading Bo's shit…"

"Bruddah's?"

"Whatever. There's a tone now. Out there. Something's shifting. And I know if it breaks—if something violent starts— with Hoeksma's political ambitions and Tuttle out there in his dark dark dark world, they'd jump right in it with the, uh, Bruddah bros."

Both thought about it. Then Benjamin said, softly, "Look. I know. I know. I know. I can't stop reading about it and them either. You got me hooked."

"Sorry."

Benjamin laughed. "Don't be," he said. "I love being part of your world."

Miky felt something stir in her chest. She tried to ignore it.

"I mean," Benjamin said, "it's my choice to visit the militia sites and read their chat and all that. Besides, what's a reformed alcoholic native American Indian with a multi-million-dollar trust fund supposed to do with his spare time?"

They both laughed. Semi-awkwardly.

"But seriously," Benjamin said, "if you feel you have to do something and that something is talking to someone in the media, so be it. I support you. And I get it. But damn, girl. That's dangerous. I mean, this is scary stuff."

"Yeah, but no scarier than seeing you in a Speedo."

They both laughed. Less awkwardly.

The day after her conversation with Benjamin, Miky agreed to an interview with a reporter from the *Denver Post*, one who had tracked her down the year before and patiently emailed her every month or so, gently asking for "her side of the story." The story based on the interview ran as a feature in the *Sunday Post*. It portrayed her accurately, she had to admit. Her criticism was blunt, honest and clear. She spared no one, including herself, for being part of the "stupid scheme" that led to the attempted Wisconsin invasion, and for perpetuating the ridiculous conspiracy theory Hoeksma, Sr. and Tuttle had used to fuel it. She once again renounced the militia movement and her ex-husband. She vilified the "conspiracy sewer that we call right-wing media." She renounced the "culture of macho, White-male-fueled violence" that was "poisoning America."

She got a lot off her chest.

The story brought a fresh wave of celebrity, demonstrated in Crested Butte by nods, smiles, and "you-go-girls" muttered in passing and trumpeted online. Her adopted town was, for the most part, with her. Elsewhere, on talk shows and across social media, the former militia princess was vilified as a turncoat and self-serving whiner.

Death threats. She'd expected them. And they'd come.

Now, as she dropped her purchases on the conveyor and nodded to the pink-mohawked clerk, she glanced toward the two men discussing a display of batteries near the checkout and felt not fear but unexpected relief. She and the people who had turned her life upside down were going to have a reckoning. So be it. She could handle it.

Miky nudged the six-pack of Sawtooth Amber Ale toward the waiting scanner.

The clerk—Raina, according to the crooked letters pasted to her plastic Safeway name badge—seemed to approve of the purchase. "Love me some Left Hand Brewing," she said softly, hair down but nodding—pink mohawk turned tomahawk.

Raina picked up a plastic bag of kale, seemed to sigh, and then spent several seconds punching through options on the scanner's touchscreen. She found what she was looking for. There was another touch, another beep from the scanner. She dropped the kale on the conveyor, where it slid toward the rest of the flotsam waiting to be bagged and reached for the beer.

You going to card me for that?" Miky said with a smile.

A snort. "I should card you for making me come out in this storm so you could buy kale."

Miky laughed. Raina's voice was soft with an edge of steel. Single mom was Miky's guess. Working on a night like this because she had to. "Sorry about that. I had an empty fridge. Poor planning on my part."

"Tell me about it." Raina sighed, finished scanning and turned to her register to read the digital display. Miky noticed a handgun on the small shelf that stuck out from the far side of the register.

"Expecting trouble?" Miky said, gesturing. "The gun."

Raina's eyes remained on the register. "I've got a permit," she said. "And a cranky ex-husband."

Before Miky could respond, Raina continued, "Looks like you owe Mr. Safeway fifty-seven ninety-two for your troubles." She made eye contact with Miky for the first time. She looked tired, a bit of the world's considerable weight on her shoulders. "Any coupons?"

Miky shook her head. "Who has time?"

"Some of us make the time."

"Oh, sorry. Yeah, I hear you." Miky smiled. "My other excuse is I don't have kids."

Raina's weary face flickered. Miky's hunch was right. "I have two. Boy and a girl," she said, a flicker of pride in her voice. "One of each."

They completed the transaction, Miky sliding her card and collecting the receipt as Raina packed Miky's reusable bags. The two men stood a few feet behind her, at the head of the checkout lane, one holding a bag of pretzels, the other a jug of fabric softener. When Miky looked at them, both turned and studied the candy display. One picked up a pack of gum and pretended to read it.

Raina topped the last of her three bags with the kale and put it in Miky's cart. She returned to her position behind the cash register.

"Uh, Raina," Miky said softly. "Can I ask you a quick question?"

Raina frowned, paused, glanced down, seemingly remembering her nametag. A grin flickered in her eyes. She looked at Miky, taking the cue and lowering her voice to a near whisper. "You just did ask me a question. You want another?"

Miky smiled. "Yes."

"Shoot."

"See those two guys?" Miky nodded toward the two men.

Without shifting her gaze, Raina said, "I'm a bi-racial chick with pink hair but that doesn't mean I'm blind."

"Well, could you do me a favor and hold them up for a minute or two while I leave? Could you watch that they don't do anything..." Miky thought for a moment. "weird?"

"That's two quick questions. We're above your limit," Raina said. Miky held her gaze. Raina smiled. "Actually, if you ask me, and you did, I'm not sure you could recognize weird if it bit you in the ass." Raina looked toward the two guys. "I mean, what's weird is you thinking I'd be legit working here in an empty Safeway in the middle of a snowstorm when the whole damn county is shutdown." She thumbed a switch. Miky looked down at the conveyor. A pack of gum moved toward her. Raina reached for the gun.

Chapter Twelve

Carpville, South Carolina

Tuesday evening

The nerve center for Project Black Dog was wired into the lead-lined walls of a small amphitheater three floors below ground, in The Will's bowels. All communications and surveillance for the secretive organization originated there. The room appeared on no blueprints or schematics of The Will. It had no name since no one ever spoke of it. It was the darkest of dark spaces in Tuttle's dark ops.

After the usual day packed with meetings, Tuttle had changed into a black jumpsuit and aviator sunglasses. The jumpsuit was his Project Black Dog uniform, but other than the color, there was no clear visual evidence that it was. Project Black Dog had a logo but only Tuttle and the designer of the logo, who'd died in a mysterious fishing accident, had seen the logo; as with much of Project Black Dog it was designated TEO (Tuttle's Eyes Only). Therefore, the Silver Eagle logo stitched over the left breast of the jumpsuit was a subtle disguise. Rumor was, the Project Black Dog logo was underneath it, but Tuttle wouldn't say if it was.

Tuttle quickly completed the security protocol to access the room; it involved a keycard, retinal confirmation, fingerprint, and Silver Eagle's exclusive breath-based DNA security analysis (BBDNASA™).

The amphitheater's lights flicked on automatically. As the thick steel door ca-clunked shut behind him, Tuttle allowed himself a moment to admire his creation: three tiered rows of theater seating, each seat fronted by tables that ran in an arc from where he stood to the far wall, fifteen seats in each tier, computer keyboards and monitors in front of each seat, all wirelessly connected to what was known as the Black Cloud, which was a server farm in Kansas managed by Tuttle's personally hired team of Serbian hackers. The room's seating faced a wall of interconnected video panels fronted by a lectern. To the right of the lectern was a tall, red, inflatable tube man, which now suddenly inflated, fueled by a softly humming fan, to its full six feet nine inches. Tuttle had seen a similar tube man at a used car dealer and ordered one for the room because it made him smile. The tube man, now dancing crazily, smiled back.

Tuttle crossed to what was known as the "commander's seat," in the middle of the second tier. He settled into the custom-made high-backed chair, which was stuffed with ostrich down and wrapped in llama skin, and he swiveled to face the video wall. From a control panel embedded in his right armrest, he chose a toggle switch, flipped it, said, "Call Bruddah, camera off, and play England Dan and John Ford Coley," then flipped the toggle off.

The video wall hiccupped, blinked once, twice. A breeze of music, audible but low, swept in through a dozen speakers secreted around the room. The satellite comm system whirred to life, and a phone number popped up on the video wall as did a satellite photo of Big Bruddah's current location and Big

Bruddah's mugshot (pulled from a police database; the photo was taken when the then-Bo Watts served twelve days in the Kent County jail for licking the face of the mayor of East Dorr, Michigan at a village council meeting during the pandemic). As the system rang Bruddah's number, it simultaneously regurgitated on-screen, personal data on him; of particular interest to Tuttle was his Internet browsing history, heavy on porn and gun sites; his recent online purchases, which included underwear (briefs, size XXL), porn, gun magazines, and a half a cow from a meat processor; and his current health information (medications for hypertension, blood pressure, an apparently persistent bout of Chlamydia, and high cholesterol).

The screen blipped once more and Big Bruddah appeared, uncomfortable and larger than life, his face pasty and unshaven, tufts of unkempt hair sticking out from his misshapen Detroit Tigers cap. White noise—rain?—bled in from Big Bruddah's world, under the England Dan and John Ford Coley. "Tuttle?" Bo said, squinting. He smiled, uncertainly. "You there?"

Tuttle savored the moment. He kept his own camera off. Big Bruddah could hear the music but could not see him.

"Shit. I've been waiting for you all day, man. We ready or what?" Big Bruddah said, his face a strobing gray-white—lightning. There was a crack of thunder. Big Bruddah jumped and looked off camera, then turned back and shot him a nervous grin. "Quite the storm here."

Tuttle looked at the tube man, who was waving and dancing like the devil. Tuttle smiled but said nothing.

"Listen, bruh," Big Bruddah said. "Sorry. I know you're busy. Just a little on edge is all. Got a lot of people who need to know, you know, what's up." The "up" was all but obliterated by another rumble of thunder. Big Bruddah jumped again, and then looked into the camera, sheepishly. "Quite the gully washer right now. Been like this forever. About to grow gills up in here."

In the video frame behind Big Bruddah, Tuttle could see the gloomily lit tableau of the militia man's miserable under-lived existence: a poster of a topless woman with two crisscrossed ammo belts covering her breasts taped to a paneled wall next to the mounted head of some animal he had shot. On the edge of the frame was what appeared to be a fish fastened to a wood plaque.

"What's that over your left shoulder?" Tuttle said, genuinely interested. "That one of those voice-activated bass; one of those fish that sings?"

Big Bruddah turned, studied the fish, which was momentarily illuminated by lightning. More thunder. This time, Big Bruddah barely flinched as he turned back to face the camera. "Yeah. My buddy Jerry got that for me when I was sick. Sings "Jeremiah Was a Bullfrog" or some shit."

"Joy to the World."

Big Bruddah frowned. "Jeremiah… whatever. That's how the song goes."

"It's 'Joy to the World' by Three Dog Night."

"Okay. Yeah. Right."

I have to give you credit. You have good taste for kitsch," Tuttle said sincerely.

Big Bruddah, looking relieved to have found a conversational starting point, said, "I can get you a few, if you want one—or a lot of them, actually. I know a guy. Gets them…" He drew air quotes. "…wholesale. If you know what I'm saying." He grinned.

Tuttle imagined a whole school of the singing fish on the walls of his office. He liked the image. "Might just take you up on that. Why don't you text me the guy's contact information?"

"Sure. Sure. Done."

From the armrest controls, Tuttle found the mute button and tapped it; hit the toggle switch, said, "Kitty kitty," and toggled off. From the right front corner of the room, there was a click, a soft whoosh, and a meow. Within seconds, a black cat was in Tuttle's lap, stretching and purring.

"Tuttle? You there, bruh?" Big Bruddah's big face was looking impatient.

For a moment, Tuttle nuzzled the cat, savoring the soft-rock duo singing "Soldier in the Rain" against the rain from Big Bruddah's side of the call. He thought about a day long ago in Saigon. It had been raining. There was danger and a girl. Helicopters thwap-thwap-thwapped the humid air of his imagination, which Tuttle savored until the thing turned sour in his gut—the girl had betrayed him.

"I am with you, big man. I have been waiting for this day for much long time," Tuttle said, his accent, in his mind, Vietnamese.

Big Bruddah laughed, a bit nervously. "You and your voices, bruh."

Tuttle laughed, Vietnamese-ly.

"Why you do that, Tuttle? Always with the accents and shit."

Tuttle laughed. "It is my way, American GI."

"What does that even mean?" Big Bruddah squinted into his camera.

Tuttle said nothing.

"I mean, this is serious. That woman, the President. She's finally gone too far. Right?" Big Bruddah began toying with something on his desk: a handgun. Big Bruddah flipped the gun again. And again. And again, all while shaking his head. "I mean, you can't even hug a cow? What kind of left-wing nightmare bullshit is that?"

Tuttle smelled fear. "Are you nervous?" he said, switching to his most gravelly, ominous Tuttle voice.

"No. Of course not." He flipped the gun.

"Because if you are, we can…"

"I'm not nervous," said Big Bruddah. He winced at another crack of thunder.

"You seem to be."

"I'm… Seriously, I'm fine. I've just been sitting here all day, you know, waiting."

"Look," Tuttle said, savoring the fact that, with his camera off, Big Bruddah couldn't look. "You told me a long time ago that you and your friends were ready to become boogaloo boys, if the situation called for it. When did we first talk about that: two, three years ago?"

"Yeah. You were still in, like, prison."

"That's right. It was right after she got elected…"

Big Bruddah sniffed and sat up. "Damn straight. We all knew from the start that once they gave her power, she was going to come after our liberties and freedoms and whatever. The cows are the straws that broke the camel's ass, as far as I'm concerned."

Tuttle smiled. "Yes. Yes. I recall those views of yours in particular. You drove across the state to see an old man in prison to tell me all that."

"Yeah. Because I figured you, you know, would sympathize. Me and some other guys got talking about you and maybe that you could help us."

"And I did."

"Did what?"

"Sympathize."

"Yes. You did."

"And it was you who suggested that maybe the day was coming when people who think like us would do something about all this."

"Or it was you who said that, I think." Big Bruddah frowned and thought, then said, "Whatever." He looked up. "We agreed that we might be led to a point where it was time to get serious about some kind of armed insurrection to protect…"

"…our civil liberties. Our homes and property. Yes."

"Exactly."

"Yes. I told you I could help. Until the time was right, I said, I could supply weapons and logistical planning."

"Yeah, yeah. I remember."

"Well…" Tuttle let the moment hang.

"Well…" Big Bruddah said, momentarily looking away, like he was leaving with the fading thunder. His eyes swung back. "Well, what?"

"You know what. This is time to fish or cut bait, my friend." Tuttle put some weight in his voice. "We have a government run amok. And my people tell me this is the time to strike. I just have this sudden sense that you might get a little weird when the shooting starts."

The cat's tail twitched. It jumped from Tuttle's lap onto the floor and walked slowly away, tail high and twitching.

Something weak flashed in Big Bruddah's eyes. Something wrong. Something, to Tuttle, dangerous. It looked like the thing he'd first seen decades ago in the eyes of a teenaged private first class during a patrol Tuttle had commanded in the jungles of the Mekong Delta. Tuttle had asked the Pfc if he was up to the job of being a soldier and the kid had hesitated before responding; for several seconds, he'd sat there, in the soul-withering heat of the jungle, staring down at the belt-turned-tourniquet and bloody mess at the end of his leg, the echo of the land mine he'd stepped on with the foot he no longer owned still fresh in his head. Tuttle had repeated himself. "You up to being a soldier, Son?" The kid had put down the kilo of heroin they'd

116

just retrieved on Tuttle's behalf from a now-dead guy dressed as a Buddhist monk, and gave Tuttle a look that, to Tuttle, was the look of doubt. Of fear. Of a… Tuttle couldn't help himself. He spit the word: "Pussy."

Big Bruddah recoiled. He leaned forward, frowning. "What did you just say?"

"You heard me," Tuttle said.

"No. It's raining too loud. Try me again."

"Pussy. Pussy. Pussy." Tuttle was angry too. The cat darted back to his feet and jumped onto his lap. Tuttle shoved the animal away.

The cat yowled.

"Don't disrespect me, man. Don't you dare disrespect—" Big Bruddah was saying.

Tuttle rolled his eyes. "So, you're giving me orders now?"

Big Bruddah looked down on Tuttle from the wall. His eyes were narrowing and Big Bruddah was starting to show the attitude of a young man who didn't know his place. "Fuckin' millennials," Tuttle said.

"What was that?"

"You heard me. All you young guys are alike," Tuttle said, his voice turning falsetto, feminine, and mocking, "'Don't disrespect me,' bro.'"

Big Bruddah's eyes were slits. "Tuttle, we need each other. But I don't need your shit. You might want to back this up and start over. I mean, I don't how we took this conversation so far south so fast, but it's up you to fix it." Big Bruddah picked up the gun he'd been flipping and gestured toward his computer's camera. "You can start by apologizing."

Tuttle smiled and shook his head. These militia types were all alike. He found the right switch and flipped on his camera. Big Bruddah blinked, jerked backward, frowning, then leaned forward.

"You know I don't need you, right?" Tuttle said.

"What's that supposed to mean?" Big Bruddah said, his gun hand momentarily limp.

"It means I put a lot of tactical elements in place, so my men would have a plausible excuse to be in Florida when our people leaked the story about an attack at what's-her-name's—the first-daughter's—school. Everything's in place. I've got assets in DC and Florida ready to trip the wire. We can use your manpower. But it's not…"

"It's Sabrina or whatever. Her name."

"Sabrina."

"The President's daughter. The teacher. At the school in Tampa or wherever."

Tuttle shook his head. He took a deep breath. "My point is, I have no use for play soldiers who aren't up to the job. You talk big until you get into a little conflict and turn into whining little pussies. I've got the firepower to start any level of insurrection I want. Without you, Mrs. Bruddah."

Big Bruddah looked like he'd been slapped. He raised the gun again and pointed it at Tuttle. "You don't got shit. You know that. You need us. Down there, in Florida. For when things get real. All along, you've said you couldn't steal Silver Eagle personnel to move on the government. That's why you've helped us, you know, train and shit."

Tuttle rolled his eyes. "You think this is my first trip around the killing field? Of course, I can't use Silver Eagle people. Which is why I've been training a separate group. Of professionals. The best of the best. Because, you know what? I knew this would happen. I knew the minute we got to this day, this call, you'd show me a reason to do this on my own. Because, in the end, you don't have the stones to do this. And I do."

Big Bruddah pulled the trigger. The connection went silent, loudly.

Tuttle stared at the gleaming black video wall. The mortally wounded audio connection whined as if in pain and then faded to a hiss.

Redneckhickhillbillytrailertrashbastardidiotmoronicassholes. The never-voiced but always lurking names for Big Bruddah and his brethren screamed from Tuttle's gut to his head and back again. These people and their pickup trucks and godawful music and dad-married-his-cousin stupidity. He was so damn sick and tired of them. Their value was in their mindless, blind devotion. And yes, in those guns. But Tuttle had guns. And he had people with the skills and the wills and the guts to do what he needed them to do with those guns. How did people like Big Bruddah ever accomplish anything without people like him?

Dumb question. They didn't.

He jabbed the off button on the communications system. The hiss crawled away. The flat screens blinked and faded off.

Tuttle thought for a moment, set his jaw, and then reawakened the comm system. The video wall brightened. He flipped the appropriate toggle and said, "Project Nuclear." Within seconds, an image of the movie poster for "Boogie Nights," altered by his marketing team to read "Boogie Knights," appeared. The campy funk of "Brand New Key" by Melanie—Tuttle's favorite song from the film—rolled in from the speakers, the poster image pulsing to the music.

"Call them," Tuttle said, suddenly gleeful, his head moving in time to the music, his aging heart feeling as though it had shed a year or two.

"Calling them." The voice was a digitally reanimated version of the late FBI agent Babsy Witt's, taken from voicemails; while Tuttle had wished Babsy dead and had served time for killing her during Operation Cheesus, he hadn't actually been the one who killed her. And he'd always loved her voice.

He forced himself to focus on the music and the soft whir of the tone beckoning his team. One by one, his seven most highly valued and lethal soldiers appeared in ultra-HD on the wall in front of him. Each was formed from the Silver Eagle mold: muscular, heads shaved or closely cropped, White, serious, male, he, him, his, himself. All were wearing tight-fitting short-sleeved black t-shirts. One had a beard.

"The beard's looking large today, Dirk," Tuttle said. He called all of them "Dirk" for Dirk Diggler, Mark Wahlberg's screen character's screen name in "Boogie Nights." He did this because he thought it was funny. And because he didn't know their real names.

"Thank you, sir," the bearded Dirk said.

Tuttle took a breath. "Project Nuclear is go," he said. He waited for a response. None of the men flinched, blinked, or "emoted in any way," which was their training manual's guidance for behavior in moments of high stress. Good, Tuttle thought. Good good.

"We will proceed, however, without the assistance or collaboration of our private militia brethren. We are on our own." He waited, looking for a reaction, for any sign of weakness.

Bearded Dirk yawned.

"This will be just us. Launching an event that will change history."

One Dirk waved at a fly or something.

"We all could die. Or be captured as traitors."

Nothing.

"This could totally blow up on us. The op will set in motion a move to oust the President. And we don't know where that will lead. We are merely the catalyst. But, if all goes well, we will be lopping off the ugly head of the government and replacing it with our own idiot puppet in hopes of eventually igniting a civil insurrection that brings down the entire government structure. With just a handful of committed men, we can do this. But the arc of the operation is uncertain. We…"

"Sir, we get it," one of the Dirks said.

"Yeah, we're good," another Dirk said.

"Absolutely," two other Dirks said. Together.

"Well then. Excellent," Tuttle said. "We will proceed with operational plan Boogie-B as outlined in our most-recent briefing. Prepare for immediate or pretty-damn-soon departure for Tampa. As per the briefing materials, I will contact our people on Pennsylvania Avenue and at U.S. Central Command in Florida. On my cue, our assets at MacDill Air Base will inform the President about a shooting involving the school in Tampa where POTUS's daughter is a teacher. Our loyalists will collaborate to facilitate a POTUS flight via AF-1 to MacDill. We will launch operation Delta Sigma Delta via our flight to Tampa Executive Airport, a feint toward the school and a move instead to secure the base and prepare for the arrest and detention of POTUS."

"If she resists, sir?" a Dirk asked.

Tuttle thought about this.

"You want her alive, right?" another Dirk said.

"Roger," Tuttle said.

"My name's not Roger," the Dirk said with a laugh.

"But it's fluid," Tuttle said.

"That's not his name either," Another Dirk said.

All the Dirks laughed.

Tuttle allowed himself a smile. "Okay. Okay." He gave them a moment as the laughter faded. "Our operational stance is to maintain maximum flexibility. Anything is on the table. POTUS is deemed a threat by millions within the country and thousands within the government. Keep your heads on a swivel and in the game and know that our nation is at steak. That's s-t-e-a-k, in this case, given the beef situation and all."

Tuttle waited for the laughs. None came. "Okay then. Do you understand your orders?"

"Yes," the Dirk who'd said "roger" said.

"I will alert our transportation personnel. We need to plan for departure within the hour. Full packs. Next-of-kin forms complete. Rendezvous in the hallway outside the comm center…" Tuttle checked his watched. "Meet me here in—"

"We're here, sir," one of the Dirks said.

There was a soft knock on the door of the comm center. Tuttle frowned, twisted to look at his armrest, found the right button, and tapped it. The video wall flickered and the feed switched to the hallway security cam. Tuttle shook his head.

"Roger that," he said.

Tuttle rose to join the Dirks in the hallway. His phone vibrated. He swore softly and answered.

"Tuttle, we have a situation." Commander Bill's voice was shaking ever so slightly. "In Colorado. I've been contacted directly on this one. Well, we were. But the request came to me. From Kelli. There's this guy from Traverse City. He's, like, a big tech guy. He's Oriental, I guess."

The tightening in Tuttle's chest tightened. "Jackson Nguyen?" The name slipped out.

"Something like that. You know him?"

"Heard of him." Tuttle's chest grew hot.

"Anyways, he was out there in Colorado with this other guy, Donovan something…"

"Donovan Reed." Tuttle said the name through gritted teeth.

Commander Bill let out a sigh. "Yes. Okay. So then, you know already."

"Well no." Tuttle ground his teeth.

"Well, I guess this Reed guy was kidnapped or something. And, like, Nguyen is asking us for help."

"Are you sure it wasn't Reed who contacted us about Nguyen?"

"No. Definitely the other way around. I mean, you might have gotten this second hand, Tut. I got the straight poop. From Simons to Kelli to me."

"It's Simmons, sir. He handles this sort of thing." Tuttle took several slow, deep breaths, eyes closed, forcing himself to descend, by reflex, into a meditative state he'd first reached in 1968 via an acid-tripping car salesman in Hanoi. Commander Bill's voice—"I mean, he's a West Michigan guy originally and I'm sure he knew of me and my dad from all we did…"—faded. Tuttle centered himself on the calm color of lavender and, paradoxically, on Procol Harum's "Whiter Shade of Pale," pushing away the negative imagery of Jackson Nguyen and Donovan Reed and Kelli and Commander Fucking Bill. His chest chilled. His pectorals relaxed. Clarity returned. As did Commander Bill's voice: "Donovan, I remember, because he was the name of a singer back in, like, the sixties, right? Seems like you would know that, right? When Kelli said, 'Donovan Reed,' first thing I thought of was that song, 'They Call Me Mellow Yellow,' by the only other guy I know of named Donovan. The singer. Only had one name. Like Cher. Donovan. Right, Tut, Mister Classic Rock?"

"Yes," Tuttle said, forcing himself to add a smile to his tone. "Yes, sir."

"So. We need to head out. To the mountain state."

Tuttle closed his eyes. He sensed the lavender and heard the echoes of the music—felt the colors of it. Calm resolve, and the outlines of a plan returned. He, Tuttle, was nothing if not agile. He'd always been proud of that. Women loved his agility. So did clients. He would be agile now. He would cope and adjust. He opened his eyes. "Yes, sir. Most definitely. I will assemble a team for us—for you, Commander."

"Excellent."

"I'll begin by confirming some details. With Simmons."

"You mean Simons?"

Tuttle blinked, breathed deeply, and said, "Let me figure it out sir."

"Roger that, Tuttle."

After shooting his computer monitor, Big Bruddah's ears were so full of sound, he couldn't hear. So, for several minutes he leaned back in his chair, gazing at the place where his computer monitor had been, waiting for the deafness to retreat. The throbbing of his heart punched blood to his aching eardrums in a painful, driving beat.

Tuttle was trying to cut him out of the damn boogaloo; worse, he'd called him a "pussy." And had he, Big Bruddah, stopped him? No, he'd murdered the monitor and seriously wounded the wall behind it.

"Idiot," Big Bruddah said, but it wasn't clear to him whether he was talking about Tuttle or himself.

Slowly, the lingering, sulphury odor of the fired gun freshened his rain-soaked, grime-smeared world. Gunpowder smoke was his happy-memory scent.

The rain on the roof crept back into his line of hearing. He thought about beef and how much he loved it. He contemplated personal liberty and what it meant to him. He squeezed his gun, remembering all the months of chatting with militia members across Michigan. The plan had always been to let Tuttle spearhead the boogaloo in Tampa, and for Big Bruddah to lead the militia assault that came behind him. But truth be told, Big Bruddah and a lot of other militia members had chafed at the backup role. He'd spent a lot of nights worrying over it. He'd even come up with a boogaloo ops plan of his own; had worked it over in his head. He'd gotten creative, thought about how to make a big, loud statement that would get the world's attention the way only his badass Michigan militia bruhs could. He'd done the initial planning and then had gotten all worried about backlash from Tuttle. Bruddah had dropped his plan. Like a pussy would.

The plan, his plan, was still in his head.

Big Bruddah sat up, rocked forward, slammed down his gun, and picked up his phone. He made some calls. Talked to militia people in other states who would talk to other people. He arranged some things and set several others in motion. Then he jabbed out the text message he'd crafted in his head forever ago.

"Get to Kalamazoo. Now. Bring AYS. Booj on," the text read. "We're Sunshine State-bound. I repeat. Booj on."

Big Bruddah hit Send. Thunder rattled the house. He looked up, pulse quickening, saw what was left of the seriously wounded singing fish, and smiled. "Bite me, Tuttle," he said. "You want boogaloo? I'll show you boogaloo."

Big Bruddah hit a key on his computer keyboard, looked up into the empty space where his monitor should have been, grimaced, and picked up his phone instead. He logged on to his blog and added a post that repeated the message: "Sunshine State-bound. Booj on."

He sent the same message via four different apps, spreading the word across the country.

His phone vibrated. An anonymous sender texting: "AYS?"

Before Big Bruddah could answer, three more texts arrived with the same question. So, he quickly thumbed a follow-up message to the original group: "AYS means ALL YOUR SHIT. THIS MEANS EVERYTHING YOU NEED FOR WAR." For a heartbeat, he second-guessed the wisdom of adding the last sentence in a text rather than via the more-secure messaging apps. He hit send anyway. Doing anything less felt like pussying out.

Big Bruddah opened the trap door to his underground bunker. Another squall rattled the windows. Trees moaned. Bullets of rain attacked the roof, matching the rhythm of his racing pulse. He hadn't visited the bunker in months, and just the act of opening the door and flicking on the lights gave him a rush. For a moment, he was once again a militia kid, rushing to get to the Christmas tree, anticipating a new gun or his first Kevlar vest.

He was three steps into the water before he registered "wet." Big Bruddah stopped. An Igloo cooler bobbed toward him. Kid Rock's autographed image floated a few feet away. Across from him, against the far wall, the tops of the two gun safes were barely visible.

"Holy… No. No no no no," Big Bruddah said. He sloshed down into chest-high water and half-swam toward the guns. He pushed away a floating plastic tote; on its lid was what looked like "Winter Gear" in unfortunately not-permanent marker. He scraped his shin on something that memory told him was a crate of handmade IEDs or a small freezer filled with Pepperoni Pizza Hot Pockets. He reached the gun safes and thanked himself for leaving them slightly ajar rather than locked—a decision made after hours of overthinking, fueled by beers, that ended with Big Bruddah imagining a moment such as this, when he'd need guns and lots of them in a hurry.

He opened one safe and then the other. For a moment, he stood there, arms held shoulder-high and cocked as though he was in the water ballet. Big Bruddah was breathing hard, swearing at f-ing Tuttle and the f-ing lord and the f-ing former engineer (him) who hadn't gotten around to installing a sump pump and building a drainage system for the property.

The water was cold. He slowly turned, studying the flooded room, arms still akimbo. He told himself there was no panic button here. And if there was, it was underwater like everything else. He could hear his father saying such things. He'd spent a lifetime preparing for a moment like this, a lifetime serving the militia cause. He couldn't—wouldn't—let that cause down. He was a soldier at heart, always had been. Sure, he hadn't served his country in a foreign land. Sure, he'd never really done the "kill" thing. But he damn sure had trained and prepared to defend and kill on America's behalf here at home. Right now, she needed him, America did. Because a crazed woman, THAT WOMAN, was using illegal and unpatriotic means to take away his rights under the guise of fake science.

Tuttle had called him a pussy.

If he let Tuttle or a once-a-century freak storm get in his way, then he needed to kick both of them in the balls and proceed toward the objective.

He was able to retrieve guns and ammo, and a Ziploc bag of homemade beef jerky that he knew tasted like cardboard, but nothing more.

Fine, he thought.

He was a solider. He'd improvise.

The Road to Insurrection Goes Past the Bidet and Through the Waffle House

Chapter Thirteen

Carpville, South Carolina

Tuesday night

Cody Marks—the son of a Fargo, North Dakota minister—drank one too many Budweisers one Friday night the summer after high school and woke up the following Monday in the front passenger's seat of the family minivan on the way to a meeting with the local air force recruiter.

He went on to serve his nation in Iraq, Afghanistan, and Syria before Tuttle lured him into the private sector.

At age twenty-six, with his portfolio and skills, Cody should have been part of a Silver Eagle air op. There were two underway, one flying support for a CIA-funded mixed bag of drug cartels and revolutionaries in Burkina Faso, the other training teenagers in Georgia (the country, not the state) in the art of aerial bombardment using Silver Eagle's exclusive retrofitted crop dusters. But the year before, Cody had been hotdogging during a test flight for Silver Eagle's procurement department as part of its back-door purchasing arrangement with the Pentagon, and he'd augured a $38 million F-14 Tomcat into a forgotten area of Arizona. Cody had been savvy enough to bail, uninjured, before the brutally expensive plane pancaked on the desert floor. That Tomcat would've been the pride of the Silver Eagle air fleet, which was why Cody was suffering through a two-year probation from all military-style flight, as well an uncertain period of seething contempt from the man who hired him. It was Tuttle who decided Cody should serve his suspension by piloting Silver Eagle corporate aircraft. This bored the bejeebies out of Cody Marks and simultaneously enraged him. Which was, of course, the point.

A takeoff from the Silver Eagle base in the high-octane winds of an approaching hurricane promised to deliver the adrenalin rush Cody had been missing. However, the Gulfstream G650ER, one of six in the Silver Eagle non-military corporate fleet (NMCF), handled the tail-jouncing, wing-wobbling conditions just fine, which was a faint disappointment.

As he engaged the autopilot, the young pilot drew some satisfaction in knowing that at least the current mission had an air of secrecy and danger. First, the weather at the mountain destination was also conveniently horrible. Then there was the lack of a crew. He was flying solo. Solo meant siloed—secret. Which was sweet. The group of men he was to deliver to a private hangar in Denver included Commander Bill, Tuttle, and a team of Tuttle's Black Ops bros with full combat gear. The mission was cloaked in wonderfully suspicious intent.

He could only hope the landing in Denver would give him the thrill he wanted. And if it made Tuttle grab for the barf bag, all the better.

In the Gulfstream's cabin, Commander Bill sat in a black leather captain's chair, his forehead pressed against the cool glass of the window. The ride through the cloud deck had been bumpy; he was queasy and grateful to be above the outer bands of the approaching storm. Command Bill searched in vain for any breaks in the clouds; he'd hoped for one last view of the fire and smoke from the wildfires that were chewing through the forestland in the east.

"No more smoke. Pretty wild that we could see all that from here," he said.

"'Smoke from a Distant Fire,' Sanford Townsend Band, 1977. Great tune," Tuttle said.

Commander Bill turned to face his second in command, who sat across the aisle in his own captain's chair. Tuttle, dressed in a Silver Eagle jumpsuit that matched Commander Bill's, stared through aviator sunglasses at an open laptop on a table in front of him. He didn't look up. "You probably didn't know Sanford and Townsend were originally in 'Heart.' Not the famous band, 'Heart.' Different one."

Commander Bill's phone vibrated. He pulled it from his pocket. It was a weather alert: a tropical depression in the Gulf of Mexico had strengthened to a category one hurricane. Commander Bill read the alert twice, then told himself that there was something probably not true about it, since there was already one hurricane approaching the southeast and a blizzard in the mountains. He rolled his eyes. He'd started to return the phone to his pocket when it buzzed again. Another alert: "Six Inches of Rain in Michigan, Governor declares state of emergency." Commander Bill shook his head. He looked at his companion. "Looks like old Ham DenBraber is overreacting to a little spring rain. State of emergency. Not what I would've done," Commander Bill said.

Tuttle didn't respond.

"What you working on there, Tuttle?" he said. "I mean, besides remembering weird old songs and stuff."

Tuttle, frowning and focused, typed for several more seconds in silence.

Commander Bill said, "Working up a plan for finding and saving this Vietnamese guy?"

Tuttle fingers stopped. His face twisted. A small sigh escaped. Then, still facing the laptop screen, he said, "I believe our mission is to find Donovan Reed, who is British. I believe it was Mr. Nguyen; who, yes, is of Vietnamese origin; who contacted us—you." Tuttle, eyes still on the screen, sat, mouth closed. He sighed deeply, opened his mouth as if to speak, and then seemed to think better of it. He resumed typing.

"Right. Gotcha. Sorry, Tut. It's been awhile since I've been on a mission, you know, with my operations guys: you and our"—Commander Bill made air quotes—"'brave commandos.'"

"You've never been on one, Commander," Tuttle said, still typing.

Commander Bill ignored the point. He stretched, lifting his arms, his hands brushing the upholstered ceiling of the Gulfstream. He looked out the window and let out a loud long sigh. "Yep. Yes, Tut, Colonel. It does me good to get out in the field like this." He let his hands flop in his lap. He turned to look at Tuttle again. "Glad I green-lighted, you know, the opera… the op."

Tuttle typed for several more seconds, then emphatically hit a key, and stopped. He turned to face Commander Bill and paused, his eyes probing through the dark lenses. Finally, in a low voice, Tuttle said, "Now. You need to listen carefully. And you need to lower your voice."

Commander Bill didn't like the sound of that. But he obeyed. "Why?" he said in a near whisper.

"Because what I have to tell you is of critical importance," Tuttle said. He looked at the luxury jet's carpeted floor, as though he was searching for a thought. He seemed to find it. He looked up. "The people behind that curtain," he nodded toward the rear of the plane, "are my very top people. They're equipped with the best tactical gear money can buy or very talented weapons merchants can steal. But if you were to look at their uniforms, you would see that they're not uniforms. They're combat fatigues without any insignias or markings of any kind. There's a reason for that."

"Sounds like one of your Black Ops deals," Commander Bill said.

"Yes, sir. The men involved are a Black Ops team within our Black Ops team. They're black black. The deepest black. On that score, it's Black Ops."

"Which, as I said, is something I'm not sure you need to tell me about, you know, for security's sake."

Tuttle seemed not to hear him. "These men are prepared to launch an operation that will make history. A very public—and, in that sense, not black—operation. And you are a central figure in it."

"Me." Commander Bill smile frowned.

"Yes. It's something I have been considering for a number of years, given the rise of socialism here and the threats to our personal liberties, as well as the opportunity these things present to my, our, operation from a security-protection-revenue standpoint."

"You're losing me here, Tuttle. Get to the 'me' part."

"Sir, the country—heck, the world—needs the right people to step up and stop this president. As you know, there's been this nonsense about cows. We've seen the movement of cattle into Mexico with the obvious Muslim factor there—the rituals with candles. Our sense is this is the tip of the iceberg."

"She wants to ban koe knuffelen," Commander Bill said.

"What she wants, sir, is to ban beef entirely and control every facet of our lives. And our belief is that certain organizations, certain people, are clearly equipped to stop her."

"My family used to do that."

Tuttle paused. "What, sir?"

135

"Koe knuffelen. During the pandemic. We'd go back to Michigan for a weekend or whatever and one of our friends has this dairy farm and he'd let us knuffel all we wanted. Very therapeutic. Google it."

"Right, Commander. It's a Dutch thing. I know. As I was—"

"There's nothing sexual about it. Some people think there it is. But it's comforting. Cattle are surprisingly soft and those big brown eyes. Very gentle. Wonderful. The feeling is pretty amazing."

"Understood, Commander," Tuttle said, sounding impatient.

"And that Mexican-Muslim deal." Commander Bill thought about this, imagining the rituals with the cow-fat candles. "They pray five times a day, you know."

"Commander, if you could just let me get back on point here."

"I'm talking about Muslims, obviously. They do. Pray. Five times. I'll give them that. I mean, I'm a good Christian, Tuttle. I am. I really am. I like to throw a little quick one up to God in the morning, sort of check-in that way. And at night, before bed. Pray for the kids, the wife, the country—that sort of thing. At church, yes. Of course. The Lord's Prayer, 'Our father who art...' the whole deal. But these people *pray* pray. They get their mats out and face Mecca and do their thing, wherever they are."

"Commander, yes. I am well aware..."

"Very devoted. Very devout. I get it. Tuttle, frankly, they're not in line with God, you know? They're all on the road to h-e-double-hockey-sticks. And that's fine. That's their choice. But the thing is, they don't value life the way we do. I mean, you don't see America killing innocent civilians. As my dad used to say, you can't name one time America took a foreign life that the world wasn't better off without. You just can't. Yes, occasionally, innocents die—but always accidentally. That's what makes war

war. The Muslims? They start their wars as some kind of holy thing. Jihad. We do wars because we want to save people. It's not a holy deal. God just put us in position to have the kind of military that can police these situations."

"Well, yes," Tuttle said. "And the point is, right now we're not playing our role in the world. We've got our eye off the ball. We're chasing this climate nonsense and every other little thing. Silver Eagle's resources put us in the perfect position to bump America back on the right path."

"She wants to get rid of all the police and let boys who want to be girls sneak into the girls' bathroom, Tuttle." Commander Bill said. "Good lord in heaven."

"That's right, sir. So, something must be done. To start, we want to make you president."

Commander Bill thought back to the recent Silver Eagle board of directors meeting, the one in which his sister and brother and a couple of other—he came close to thinking "assholes" but he mentally swerved to "jerks"—had insisted on keeping his title as "commander" despite a motion from one of the other powerful and faceless people on the board who'd thought it was contrary to the company's brand ethos to be led by a man without what this board member called "corporate leadership credibility." Commander Bill usually hated the board meetings but he'd hung on the debate, which had rattled back and forth for an hour or more, primarily focused on striking the right balance between a title that portrayed a leader who could deliver shareholder value and one that exuded the persona of a blood-and-guts kicker of ass with the bummer reality that Billy Hoeksma Jr. was neither. In the end, "commander" was deemed sufficiently not overpromising.

"President?" Commander Bill said. "Seriously?"

"Yes," Tuttle said. "I would not shit you about this, sir."

'But the board."

"Screw the board."

"Tuttle, the language. Jesus."

"Commander, we're talking about a situation of national—international—import. Do you understand what I'm proposing?"

Commander Bill smiled. "Well, yes. Of course."

Tuttle eyed him. He frowned. "I'm not sure you do."

Commander Bill felt a familiar stirring in his chest. His dad and Tuttle had had a way of talking to him, a tone he despised. "Oh, for gosh sakes. Yes. I completely… You don't have to treat me like an idiot."

Tuttle's tinted glare held his gaze for a moment, then another. And another. The gaze reminded Commander Bill that Tuttle could snap his neck like it was a chicken's. He knew this because Tuttle had told him he could. Also, Tuttle raised chickens. He practiced.

Tuttle cracked the tension with another smile. He sat up slightly. He held up a hand. "Okay then. As long as you understand."

"I do. Understand. Perfectly." Commander Bill said, his voice wobbling. He hated that it did that when he was nervous. His dead dad had hated it even more, which was why William Hoeksma, Sr. rarely let William Hoeksma, Jr. handle high-pressure situations on his own. This, Commander Bill vaguely knew, was one of the big reasons he got so nervous in high-pressure situations.

"Good. That's settled. We'll proceed then," Tuttle said. He twisted in his seat and pulled something out of the right pocket of his jumpsuit. It was a small orange. He held it up for Commander Bill to see. Without peeling it, Tuttle took a lavish bite. He chewed for several seconds, the scent of the fruit drifting to Commander Bill, triggering a memory of his father washing Bill Jr.'s mouth out with an orange-scented soap after he, elementary-school-aged Bill Jr., had said how cool he thought it was that Jimmy Carter was a peanut farmer. "Clementine, Commander?" Tuttle said, reaching for his pocket and talking around the citrusy smell and pulp. "I have a couple in here."

"Uh no. No thanks," Commander Bill said.

"You don't know what you're missing." Tuttle took another bite. Commander Bill wanted to ask something but he wasn't sure what it was.

Tuttle sniffed, finished the last of the fruit, swallowed with a bit of difficulty, cleared his throat loudly, and licked each of his fingers before wiping them off on his thigh. He belched and smiled. "Just needed a blood sugar boost there, sir."

"That was weird, Tuttle."

"Well, sometimes it just hits me. Besides, it's going to be a long night, sir. Once we've handled your problem in Denver, we're history-bound to the Sunshine State."

"Whoa. Hold on. Florida? We got kind of a full plate right here, what with the snow and the missing computer guy and all." Commander Bill thought for a moment. "And, and there's the weather back home plus something… I just saw on my phone something about another hurricane in Florida, too. I mean, not that I believe it, but you know it just… I don't think this is the ideal time to head down there."

Tuttle's eyes stared through his sunglasses. The way his lips were set made Commander Bill think "Shut up. Shut up, Commander Bill."

Commander Bill shut up.

Chapter Fourteen

Arkansas airspace

Tuesday night

Tuttle closed the door to the Gulfstream's bathroom and sat on the leather chair next to the bidet. He swiped his phone's screen. The plane shuddered with what would likely be the first of the turbulent air they would ride into Denver. He barely noticed.

He pressed the button on his iPhone and said, "Call the pink-haired chick."

On the screen, a circle swirled. The voice assistant, Siri, was chewing her lower lip and trying to translate his voice into a code she could understand. Finally, a nanosecond before Tuttle said, "C'mon, you idiot," an Australian-accented woman's voice said, "I don't see a 'pink-haired stick' in your contacts."

Tuttle grimaced. He pressed the button again. "I said, call pink. Haired. Chick."

The swirling turned like a wrench in Tuttle's gut—the code apparently too tough for Siri to crack. He pressed the button again to stop the nonsense. He thumbed the phone icon, scrolled through the recent calls, and found the number he was looking for.

A woman answered on the first ring. "About time. We've got her. What do you want us to do with her?"

"Where are you?"

"We're in a Jeep in a parking lot. In a damn blizzard. Waiting for you."

"Is she well?"

"She's plenty pissed is what she is. One of the boys here had to get pretty rough with her to shut her up and get her into the fucking vehicle. Duct tape works wonders on a mouth like that." The woman chuckled. "Want to talk to her?"

"Not really."

"Here. Say something," she said, her voice fading.

Tuttle said nothing. He heard a duct-taped voice mumbling loudly and smiled.

"Now," the woman said, her voice returning to full volume, "we need instructions. Before we freeze our asses off."

Tuttle tried to recall the pink-haired woman's name. Raisa. Rianna. Something like that. She was a rarity in the militia world; a Black woman. More important to him, she was a multiply pierced, tattoo-heavy Colorado militia godsend, a member of the High-Country Mountaineers who had a job at the Safeway where Miky Spike shopped; hell, high water, or polar vortex; the same evening every damn week. They'd planned the op via secure video conference, Tuttle letting her pick two other militia members to help. He hadn't briefed her on anything beyond the kidnapping. She'd been curious, but he'd convinced her she'd be better off not knowing.

"Okay. Listen…" The name came to him. "Raina. I need you to—"

"Pink," Raina said. "You're supposed to call me fucking 'Pink.' No real names because of the g-u-v-e-r… the government. They've tapped my phone before. They could be on here right fucking now. If you don't want me to cut her the fuck loose or

141

slit her damn throat, you best remember that and you better hurry and tell me where you want us to go. I'm about to die in here of the carbon monoxide or some shit."

Tuttle smiled. He liked Raina. A fantasy flickered and he forced it away (for now). "Okay, Pink," he said, drawing out the name. "You and your boys need to help us get our friend there to Denver."

Raina cackled. "How the hell are we supposed to do that? We'll be lucky to get out of town in this piece of shit car in this fucking weather."

Tuttle loved a good swear from a woman, but he couldn't relish it. He had to think. He took a moment, staring at himself in the bathroom's mirror, reviewing options, playing out scenarios, admiring his look. Finally he said, "Get her to the airport, there, in Gunnison. Can you do that?"

"Hold the fuck on," Raina said.

There was a muffled conversation from Raina's side. Then her voice, full volume: "We're like five minutes away. So, yeah." She laughed. "God knows how you're gonna land and take off again in this weather."

"You let me worry about that," Tuttle said.

Tuttle ended the call and then pressed the button to summon Siri. He stared at the swirl on his screen for too long, growled, pressed the button again, returned to his "recent calls" list, and found the number.

"Cody Marks."

In the mirror, Tuttle's face went from a scowl to a smile. "It's me, sunshine."

"I know who it is," Cody Marks said.

"How'd you like to get a little taste of that adventure you've been looking for and earn your full flight status back in the process?"

The hotshot pilot paused. When he spoke, his tone was significantly softer. "What do you have in mind?"

Tuttle winked at himself in the mirror. "We're gonna need to change our flight plan a bit."

Before Tuttle could return to his seat, his phone whirred. It was his other problem, in Boulder. Jasper Joyce's text glared at him: "Teammates snatched wrong target."

"Tell me something I don't know," Tuttle said. His thumbs jabbed angrily at his phone's keys: "I know, idiot! Tuttle."

From Joyce: "You know?"

Tuttle resisted the urge to throw his phone. Instead, hands trembling, he texted: "Nguyen contacted S Eagle about Reed!!!! We are inbound. Tuttle."

"Inbound?"

"To Denver, with a side trip. I have full team. And Commander Jackass. Tuttle."

From Boulder, the hired kidnapper texted: "I've got this. Know Nguyen's location. Planted GPS."

Tuttle thought for a moment. "Where? Tuttle."

Seconds later, Joyce texted: "In his coat."

Tuttle forced himself to exhale. Slowly. "Where is target? Tuttle."

"Borrowed home for weekend. Not far away."

"Can you handle your team-mates? Tuttle."

"Benched. Both."

"Benched. Permanently? Tuttle."

"Forever young."

Damn, Tuttle thought, *this guy*. He texted: "Murders are messy. Tuttle."

"You paid for messy."

Tuttle smiled. You met a lot of horrible humans in this line of work; this time, he'd found one of the talented horrible humans. He texted: "Just you and DR now? Tuttle."

Joyce texted, "DR?"

"Brit Boy. F-ing Reed. You two alone? Tuttle."

"Y."

"Why what? Tuttle."

"Y as in yes."

Tuttle said aloud, "Speak English, asshole," then texted, "Did you tell him I hired you? Tuttle."

Joyce texted, "N."

Tuttle growled. He waited.

Joyce texted, "No."

Tuttle texted, "Tell him. Tuttle."

The airplane shivered. The screen seemed to hold its breath. Tuttle stood, his jaw set. He fought back panic, unzipped his pants, positioned himself at the toilet, and waited impatiently for his prostate to allow his bladder to empty. It didn't. He flushed, zipped, washed his hands at the sink and meticulously dried them with the Silver Eagle-branded red cloth towel. Tuttle looked at his phone and growled, shoved his phone in one pocket of his jumpsuit while fumbling with the contents of the other. His fingers groped the tube of lipstick and he was caught briefly in a drowsy memory of the woman from whom he'd stolen it. LaDonna was her name, or Stephanie. They'd met at a church holiday potluck in Bangor, Maine, Tuttle working undercover for Silver Eagle as a Methodist; LaDonna-Stephanie, with her dazzling cherry-red lips, was there to handle the coffee urn. After a tryst in a mostly private corner of the church narthex, the two had gone their separate ways, but not before he'd pilfered the tube from her open purse. It was a badge from a conquest. A sentimental token of an all-too-brief romance. It was also a color that went well with his eyes.

Tuttle uncapped the lipstick and wrote on the mirror: "Situational Analysis." Below this he added:
- D. Reed supposed to connect with J. Nguyen
  ◦ Done

- J. Joyce supposed to detain J. Nguyen
  ° Took Reed instead (WTF?)

Tuttle reached again into his pocket, found his last clementine, bit into it, and chewed slowly, staring at the cherry-red list. He added:

- Need more clementines

His mind drifted. He thought about the decision to worm into a relationship with Donovan Reed. He recalled it as a long and winding road, and immediately the Beatles' "The Long and Winding Road" drifted into his head which crossfaded to "Knock Three Times" by Tony Orlando and Dawn, an earworm connection that only made sense in the context of his enthusiastic embrace of LSD in the late 1970s. Tuttle forced his way out of the mind muddle by destroying the clementine in two aggressive bites. He tilted his head back and swallowed hard, coughed, coincidentally, three times at the ceiling, and swallowed again. After a moment of studying his now red-rimmed eyes, Tuttle turned away from the mirror and sat in the chair. He slogged back through the swamp of his memories to the day his three-man Black Dog Intelligence Team (B-DIT) discovered that Jackson Nguyen, the Michigan-born tech entrepreneur, was the brother of Lalani Nguyen, the sixteen-year-old lust-of-his-life who'd metaphorically ripped out Tuttle's heart in a helicopter over the Gulf of Thailand in 1975. His rage over the loss of Lalani—well, okay, over her betrayal— still tasted like the bad Thai food they'd shared one steamy weekend. The B-DIT commanding officer; a burly, bearded former National Security Agency employee whose name now escaped him; had marched into Tuttle's office while Tuttle was shaving his head and delivered the news: Jackson Nguyen, Lalani's brother, lived in seclusion somewhere in Silicon Valley but his family, Lalani's family, lived in Traverse City, Michigan, a two-and-a-half-hour drive from Silver Eagle's former home base. Jackson Nguyen's parents confirmed Lalani was their daughter. They said she had left the U.S. years ago to become a nun and had fallen completely off the radar. That left the first American-born Nguyen, the famous tech wonder boy, as the only source of information. But damnit, the family couldn't reach Jackson either—hadn't tried in years. He was a public figure, yes. But he was a very private one with a tough, loyal security team who rebuffed every attempt at contact. Letters were disregarded. Visits to his gated home were spurned. He wouldn't return emails. Tuttle refused to call him. Finally, in a fit of pique, he defaulted to his forte, a confrontational and somewhat criminal approach. He would coax Jackson into the open and then detain him. B-DIT found Donovan Reed, a totally pliable man whose infidelities, backdoor dealings, and nightmarish personal finances would nearly but not quite make Tuttle blush. Compromising photos and hacked financial records gave Tuttle's team what it needed: Reed agreed to get together with Jackson. Hiring Jasper Joyce to "secure Nguyen" had been Tuttle's idea.

Now, the op was off the rails. Because of Joyce's now-retired teammates.

Tuttle's phone vibrated.

"Told him." Joyce's text read.

Tuttle typed, "He happy? Tuttle." And sent it.

Joyce responded with a blown-up-head emoji. He then texted, "I can still deliver Nguyen. And rendezvous with you."

Tuttle sighed and texted, "Give me a minute. Tuttle."

He looked at his messy list on the mirror and the messier list in his head. A brief, unfamiliar feeling, which Tuttle vaguely understood was doubt, snaked through the messiness. His famous inner strength wobbled. This moment, this day, was to have been about Silver Eagle and, more important, Project

Black Dog firmly leading America back on the right path. This was supposed to be the day the right people punched back against the meat banners and the socialist global-warmists, the gun-hating queers and pussies, the quinoa-eating east-coast media morons, the Tesla-driving Hollywood woke wackos, and the tattooed illegals and dealers and bangers who had been quietly drowning America in an f-ing melting pot since forever. For Tuttle, deep down, it was also to be the day he rose above the embarrassment of Operation Cheesus and, deeper down, of the father who had walked out on his mom and toddler Tuttle to go live with a man Tuttle's mom would thereafter call "your Uncle Steven" but Tuttle doubted was his uncle or even Steven because who knew any Black guys named "Steven" who also wore dickies? This last part, about his father and the dickie-wearing not-uncle had not appeared in his conscious mind in decades, which made the moment feel even more precarious.

Tuttle closed his eyes.

At the bottom of the mirror, he wrote:

- GET CONTROL/FOCUS
  ° Contact people in DC
  ° Draw POTUS to Tampa
  ° Launch BOOGALOOOOOO
- Eliminate problems
  ° Joyce's team
    - Done
  ° Reed?
  ° Joyce?
  ° Nguyen
  ° Spike

Tuttle's phone vibrated and kept vibrating for several seconds. He looked at the screen, swore, and answered the call, "I said to give me a minute."

The response came with a British accent, "Just what in bloody hell have you got me into?" Tuttle winced and held the phone away from his ear. The tirade continued, Donovan Reed spewing about "blizzard" and "kidnapping" and "rat bastard gun crazies" with a "we had a deal" and "my lawyers" thrown in for good measure.

When Donovan finally stopped for a breath, Tuttle pressed the phone to his ear and said, "You need to…"

"I need to do nothing. I already did everything. We had an understanding," Donovan Reed said, his voice boiling, "an understanding based on blackmail, I might add. Black. Mail. You dredged up all of this muck, all of these personal… these things about me, and threatened to spread all of it to the authorities and press and most of it is rumors and lies."

"One of those 'lies' happened to involve a sixteen year old."

Donovan ignored him. "I re-connected with Jackson. I gave him your tracking device, let me add, and suddenly these goons, these imbeciles, kidnapped me; that's what it is, kidnapping; and they brought me here and now this man murdered them right…" Donovan paused for a moment. When he spoke, his voice was shaking, "He murdered them in cold blood right in front of me." He paused again, collecting himself, "And now, NOW, I discover this awful man is also, what, working for you too?"

Tuttle stared at his lipsticked analysis of the situation. When Donovan at last talked himself out, Tuttle said, calmly, "Give the phone to Mr. Joyce, please."

"I'll do no such…"

"Give. The phone. To Mr. Joyce. It will only be a minute."

There was a pause followed by a muffled, "He wants to talk to you, apparently."

Jasper Joyce came on the line. "Yeah?"

Chapter Fifteen

I-75 in Georgia

Tuesday night

Zip Pierce; former major league baseball player, retired high school athletic director, and avid doomsday prepper broke the drowsy quiet in the crew cab of Big Bruddah's Ford F-350 pickup.

"Yo, Bruddah boy," Zip said. "You been behind that steering wheel for hours. What do you say we find us some food for this little army? The athlete in this old man needs to refuel and I need to drop the kids off at the pool, if you know what I'm saying, big man."

Big Bruddah glanced in the rearview mirror. Zip was crammed into the backseat between Corky Vanderlaan, a graying Gulf War vet from Dearborn, and the black-bearded, shaggy-haired bear of a man from suburban Grand Rapids whose name no one knew but everyone called Nunchucks. "Tampa is still quite a ride from here. There's a lot of I-75 to eat," Big Bruddah sad.

"Yeah, and we need to eat something besides road, Bruddah buddy," Zip said. "Am I right, boys?"

No one responded.

"C'mon, guys," Zip said. "Little help here."

Big Bruddah shook his head. "From where I sit, your athleticism will not be affected by a missed meal, Zip," he said, drawing a rumble of laughter from Corky, "If you're that desperate, I can pull over. You can take care of your business in the ditch. We got freeze-dried rations in the back. At least everyone should have it—in their packs."

They drove another mile or so in silence, except for the hum of the truck's massive tires and Charlie Pride on the radio singing about an angel. Then Corky shifted in his seat and said, "Gotta admit. Need to eat. Need to whiz."

Big Bruddah groaned and shook his head; Corky was the last guy he'd figured would stop on the way to a serious operation. "Sounds like I'm driving into a war with a bunch of girls, Jerry." He glanced to Jerry Plannenberg, a pony-tailed ex-murderer and Bruddah's long-time buddy. Jerry was trying to doze. Face lit by the glow of the dash, he opened one eye. "An army runs on its stomach," he said to the windshield. "And we got us some stomachs."

Big Bruddah glanced in the rearview. "I'm betting Nunchucks is with me at least. Need to make time, am I right Chucksman?"

"I don't give a shit," Nunchucks said from the back seat. Big Bruddah shook his head. Nunchucks didn't care to tell anyone his real name, what he did for a living, or if he had, as the militia rumor mill claimed, killed his family. His feelings about a snack were, not surprisingly, kept to himself.

They were nearing an exit. High in the night sky, the yellow, lighted letters "Waf fle Hous" beckoned. Bruddah sighed and hit the turn signal.

"There you go, Bruddah man," Zip said.

Their waitress, a thin woman named Brenda who reminded Bruddah of a girl he once liked but never dated, led Bruddah and his men to a table. Corky and Nunchucks sat first, on opposite sides of the table. Bruddah plopped down next to Nunchucks. Jerry sat next to Corky. Zip took the head of the table. Brenda handed them each a menu and smiled as they pulled their sidearms from holsters and placed them on the table next to their paper placemats.

"You got a problem with this?" Nunchucks said, nodding to his weapon.

Brenda the waitress barked out a husky laugh. "Well, we do got a policy," she said.

She held their collective gawk for a beat, then said, "We say 'no guns, no guts, no service.'"

Bruddah, Corky, and Jerry laughed. Nunchucks frowned, picked up his gun, and stared at it long enough to kill the laughter. Something dark fluttered through the big man's eyes. "What is that supposed to even mean?" Nunchucks said, eyes locked on the gun in his hand. "No guns, no guts…"

Big Bruddah shot a raised eyebrow at Jerry.

Jerry said, "We're cool here, Nunchucks. She's saying she's one of us. It's a play on words, kind of. They're, like, pro-gun here, you know?"

"Yeah, relax, dude. We're all good," Corky said.

Nunchucks slowly put down the gun, eyes still locked on it. It was a nice gun, Big Bruddah couldn't help but think, the words slipping out, "Sweet piece there, buddy."

"Sig Sauer P226," Nunchucks said. "Like the one the SEALS use. I stole it off one of them in a bar." He looked at Brenda. "What's your special?"

"Well, hon, let's see," Brenda said in a voice tinged by a lifetime in Cobb County. "It's way past suppertime, you boys are packing, you're the only customers in 500 miles, and it's colder than a witch's tit out there." Before Nunchucks could respond, she added, "I like your company is what I'm saying, so let's just consider everything on special and start with coffee."

Big Bruddah smiled and turned over the upside-down coffee mug next to his gun. "I take mine black."

"It's not all he takes black. Just ask all his lady friends," Zip said with a wink at Brenda. "Big daddy here takes his with a little sweetener, Sweetie."

"Walk that 'black' comment back, asshole," Big Bruddah said. And meant it.

Brenda filled Bruddah's cup, turned over Corky's and Nunchucks' and looked at Corky, who said, "I believe we both will take ours straight." Nunchucks' grunt seemed to affirm this.

Bruddah's gun, a Beretta 9A-1, was up and pointed at Zip's smirk before he could make his next predictable comment about "taking it straight." Through clenched teeth, Bruddah said, "Zip here will take his with some fucking Sweet 'N Low, and will apologize to me before I shoot his empty head off. And then he will zip his mouth."

Brenda finished pouring Corky's and then filled Nunchucks' cup of black. She eyed Zip. He winked again and held his palms up. "I give," he said and turned to Big Bruddah. "My deepest apologies, amigo."

"What an asshole," Big Bruddah said to himself. He leaned back, his gun still in his hand.

Zip flipped his coffee cup and forced a laugh, "If I don't watch it, I'll get myself shot before the boogaloo." He looked at Brenda. "Trust me, honey. I played pro ball and missing the big boogie would be like taking a ninety-five-mile-an-hour fastball right down the poop chute after all the training we've done."

Brenda froze, coffee pot in hand, trying to act like she hadn't heard. She was not a good pretender.

"Zip," Jerry said.

"What?" Zip said. He looked around the table, his gaze stopping at Big Bruddah. "I'm just saying it would be nice to actually make it to Florida. I been waiting for this since 'Nam, which I didn't get to go to because I—"

Big Bruddah slammed his pistol on the table. Coffee sloshed, silverware rattled. "Zip."

"Zip what? A lot of people say I deserve this chance, you know. I mean, Tigers won the World Series last year. Lions won their first Super Bowl. My bucket list is missing one thing. The big, fat boogaloo."

"Zip," Corky and Jerry said, simultaneously.

"What?" Zip said.

"Shutthefuckup," Nunchucks said.

Brenda, her face a fragile mask, filled Zip's mug to the rim in one pour. "Sweetner's right there," she said, pointing to a small wicker basket in the middle of the table. Corky grabbed a packet of Sweet 'N Low and flipped it to Zip, who tried to catch it and missed.

"I'll give you a few minutes," Brenda said, and walked toward the kitchen.

"No. Hold on," Big Bruddah said. "Let's go ahead and order. We need to get this show on the road."

Brenda shook her head, shrugged her shoulders. Her smile returned. She pulled a pad of paper from her apron pocket. A pen appeared from somewhere.

"Don't pay attention to shit Zip says," Big Bruddah said. "Dude hasn't said anything relevant in, like, thirty years."

Brenda patted Big Bruddah on his forearm. "I got this," the forearm-pat said. Then she looked at Zip and said, "So what'll be, Mr. Boogaloo Baseball Star?"

It was way too late, according to the glowing dial on Big Bruddah's military-grade watch. Bruddah and Jerry were sitting on the rear bumper of the truck, Jerry smoking and Bruddah tapping his army-booted foot, the Waffle House parking lot lights quivering and shadows dancing across the glistening asphalt. "They better hurry their asses up or I'm leaving without them," Big Bruddah said.

"It's not necessarily all of them I'm worried about. It's him. Swear to god I'm gonna kill him," Jerry said. "Why he had to come I have no idea."

Big Bruddah shook his head. "He came because he's committed. He knows his weapons. And he's loyal as a brain-damaged golden retriever. Besides, he gives us a brand-name personality if shit goes sideways. People have heard of him."

"A few people. For, like, the two good seasons he had in the 1970s."

"All those years he was athletic director at that school in Farmington—that, too. What I'm saying is, he's got a profile."

"I can't believe you defend him."

"I don't. I manage him. It's what you do with dudes like Zip."

Jerry shook his head, gray ponytail dancing in the wild wind. He took a long drag on his cigarette. "What he said about boogaloo. That puts this whole deal in, like, jeopardy."

"He's the least of our problems."

"People knowing about us is a pretty big problem."

"Yeah, well, good news is I got something else up my sleeve. Something pretty awesome." Big Bruddah's smile glowed in the parking lot lights. "For when we get down there."

"What?"

"You're gonna love it. Trust me."

"Oh, you're about the only one I do trust."

"And seriously, we'll deal with Zip."

"You'll deal with Zip."

"Fine. But big-picture problem is we're going to need munitions. Had a shitload of pipe bombs and grenades and shit down there in that bunker."

"You said that to me earlier. You're making me nervous. Are you nervous?"

"No. Not at all. Just trying to play three-dimensional chess or whatever." Big Bruddah hated the way his own voice sounded—defensive. He tried to smooth it out, to lower the octave. "There's a lot to think about. I mean, we're heading into this thing hot and fast and blind."

"This was your call, Brother."

"What does that mean?"

"I'm just saying."

"Tuttle's the one that messed this up."

"You're the one that got us in bed with a crazy man. Now you got your underwear on backwards and don't know how it happened."

Big Bruddah swallowed a chestful of anger. "Just like with Zip, you need to work with some guys because of what they bring to the party. Tuttle having his own private militia with a multi-million-dollar budget and weapons up the yin-yang, that's a heckofa party."

"Money comes with a price, my grandma always said."

"I didn't expect he'd start calling me a pussy," Big Bruddah said, the heat rekindling in his gut.

Jerry looked at his cigarette. "You know as well as I do that this isn't the first time people like you and Tuttle had disagreements. Militias are always splitting apart for one reason or another. I mean, hell, I never considered myself a boogaloo boy really until now. I know some people back in the day that would've thrown us out of Red Sky for thinking about taking down the government or whatever we're doing."

"Oh, that brings up a whole 'nother issue right there. Not sure Tuttle has an end game or that we do. Didn't exactly talk that through."

"I don't have a problem with that. We get down there. Set it all in motion. Chips gotta fall. See where they land."

"Yeah, I guess."

Big Bruddah stared off, searching the night for answers. "You're right," he said. "This isn't the first time people were fighting inside, you know, the movement. There's always been this, like, ideological battle."

Jerry snorted smoke out of his nose. "Listen to you. Talking 'ideological.' Now you're making my head hurt, college boy."

"I'm just saying I get your point." Big Bruddah said.

"Right. And then you throw in a guy like Tuttle and that walking coma Billy Hoeksma, you got a whole buttload of ideological whatever." Jerry started to laugh but it turned into a phlegmy coughing jag. When he recovered, he said, "We could end up fighting, like, a civil war against each other. So, you're saying that could be a problem?" He ran through the laugh-cough jag again.

"All that said," Big Bruddah said with a sigh. "That waitress is not a problem."

"You're sure about that."

"Positive," Big Bruddah said.

"I could take care of her, you know. Wouldn't be but a thing."

"She gave me a nod when I paid. She's cool. A sympathizer."

"So we're figuring our security status on a nod basis."

"I asked her if we were good. She said we were. She's cool. She and Zip don't worry me like the others do."

Jerry took another drag and shot the smoke into the wind. He stood, shoulders bent, shivering, skinny fingers holding the cigarette away from him, hopping from one foot to the other. "You're thinking about Nunchucks."

"I mean, I let him on the team because he's supposedly got that murder streak in him, know what I'm saying? That's gonna come in handy at some point."

156

Jerry crouched against the icy wind and let out a brittle laugh. "Hey, I killed a complete stranger in a factory because a guy paid me to do it. And I don't act batshit crazy like this guy."

"You were professional about it. I would expect a guy who murdered his family to be crazier than your basic hired murderer. Doesn't make him less valuable to us."

"I didn't use a gun. Drugged his drink then punched him a lot. Guy didn't suffer, I tell you that. It was over fast," Jerry said. "Didn't feel a thing."

There was a long silence. The wind whistled, chasing a truck on the interstate.

Bruddah looked toward the restaurant. "All I know is they better hurry up. And lord help whoever goes into that bathroom once Zip's done with it."

Jerry got the hint. Conversation over. "Damn, it's cold," he said. "We got past all that rain in Michigan and Indiana but now we're freezing our asses off in Georgia. Thought it was supposed to be warm down here this time of year. Radio said they could get snow. Like a few inches. Insane weather."

"In about two seconds, I'm leaving without those assholes."

Jerry chuckled. "Yeah, turns out the ol' 1990s-era battle dress uniforms aren't all that warm. Buy shit on the internet, you deal with it."

"It'll be warm in Florida," Bruddah said, his teeth chattering. "And it's damn warmer in the truck." He started to walk around Jerry. The two men bumped into each other. Jerry's cigarette flew from his mouth in a shower of sparks; he lunged for it and tripped over Bruddah's leg. To right himself, Jerry grabbed Big Bruddah around the waist. Bruddah tried to shove his skinny friend away.

From the restaurant entrance, a voice boomed. "Look at this, boys. The minute our backs are turned, they go all gay for each other."

The other three militia men; Corky, Zip, and Nunchucks; were jogging toward them, a wheezing Zip in the lead with a big smile.

Big Bruddah, unsnapped his holster and drew his Beretta. "Who's calling me a faggot?"

"Don't shoot, my fairy good friend," Zip said with a mocking lisp.

Corky Vanderlaan, reading the parking lot, said, "Zip it, Zip."

"I'm just saying…" Zip said with a running shrug.

"Shut the F up, Pierce. We gotta move," Nunchucks said. "Sun'll be coming up soon. Gotta make time."

Big Bruddah looked past the men. Inside the Waffle House, Brenda the waitress stared, open-mouthed, at him. The front of her uniform was soaked; she was holding her arms out and sucking in her stomach as though her body was in retreat. The tile floor in front of her was puddled with brown liquid and the shattered remains of what had to be a coffee pot.

"What the fu—?" Big Bruddah said.

"Nunchucks didn't like the coffee," Corky said.

The other men scrambled to get into the truck. Big Bruddah took a step toward the restaurant, figuring maybe he should go back inside, explain Nunchucks and offer to pay for her uniform and the coffee pot. But Brenda turned and walked toward the kitchen, cell phone in hand.

Chapter Sixteen

Boulder, Colorado

Tuesday night

Donovan Reed wasn't dead; he just felt like he was. He wished he could say the same thing for Jasper Joyce.

Donovan was driving Joyce's rented SUV, following the directions supplied by the vehicle's onboard navigation system. It had, indeed, been a long time since Donovan had been behind the wheel. The sky was brightening in the east, which improved visibility a bit. He tried to convince himself to drive faster, but it was still snowing lightly and the road to Jackson Nguyen's friend's mountain home was a twisty frozen snake. To complicate matters, Donovan kept glancing in the rearview mirror, fearing police lights would appear. He couldn't shake the image of those lights catching up to him, a Colorado cop forcing him over and approaching the vehicle with his gun drawn, ready to shoot him the way American cops liked to shoot Black men and maybe foreigners like Donovan Reed. Donovan imagined buzzing down the window, and yelling, "I'm unarmed. I'm unarmed," even though Jasper Joyce's gun was jabbing his ribs, reminding him—nagging him—that it was in his pocket and no longer in the bloody grip of its owner. In the best-case version of the scenario, Donovan saw the cop believing his lie about not being armed, and not asking for the license he didn't have.

"Tough weather for you to be out in," the cop would say.

"Oh yeah. A real bugger," Donovan would say.

"That's a great accent you got there." The cop would smile, the lights going red blue white red blue white on his ruddy face, his eyes squinting against the biting wind and snow. "Where'bouts you from?"

"The UK, I'm a Brit here on business, mate," Donovan would go full Liverpool—a ploy that always took the tension out of an encounter with an American authority figure, because Donovan really sounded like Sir Paul when he talked like a Liverpudlian and Sir Paul was number one on all the Brit accent charts among a certain American demographic.

"Well, it's certainly good that I stopped you," the cop would say. "My great grandfolks happen to be from over there in England themselves. Maybe we're related." He'd chuckle then, and Donovan would respond with a chuckle of his own. The two of them would laugh and laugh, warmed against the brutal night by the bond of an imagined genetic tie. And the encounter would end with the cop promising to come visit when he got a chance to bring "the wife across the pond to the homeland."

"Oh, one last thing," the cop would say, wagging a big, wind-raw finger in the air. "Best be careful out here. The weather's bad. And we've had a murder and fire over in town. Some crazy is on the loose. Found three dead bodies in the house."

Donovan tried to shake loose the image, tried to focus on the two-track tire trail cut through the snow, but it was difficult. He glanced in the rearview, lingering a bit too long on the frozen world behind him, and felt the big SUV wander to the right. He jerked the wheel, which sent him toward the left shoulder and a great chasm of nothingness beyond it. He braked. The vehicle slid sideways for one, five, eight, 10 seconds, and stopped. He sat there, on the left shoulder, listening to the heater fan and the wipers ka-thunk ka-thunk as adrenalin hit his heart like an inflamed fist and another image, this one of Jasper Joyce setting fire to the house and then turning to point the gun at him and headlights appeared, coming toward him, so Donovan took his foot off the brake and quickly guided his vehicle into what looked like the right lane and slowly continued driving, the ghost of Tuttle's hired hit man telling him to look behind him. He tried to resist it.

Jackson was startled from his dreams by Kanye, the resident cat; the thing was sitting on his chest and batting his face with a declawed but earnest paw. The guy who owned the house and Kanye, Christopher Sticknor, was another globe-traveling entrepreneur with his fingers in a zillion highly profitable pies. He was in Singapore for the month. Christopher had emailed that a cat daycare provider would stop by twice a day but apparently Kanye hadn't read the email or noticed the depth of the snow in the driveway. Jackson covered his face with his hands, but that only seemed to incite more batting. He groaned and swatted at the now growling animal and, in the ensuing commotion—Kanye hated to be swatted as much as Jackson despised cats, particularly batting ones—Jackson rolled off the leather couch on which he'd fallen asleep. He landed, face down, on the glossy wood floor as Kanye jumped to the coffee table.

'Stupid animal. It's still night-time." Jackson said, his voice muffled by the cold hardwood. After a few moments, he rolled to his back with another groan. He needed to pee and, like the cat, he was hungry. Had he forgotten dinner the evening before?

Yes, yes he had. Breakfast sounded good. Jackson struggled to his feet.

Kanye jumped from his perch, stretched languidly, and trotted off. Mission evidently accomplished.

After he'd visited one of the five bathrooms, Jackson walked into the kitchen, turned on the outdoor floodlights, and surveyed the storm's damage through floor-to-vaulted-two-story-ceiling windows. In the pre-dawn light, snow was still falling in thick flakes; the staggering height of what had already accumulated stirred a familiar buzz of excitement in his gut.

Jackson found in the pantry, on a rubber-coated-wire shelf, a clear plastic tote marked "Kanye Food." Jackson opened it and selected a packet marked with the day's date. Suddenly, Kanye was underfoot. Jackson stumbled, took a wild kick at him, missed, almost fell, and then righted himself. Kanye made a weird cat noise and scampered away.

Grumbling, Jackson found a set of dishes on the floor near the back door. He poured the contents of the day's packet into a gleaming gold dish—"Kanye Food" was etched in the side—and added water to the silver dish next to it inscribed with "Kanye H20."

The kitchen, as promised, was fully stocked. "Thanks, Chris, for bringing an entire Whole Foods onto your mountain," Jackson muttered.

He chose a locally made granola, poured some of it in a bowl, added almond milk, heard his father mutter in his old-world accent about "milking almonds," and brewed drip coffee. Jackson turned to watch the snow through the glass wall, the rich Italian roast filling the kitchen with the scent of morning, the gurgling machine bringing life to the large, empty house.

Then he remembered. Donovan. Damn.

He hurried to the living room, found his laptop, and checked his email. His inbox was, as usual, packed. He scrolled past messages of worry and woe from work and stopped at one he'd been waiting for, from a friend. He lingered for a moment, finger tapping lightly on the trackpad, and continued on without opening it. He found several messages from Bill Hoeksma's aide, indicating interest and asking for a response. Jackson quietly cursed himself for falling asleep. Near the bottom of the inbox, he found what he was hoping for: Hoeksma and a team led by his second in command, Wilbur Tuttle, were on their way. They'd contact him upon arrival.

Jackson rekindled the fire and fed it new logs. When it was roaring, he sat again on the leather couch. He ate the granola and drank his coffee. When he was finished, he returned to the laptop. Another Google search turned up no new stories on Donovan or on him. The kidnapping of Donovan Reed was his secret for now, but with Silver Eagle involved, people would tell people. The story would go public within hours.

This time, Jackson attacked his email inbox. He responded to the notes that needed immediate attention, filed away those he would need to manage later, and deleted the ones for which no response was the appropriate response.

He was writing a response to his friend, who was hoping to go skiing with him that weekend, when someone pounded on the front door. Jackson jumped to his feet, suddenly wary.

He waited, quiet as a whisper.

More pounding.

Jackson turned to look through the front windows. There was a black SUV in the driveway. The snow had muffled the vehicle's arrival.

More pounding.

Kanye appeared from nowhere and darted past him. Jackson's gut told him no way this was some stupid feeder of cats coming out in a storm. He shooed the animal away and opened the door.

Donovan Reed fell into his involuntary embrace.

"Holy shit," Jackson said, trying to extract himself. He kicked the door shut.

Donovan held on. He began to sob. "Sorry. I know you're not a hugger," Donovan Reed said into Jackson Nguyen's chest. He twisted free, stumbled to the couch and sat like a man who didn't want to sit but had no better idea.

Jackson sat on the coffee table, back to the fireplace. Donovan was grayish pale, his hair tortured, angst bleeding from his face.

"He was a hired killer. A bloody hired. Killer." Donovan said. "What the bloody hell? What was I supposed to do? I mean, I was trapped. And here he was, coming at me with that… and the house was… He'd set fire—"

"Whoa. Wait. Who?"

"The guy who looked like John Lennon. Him. He killed them and then set the house on fire…"

"Killed who?"

"The two… the other men. The ones who took me. They called themselves Bunker and Owen. But those probably aren't their real names."

"Probably not. No."

"They took me to this… this hellish house on the other side of Boulder. And we get there, and it's cold. And awful. And smelled like rubbish. They were eating fruit—fresh fruit—like we're on a walk in the park. And all of a sudden they realized they'd taken the wrong fellow. Apparently, they got confused somehow and grabbed me and when this monster, this Jasper Joyce, saw what they'd done, he confronted them with their mistake," Donovan Reed's voice began to tremble. "The Americans and their guns. Their bloody fucking guns."

His eyes were brimming. "He killed them. Right there. With a gun. In front of me. And when he set fire to the house, he was going to shoot me, and I reached for the thing… for the bloody gun. It went off." His bloodshot eyes told Jackson the rest.

Jackson put a trembling hand on Donovan's knee. "Look at me."

Donovan raised his eyes.

"This isn't your fault. None of it. We can talk to the police. Whatever those men were doing, whoever they were… whatever they were looking for, it wasn't about you. You were kidnapped. That's a crime. Then the rest is clearly a matter of you saving yourself."

Donovan Reed's face flinched. He pushed away Jackson's hand. Something in his loud, jagged breathing sounded like a warning.

"Someone. Someone hired them."

"Obviously, someone… yes. Had to have…"

"It was the same gentleman," Donovan's voice shrank, "who hired me."

Before Jackson tried to respond—he couldn't—Donovan spit out the story. "He came to me and demanded that I help him. He had pictures, affidavits, of certain indiscretions." Donovan Reed looked at the floor. "He was going to ruin me. He wanted me to get together," his voice dribbled away, "with you. Out in public somewhere. It seemed like a simple enough request."

Jackson closed his eyes and counted slowly to one hundred by threes, a habit he'd developed as a young math whiz when trying to respond to his first-grade teacher, Mrs. Feely, who always called on him with an otherwise never apparent Asian accent. He opened his eyes. No luck. He was still in the house, still the only Asian in the room, still had no answers.

"Why me? Why so—cloak and whatever? I mean, is there like a hit out on me or something?" The thought made the granola churn in his stomach. "This doesn't make any sense."

"Oh, I think he's just this way. With these types of people. A bid for drama so he can get whatever information he needs. He's that awful crazy man who tried to invade Wisconsin a few years ago with your godawful governor. He's with Silver Eagle. The security guys."

Jackson was standing, staring into the fireplace. Too close to the fire. The cat, Kanye, was in his hands. Jackson didn't know how he'd gotten there, cat in hand, but he knew he was hot. Very hot. And he couldn't move—couldn't turn. This was messed up.

"Wilbur Tuttle," he said the name he'd seen in the email just moments before.

"Yes, apparently, he had a… a situation with your sister in Vietnam from back before you were born and I simply complied with his demands because I felt…"

"My… my sister."

"The sister born over there. In Vietnam."

"Lalani."

"Yes. If that's her name. Yes."

Jackson stood there with the hot fire and the now-squirming cat. "What does that have to do with me?" Jackson said to the fire, which didn't answer.

He turned to face Donovan Reed. The cat squirmed free and darted off to find a cooler place to be. "I mean, is this, like, extortion or whatever? I don't even know the woman."

"I… I don't know."

"Wrong answer. What did he tell you?"

"That he… he wanted to find her and he was having trouble finding her and then he found out that you were her brother and he was getting nowhere so he decided to…"

"He could have just, I don't know, contacted me."

"His people tried."

"So instead, he wanted to lure me out to kidnap me?"

"More like 'engage you,' I suppose. The men involved, as I say, are a certain kind of people. Long on menace. Very very short on execution."

"Nice choice of word."

"Apologies."

"That's the best you've got? 'Apologies'? You could have called before it came to this. Told me what he wanted. I would've told you I don't know where she is. She left. Went to serve the Lord and never came back."

"I… I couldn't. He has a way. A really really persuasive way about using information and threats of physical pain to get what he wants. And he made it clear he didn't want me to talk to you about any of this. He wants to talk with you."

Jackson pondered the absurdity of it all. Then he laughed. "Well, he'll have his chance, I guess. He's on his way here."

"Who?" Donovan's bloodshot eyes bulged.

"Tuttle. Hoeksma. Silver Eagle. They're coming here."

"How on earth would you know that?"

"Because I contacted them." Jackson was standing over Donovan Reed, who seemed to be retreating, back first, into the leather couch.

"Whatever for?" Donovan's hit a new level of shrill.

"To find you."

"That's not true. You didn't. It's too bloody…"

Jackson shrugged. "What? Too unbelievable?" He laughed dryly. "Oh you're perfect."

Donovan stood. He began to pace. "We can just get out of here. Right now. We can go. I'll disappear somewhere—Fiji or whatever. You can take a vacation, too. Disappear. Heck, go back to the homeland for a while. Find that sister." He laughed with the certainty that he shouldn't laugh.

The ringtone was foreign to both men.

"That's you," Jackson said.

"No. No. That's. That's not me," Donovan said. He angled his head, his ear searching for the source of the tone, which was playing again, begging for an answer.

"It's coming from your coat," Jackson said. "And if has anything to do with this… this situation we're in, then I would hope you'd get your act together and answer it."

The tone played again. Donovan began panic-patting his pockets.

"Oh," Jackson said, "and just keep in mind that this Tuttle, I assume, wanted you dead and probably thinks you are."

The tone played again, and Donovan reached for it, pulled a phone from its hiding place and stared at it. Bewilderment quickly became recognition. "His phone," he said. He held the thing away from him. "It's not mine. It's his. The… John Len… Mr. Joyce. I took it. After."

Jackson took the dead man's phone. "Probably a burner. Prepaid." He flipped it open and held it to his ear. "Yeah," he said in a voice he thought was suitably like the voice of the guy who looked like John Lennon but was now dead.

There was a pause, and then a tinny female voice: "Hi, this is Donna from Credit America and we are calling to offer you an amazingly great rate on our no-fee credit…" Jackson flipped the phone shut, whirled, and cocked his arm to throw it into the fireplace. Donovan fell to the couch, the back of a hand over his eyes.

As if pleading for mercy, the phone chirped. Jackson fought back his rage, and flipped it open. A text. Jackson read it aloud, "We are outbound to Tampa. Things are messy. Get to DIA as soon as possible. I have a charter waiting. Bring JN. Tuttle."

Jackson stared at the screen. At the name.

"Tuttle. He ends his texts with his name," Jackson said softly. He looked at Donovan Reed, who'd taken the hand from his eyes. "My dad always does that. Like I don't know who's texting."

"He thinks…"

"Yeah, he thinks he's texting the guy…"

"Jasper. Jasper Joyce."

"Whatever. Him. Yeah." Jackson scrolled back through the text string between Jasper Joyce and Tuttle. He stopped. Frowned. Read one text four times. "You planted some kind of tracking device on me?"

"I… I… he wanted. Well, yeah. I did. I did."

"Where?"

"It's in your… your coat."

Jackson thought about this. He looked at his definitely-ex friend. "Let me guess. The thumb drive."

Donovan tried to speak, but only a nod came out.

Jackson smiled. "So, that's your next big idea, uh? Our next great joint venture?"

The phone chirped again. The text said: "You have JN, right? Tuttle."

Jackson looked at Donovan Reed. He looked at the phone. He looked at Donovan Reed. The cat, sensing trouble, darted off.

Jackson shook his head and texted, "Oh, I have him all right." To Donovan he said, "C'mon. It's going to take a while to get to the airport."

"But we can just go." Donovan's eyes were pleading. "I'll pay. Wherever you want to go."

Jackson ignored him.

PART SIX

Flight Zero Zero Zero To Boogaloo

Chapter Seventeen

Gunnison, Colorado

Tuesday night

Raina's accomplices and their rust-bucket SUV were gone. They'd rattled off into the swirling snow after depositing Miky and Raina at the tiny Gunnison-Crested Butte Regional Airport's terminal.

Two TSA men greeted them at the check-in area, one going to great pains to say they'd stayed behind to help with the inbound private jet "even though the airport was technically closed." A lone video monitor confirmed his claim: There were six canceled departures and six canceled arrivals.

Raina reached in her camo backpack, pulled out a wallet, flashed a badge and said something about "FBI emergency, national-security-related..."

Despite Miky's emphatic protests to the contrary, the men accepted Raina's credentials, one saying, with a slight guffaw, that she "definitely looks undercover, with that hair," the other guy muttering about "weird chicks trying to catch a friggin' flight in this weather" and that the whole thing sounded like a major "government screw-up" to him.

The TSA guys made a big show of walking them through a security check, Raina's Glock 23 drawing some quickly disregarded consternation. ("She's FBI, dude.")

At the gate, Raina zip-tied Miky's hands and forced her to sit. Raina plopped down her backpack, removed her parka and draped it on the back of the chair next to Miky, then sat too. The mutterer TSA guy said he was headed back to the security checkpoint to wait for nobody as the other agent positioned himself as a sentry behind the gate's desk. He pretended not to watch them. He was definitely watching them.

"I'm sweating," Miky said, trying vainly to flip her coat's hood off her head. "At least let me take this thing off."

Raina eyed the TSA guy. "Felons these days," she said.

The guy laughed. "Yeah. See it all the time. They do the crime but don't want to pay the fine." He thought for a moment and said, trying in vain to sound casual, "What did she do?"

Raina rolled her eyes. "You remember a few years back, when some of those militia dudes went all crazy up in Michigan and tried to invade Wisconsin?"

"Sure do," the guy said.

"She was one of the leaders."

The guy's eyes widened. He jabbed a finger at Miky. "My partner said it when you pulled up. You're that Spike, that teacher," the guy said, his voice rising. "You're the one that was part of that whole deal and then moved to Crested Butte."

"Hold up." Miky said. "I was the one that ended the thing."

Raina snorted a laugh. "Right."

Miky swallowed the urge to kick her.

"I read you turned against the other guys at the trial," the TSA guy said.

"No honor among thieves." Raina smirked.

"Wait. Stop. Just," Miky said. "Please, officer."

"Brady. Officer Brady. Hoots Brady." Hoots Brady smiled, seemly pleased with his own name.

"If you know my story you know I'm one of the good guys."

"You don't look like any guy I've ever met," Hoots said with a leer.

"Listen. Just. Call the police. Call the FBI, the field office in Denver. Ask if they have an agent named Raina-anything working around here."

"I told you to sit," Raina said, her voice suddenly brittle. She pulled Miky back her into her chair.

"Holy shit," Miky said to Hoots Brady, who was pointing a gun at her. "You can't have a gun."

"Oh, but I do," Hoots said.

"And so do I." It was the other TSA guy, who'd quietly returned. He offered his non-gun-carrying hand in a fist bump that Miky ignored. "Steven K. Pettibone, at your service." He nodded at Hoots. "We're TSA. But we're cleared to carry these bad boys, on account of the airport's so small." Pettibone sniffed and gestured with his handgun. "Sig Sauer PT250 Compacts, government issued."

"Put that thing away. This is ridiculous," Miky said. "I am not a criminal. And she is not FBI."

"Hold on with that smart mouth of yours, honey." With his left hand, Pettibone reached across his substantial belly for something in his right pants pocket. After several failed attempts to free the thing, he held the gun out to Miky. "Hold thi…" he said, but then thought better of it. He clamped the Sig under his left armpit, reached in the pocket and extracted his phone, swiped it on, paused and then snake-eyed Miky. "Watch her, Hoots," he said.

Hoots watched her.

"FBI website says," Pettiibone said, reading from the phone: "'Raina Richter, special agent based in the Western Slope region of Colorado.'"

Miky squinted at Raina, who avoided eye contact.

A muffled Glen Campbell sang "like a rhinestone cowboy" from Hoots' pocket. Hoots dug out his phone. "The plane is fifteen minutes out," he said.

Pettibone, gun still under his arm, slipped his phone back in his pocket. He eyed Raina with a know-it-all-smile. "So, Agent Richter, you've got a flight coming in. You've got a prisoner we recognize. Just for yucks, why don't you tell us what the Federal Bureau of Instigation is really doing in my airport on a night like this?"

Hoots chuckled. "Good question. I mean, hate to break it… we're no fans of the FB-fucking–I. Am I right, bruh?"

"Right as rain." Pettibone said. "I half hoped you were something other than FBI."

"Yeah, guess we should tell you we're what'cha call Sons of Liberty," Hoots said. "On top of these day jobs we got."

Miky's gut twisted. "Oh good lord," she said. "Let me guess. You guys are some kind of Colorado militia?"

"You got that partly right. By coinkydink, we're with a militia that's still based in Michigan. Your old stomping grounds," Pettibone said.

"For the love of all that is good and holy," Miky said. "Why can't I get away from you people?"

"There are millions of us now. Movement is huge," Pettibone said. "Since this administration and all that happened over the last few years. It's a deal. You're part to blame. You made that big splash and all at the Cracker Barrel."

"Yeah, can't spit without hitting someone who's militia. Friend of ours from back home, from Oscoda, was in a Netflix documentary they did on it."

"Hulu, I thought," Pettibone said.

"Whatever," Hoots said.

"I don't got Netflix," Hoots said.

"Who doesn't have Netflix?" Pettibone said.

"This guy," Hoots pointed a thumb at himself. "On account of the founder's a crazy liberal. You should look into it. Don't got Amazon Prime either. Same reason."

"It was on Hulu," Pettibone said. "The documentary."

"Fine. Whatev. You should for sure look into Netflix, though," Hoots said. "And I assume you already know about Amazon. Bezos, dude. He owns, like, the *New York Times*."

"*The Washington Post*," Miky said.

"I love me some Netflix, to be honest," Pettibone said. "Tough to give that shit up. *Mrs. Maisel*'s a damn fine show. I know she's, like, Jewish. But hot, you know. In a Jewish way. It's a show on there."

"What is?"

"*Mrs. Maisel.*' On Netflix."

Miky shook her head. "It's *The Marvelous Mrs. Maisel*. And it's on Prime. Amazon Prime Video," she said. "Listen—"

"Welp, can't watch it then," Hoots Brady said. "Guys like Bozo Bezos are what's wrong with this country."

"Him and a million other things."

"Which is exactly why we started this group," Pettibone said.

"Exactly," Hoots said.

"Yeah," Pettibone said, sidearm still clamped under his arm. "At first, it was just with some dudes Hoots knew over there in Afghanistan and some of my buddies here. Things got rolling once he come home. I was working at Simpson Machine in Newaygo—shift manager. Where my folks are from—Newaygo, you know, Michigan."

Miky closed her eyes. "Please, please. We all know the story. It's always the same. You don't have to share."

"Grew up on a celery farm, which we made home base for the Sons."

"Apparently the man is going to share," Miky said to Raina, who was studying the men with an oh-my-God look on her face.

"We did our training and planning there," Pettibone said. "My old man, he was committed to, you know, personal liberty and the right to bear arms—all that. But he died in 2012. Killed by some Black guy who hit him and drove off. Never caught the dude on account of my dad was alone, just walking to his mailbox, when the Black guy hit and run; so, no witnesses. And my mom, she's still with us but she's in assisted living. So I had the run of the farm. Alzheimer's, my mom has. I saw her every week or so, until I moved out here. Now my sister has to deal with it. Because I moved. But whatever. The farm's all hers, my fat sister's, now. Hers and her lazy-ass Mexican husband. Mom, she doesn't even remember she's got a farm. Or a Mexican for a son-in-law."

"She also don't know what we were up to with Sons of Liberty," Hoots said.

"Got that right." Pettibone looked at Miky, clenched the gun tightly with his arm and hitched up his pants. "Unlike your old Red Sky Brigade and such, no one knows what Sons of Liberty have done. Very low profile. You heard of Proud Boys and all them? We been right there with them when shit went down."

Miky let out a strangled sigh. "Oh I'm sure you have been." She looked at Raina and rolled her eyes.

"Yep. Oath Keepers, Three Percenters—all our bros," Hoots said. He paused, thought for a minute. "It got rough for us back home, lots of people infiltrating. So, about a year and a half ago, Petts convinced me to move out here."

"Michigan's loss, Colorado's gain, I guess," Miky said. She thought she heard Raina chuckle.

"Actually, I had lost my job back home and come out already," Pettibone said. "Originally was because of a woman I was seeing—the job loss—a story best left for another time."

Raina coughed and covered her mouth. Miky swallowed a "do tell" out of fear Pettibone would.

"Yeah, so, I crashed on Petts's couch," Hoots said, "until I got this gig here. He got hired first and then, you know, hooked me up."

"Good job for both of us, being hardcore patriots and all. Like you used to be, Miky Spike."

Both men glanced at Miky. She suppressed another eyeroll, poorly.

"Always figured we'd maybe run into one of those Jihadi motherfuckers trying to sabotage a plane or some shit," Hoots said. "Then we'd pop 'em."

"In Gunnison, Colorado?" Raina had found her voice. "Really?"

"Military aircraft always testing here. On account of the attitude," Hoots said to her, his chin jutted out.

"Altitude," Miky said softly.

"Yeah, it's, like, seven thousand feet. Above the sea level."

"You don't say," Raina said.

"Like, tonight, we were expecting maybe military types or national security folks—testing some kind of blizzard aircraft," Pettibone said. Then we saw you guys waltz in the door and I says to Hoots, I says, 'Hold on here, amigo."

"Yeah," Hoots said. "Being Michiganders originally, he recognized your prisoner here right off." Hoots looked at Raina. "I tell you what, back in the day, she was, like, the militia queen. Couple guys I know had a poster made up," Hoots said. "It was from a picture someone took of her in, like, running shorts and a sports bra."

Raina glanced at Miky—a flash of empathetic disgust.

"The one with the AK?" Pettibone said.

"Yep. She was holding an AK-47." Hoots said, his leer now more of a gawk.

"Give me a fucking break," Miky muttered.

Pettibone snorted. "But then her man, Bo—Bo Watts— found out about it and shot the guy who made the poster."

"Yeah, guy about died," Hoots said. "All the posters disappeared real fast. Bo was all, like, 'you don't mess with Miky.'"

"A lesson not learned by some, apparently," Miky said, her voice a low growl.

Pettibone had crossed his arms, the gun now apparently comfortable in his armpit. He said to Raina, "Gotta admit, we all figured Miky F-in Spike had gone underground with that Indian guy she had with her in Wisconsin."

"Tonto or whatever his name was," Hoots said.

Both men laughed.

Raina's mouth opened. She raised an eyebrow. Her right hand came up, index finger in the air. She seemed caught in internal debate, then lowered her hand. She bit her lip, as though preventing words from escaping, but a hiss of a sigh managed to leak out.

"I heard a rumor this Spike chick here was some kind of government informant," Hoots said.

"Also heard she was, like, killed in one of those Black Lives Matter deals. Attacking the police, you know. Or some other radical socialist bullshit," Pettibone said.

Miky had heard enough. "You guys are morons. Dirtbag, racist, sexist—"

"Figures she'd say that," Pettibone said, eying Raina. "Maybe you feel the same way, little Miss FBI. Or is it Ms.? Gotta be Ms., I'm betting."

Raina's brown eyes flashed. A muscle twitched in her jaw.

"That's beside the point right now," Hoots said. "Totally besides what we're getting at." He scowled at his partner.

"Yeah, yeah. Just saying, these lesbos don't want to be called Miss," Pettibone said. He grinned. "Then again, I've never met a hot-looking black momma lesbo federal agent with pink hair. Just trying to confirm."

Hoots sighed and looked at Raina. "You want to answer that?"

Raina shook her head, her lips pressed into a thin line, her jaw still twitching.

Hoots glared at Pettibone. "Anyways…"

Pettibone shrugged and nodded. "Go ahead."

"Anyways, Petts was online the other day and he ends up calling me, because who's back from the dead and in *The Denver Fucking Post*?" Hoots said. He looked at Pettibone.

Pettibone thought for a moment. "Oh, uh, Miky Spike," he said with a smile.

"Which gets us to today and who's coming into Gunnison International?" Hoots said.

"Miky Spike," they said in unison. They bumped fists.

"I mean, unreal, right?" Pettibone said, fumbling to secure the gun in his armpit, which appeared to be slipping. "I said to Hoots here, 'that's that Miky Spike chick. And the other girl is some kind of lover or something.' But now we see you're FBI and I'm back to wondering whether you two are up to something together. Like maybe you're acting like you're arresting her only you're not. Like maybe this whole deal is a setup for those guys on the plane."

The bang of Pettibone's gun was muffled by the generous body fat under his left arm. It was followed almost immediately by a low rumble of thunder and a flash of lightning, which would've gone unnoticed if not for Hoots Brady stepping around the desk, his eyes wide.

"Thunder snow," Hoots said.

"Aaackk," Pettiibone groaned, doubling over.

Raina's perfectly executed army-booted sidekick caught Hoots in mid-meteorological awe, sending him and his sidearm to the floor, the Sig Sauer tumbling across the carpet. Miky stood and shoved the wounded Pettibone to the floor with her zip-tied hands.

Hoots struggled to his knees. Pettibone, his face ashen and blood dripping from his wound, crawled to Hoots's gun, picked it up, turned and fired in the general vicinity of Raina. Hoots went down with a sound that reminded Miky of a retching cat.

Chapter Eighteen

Gunnison-Crested Butte Regional Airport was a challenging place to land a jet, even in typical winter conditions. The West Elk mountains rose to 15,000 feet to the south and 14,000 feet to the north. The airport's 7,680-foot elevation required a faster approach than at sea level, over rough terrain, with ice and snow making the 9,400 feet of runway feel a few heartbeats short of sufficient. The inevitable wind scouring the mountains made for a bumpy ride. While Cody Marks would have loved to take on the worse-case option, Runway 24 was the RNAV (RNP) approach and, therefore, the tower's choice, given the conditions; it offered the lowest minimums and Cody could depend on his GPS and onboard nav to help get the Gulfstream on the ground.

To Cody, aborting a landing was a shameful act equivalent to taking a dare to jump off a high ledge into an icy reservoir at midnight when you were, say, twelve years old and sucked at swimming, and then claiming you'd pulled a hamstring on the walk up to the ledge and wimping out on the jump, the kind of situation your dad would follow through on by cannon-balling off the ledge so he could spend the rest of his miserable life calling you a "fairy" whenever he brought it up, which would be often. But, in this case, while Cody was ready to man up and land on the runway he couldn't see, the air traffic controller thought the last second, 40 mph gust of crosswind worthy of respect, so the dude in the tower waved him off. It was not a fake-hammy-ledge-jumping situation, but emotionally similar.

With engines screaming and the aircraft groaning like a never-quite-forgotten interrogated Taliban fighter, Cody Marks gritted his teeth and circled back for another go at it, his only consolation that the longer he rode the storm, the more likely Tuttle and Commander Fucking Bill were puking into the airsickness bags.

The door to the flight deck swung open. Someone entered and sat in the co-pilot's seat.

"What the fu—" Cody said. He glanced up. "Tuttle?"

"Peanut?" Tuttle said, offering him a small open bag.

The scent set off alarms in Cody's head, which he shook vigorously. "I… I'm a little busy here. And peanuts, sir, please, I can't be around…" He tried to hold his breath and focus on his job at hand.

Tuttle pulled the bag back. "Oh, right. I read that someplace about you. Okay, suit yourself," he said and then reached in, got a nut, popped it in his mouth, and began crunching. After several peanuts; reach, pop, crunch, repeat; just as Cody was preparing for another descent, Tuttle licked his fingers, wiped his hand on a thigh that was not his, dropped the bag in his lap, and said, "I'm going to need you to hand over this bad boy." He picked up the co-pilot's headset and put it on. "You lost your nerve on the first go-round." Tuttle snapped his fingers. "Give it up." He settled in, faced forward, and reached for the co-pilot's yoke. "C'mon. Let Daddy handle this. This bird needs to be on the ground so we can pick up our cargo and turn her right around."

"If I may, on the peanuts, I'm severely aller… Just being around them…"

"Tower, this is co-pilot Tuttle for Silver Eagle…" Tuttle said into the radio.

"Roger that," the guy in the tower said.

"I roger your 'roger,'" Tuttle said. "Tower, I am taking control from our pilot who is encountering a health episode."

Cody Marks, his throat itching and panic clawing his lungs, ceded control to Tuttle and tried to stand. His seatbelt refused to let him go. The plane dropped, the tail canted, and Tuttle let out a chortle that sounded like glee trapped in a bag of fear. For an instant or, perhaps, half of one, Cody Marks was jealous. He'd wanted this landing. He'd earned the sheer, raw, butt-clenching joy of it. But the scent of peanuts held an even sheerer, rawer, more clenching terror for him. It took him back to the emergency rooms of his childhood—places of intensely bright lights shined by doctors with bad breath while his mother ranted about what the hell he'd gotten into this time. Tuttle's eyes were glowing, the skeleton of the aircraft was trying to free itself from its skin, and the damn peanut air poisoner was closing Cody Marks's airway as surely as if it were again gripped by an ISIS fighter in Damascus.

Through the cockpit windows, there was nothing to see except snow and dark threats. The crosswinds occasionally upped the danger quotient with an angry jolt. Even so, the plane continued a relentless dance and descent, the sober, southwestern twang of the tower guy in Gunnison offering ridiculously calm support to Tuttle.

"People forget I flew jets before I got into choppers," Tuttle said, yelling to be heard. "I was napalming Cong in the Mekong Delta when you were just a rumor in your pre-school daddy's not-yet-sexual brain."

Somehow, Cody's fumbling fingers found the release for his lap belt. He struggled to stand. A particularly strong gust threw him back to the seat. Tuttle laughed.

"Don't have your sea legs yet, eh?" Tuttle said, his eyes fixed forward.

Cody gripped an armrest, stood, and managed to retrieve an EpiPen from its usual place in his left breast pocket. He jammed the needle into his right thigh and fell into his seat. The rush of the epinephrine had its usual miraculous effect: it pulled him out of the fever dream that is near-death by suffocation and pushed him into the possibility of death by an overly accelerated airplane when runway lights suddenly appear. Right below you.

"Ahhhhhhh," Tuttle said. "Mother Earth." The landing gear hit the tarmac, bounced off, made contact, and bounced again.

"You're too fucking hot. Toofuckinghot." Cody heard his voice and was instantly ashamed of how high and frantic it sounded.

They hit again. Through the snow, a blast of brightness didn't register as lightning until a crack of way-more-obvious thunder. Tuttle let out a maniacal laugh and the plane slammed down on the landing gear with a sharp whoomp, which drew a shout from the passenger cabin. Cody fumbled with switches, set the auto brakes at medium and the thrust reversers at max, and they began the whistling slide down the snow-slicked runway, Tuttle howling like a horny coyote all the way.

Pettibone, gun in hand, blood wrecking his uniform shirt, was groaning and trying to stand. Hoots Brady was sprawled, face down. He seemed dead, until he swore quietly into the floor and tried to roll over, but failed, and made a noise a dead man would never make.

From somewhere in her heavily pocketed camo uniform, Raina Richter produced a box cutter. She slit the zip ties binding

Miky's wrists, returned the box cutter to the pocket, withdrew a 9mm Glock, and said, "Sorry about your groceries."

Miky frowned.

"The stuff you bought at the store. We left it all." Raina was fumbling with something in another pocket, another Glock. She took a deep breath and eyed the wounded TSA men. "Here," she said, handing Miky the gun butt-first, "you're going to need this."

"What I'm going to need is some kind of fucking explanation," Miky said. She snapped the gun away, checked to see if it was loaded, and turned to Pettibone. He was standing, but not well, his eyes glazed; the pistol in his hand was quivering. Miky pointed the Glock at him. "Drop that thing. You've done enough damage." Pettibone obeyed.

"Understood. About the explanation." Raina was suddenly all business, the back-country vibe gone from her voice. She walked over to Hoots, nudged him with a boot. "Where you hit?" she said.

Hoots twisted toward her. There was a green gummy bear stuck to his face. "I don't know," he said.

Raina knelt next to him, flicked the gummy bear away, and looked him over. She put down her gun and said, "Let's roll you over."

With some reluctance, Hoots rolled. Raina picked up her gun and stood. After a brief inspection of the TSA agent, she shook her head, looked at Miky, and made a face. To Hoots she said, "Get up."

The suddenly healed Hoots got to his feet and spent several seconds looking for damage. "I thought for sure he had me."

"Shut up and put your hands behind your back," Raina said. The still stunned Hoots complied. She zip-tied his hands. Hoots winced. "Sit," she said, and pushed him toward a chair.

Miky walked to Pettibone, kicked his gun away, and grabbed him by his non-wounded arm. She led him over to Raina, who repeated her zip, sit procedure. Pettibone protested loudly, to no avail.

Raina carefully plucked Pettibone's shirt away from his bloody skin and squinted through the short-sleeve arm hole. "The blood makes it look worse than it is."

"Hurts like a son of a bitch," Pettibone said.

"Bleeding has almost stopped. You're lucky that gun had slipped as low as it had."

Raina walked away from the men, motioning for Miky to follow. Raina stopped on the other side of a soft-pretzel vendor cart, turned and said, "We've got to get on that plane without any more interference from these guys."

"How about I get my explanation first?" Miky said.

Raina sighed.

"Start with an FBI agent assaulting an innocent American and kidnapping her."

"First, let me be clear. We're on the same side. But I'm not an FBI agent," Raina said.

Miky took a minute. "You know, you're really starting to piss me off."

"I understand. Listen—"

"So, you're not some grocery store militia chick. You're not even FBI, even though the FBI website says you're FBI. Because, you're—"

"ATF. The Bureau of Alcohol, Tobacco and Firearms."

"I know what the ATF is."

"Yeah, the FBI thing was just a ruse."

"You covered up being an ATF agent by saying you were FBI."

"Yeah."

"And this thing. You threw me in a car with some idiots and drove me here to get myself nearly killed by more idiots?" Miky glanced around the pretzel cart at the men. Both were rising. They saw that she saw. They froze, mid-stand.

Raina looked through low-hanging pretzels at the two men. She raised her gun. "Sit," she said to them, underlining the word by racking the slide on the Glock.

Hoots sat like an obedient Labrador. Pettibone, lower jaw thrust forward, legs wobbly, straightened to his full height.

The warning shot cracked past Pettibone, transformed a pretzel into brown mist, sliced off a chunk of brick from a pillar, crashed through distant glass, and sent the bleeding man into his seat.

Miky turned back to Raina, who lowered her gun. "You got some balls on you, don't you?" Miky said.

"Well," Raina said with a wisp of a smile, "more like ovaries. But I get the point."

Both laughed.

Miky took a deep breath. "Okay, so let me lower the hostility a tad."

"Cool," Raina said. "Cool cool. As I was saying—"

"Just don't. Just don't do the 'cool cool' thing. I get it. It's hip and so Gen Z or whatever. Just don't," Miky said.

Raina frowned. "Fine. Whatev."

"And not that either. 'Whatev.' You're killing me. I teach high school."

"Okay. Whatev… I mean, sure. Fine."

Miky smiled. "I'm just busting your ovaries."

Raina studied her face for a moment. "Okay okay okay," she said. "So, here's the deal: I've been, like, undercover for months. Thing was, when I first arrived, I had to tell local law enforcement what I was up to. But half of them have connections with militias and survivalists and anarchists. You know how it is."

"You assume I'd be some kind of expert?"

Raina smiled. "You're Miky Spike, damn it. Woman, you're a legend. When I was teenager, growing up—"

"Don't give me that. I'm not that much older than—"

Raina waved her off. "No, I know. But you were a deal for a high school kid living in Kansas. When that story came out about the guys wanting to invade Wisconsin and you saving the day. A lot of my friends—we just ate all that up." She stopped. "Sorry, that all sounds a little groupie-ish."

"Yeah, it does."

"It really wasn't creepy or anything. We just admired you, you know?"

Miky decided to accept that.

"So, anyway, when I got the chance to come out here to work this case, the fear was that if any locals—cops, whoever— figured out I was ATF, they'd think I was coming for their buddies and their guns, and they'd blow me away and drop me into Black Canyon." Raina glanced toward the men, who were obviously listening. "So, the cover to my cover was FBI. They're suspicious of FBI, but they typically don't shoot them. Not right away, anyway. Hence, my name on their website—a bit of inter-agency cooperation."

Miky chewed on this. It made no sense, which made perfect sense.

"Okay. And before you freak when you find out, I used to be NSA. I still have close ties with them."

"The National Security—"

"Agency. Yep."

"Also did a stint in the USMC, if you really want to know."

"A marine." Miky was trying to control the moment but felt it spinning away.

"Yes, and as long as we're coming clean, I don't usually wear my hair this way. And I'm half Kenyan. And, okay," she said loudly, "I'm probably related to a certain former president. There, I've given you the whole Raina Richter profile."

"Wait. Back up."

"What can I tell you? His dad got around. There's talk of a DNA match."

"Barack Hussein Obama," said Hoots Brady. He'd crept over to them and was standing at the pretzel cart. "You're, what, his little sister?"

Before anyone could respond, Glen Campbell sang from Hoots Brady's pocket, Steven Pettibone's phone trilled, the public address system crackled, and the voice of the guy in the tower said, "Attention in the airport."

The flight from South Carolina had landed.

"Grab him," Raina Richter nodded at Hoots and walked quickly toward the now-cowering Pettibone. Hoots said something about Obama that Miky didn't take time to understand. She took him roughly by the arm and walked him over to Raina and Pettibone.

Raina unzipped her backpack, rustled through it, and found a roll of duct tape. In minutes, the men's mouths were taped shut. Hoots Brady sneezed, which led to a tape-suppressed coughing jag. Nose running and his eyes tearing, he tried to speak, the result comedic enough that it made Miky smile despite the situation. Pettibone looked pale and scared in his bloody shirt, like a man who suddenly just wanted to go home.

Jet engines, whining above the wind, drew their attention to the windows. They all were momentarily transfixed as the taxiing plane appeared, turning from the runway and approaching the gate, a broad-winged ghost in snow.

It took several seconds for the plane's insignia and color scheme to register.

Miky turned to Raina. "Areyoufuckingkiddingme?"

"The not-FBI-former-NSA-former-marine ATF agent was smiling like a sad aunt at a funeral. "Yeah. Sorry to do this, but I'm going to need that gun back for a bit. I mean, thanks for the help here, but we're now back to the play-acting portion of our show."

"You can't be serious."

"I know. I know." Raina lightning-grabbed the gun and had Miky's wrists tied again before she could break away. "And for the record, I'm tying your hands in front of you in case I need your weapon skills in a hurry."

"You know, they very likely want me dead," Miky said. She looked at the jet, now braking to a stop fifty yards or so from the terminal, its company of origin plainly visible.

"I am aware," Raina said softly. Raina's eyes were a deep brown that didn't go well at all with the scruff of pink hair. Those eyes begged for trust. Miky found herself thinking Raina was trustable and that Raina's eyes were pretty damn beautiful.

The plane's airstair had lowered and was wobbling in the wind. Two men, uniformed in colors that matched the jet, were talking just inside the Gulfstream's doorway, oblivious to the snow. Miky's mind drifted back over the evening's events, from the moment she reached the Gunnison Safeway, through the mess with Pettibone and Hoots F-ing Brady, the revelation that Raina was FBI but wait not FBI, actually ATF, former NSA and former USMC and supposedly related to Barack Obama. To Silver Eagle's jet sitting in front of her. It was a lot.

"Listen, honey," Raina said, seemingly reading her mind, "In about two seconds, Wilbur Tuttle is going to come through that door. He's going to expect to take you and get back on the jet. I am going to convince him to take all of us, including these two yahoos, since it's the only way I can control everyone involved here and stop whatever Tuttle's up to." Her eyes grew a lovely shade of authoritarian. "You were raised to be a soldier.

You know how this plays out. You are going to follow my lead. And we are going to kick some ass."

Miky looked around her. Pettibone seemed resigned to his fate. Hoots was sitting forward in his chair, agitated. A snot bubble appeared in a nostril and popped. He wiped his nose on his right shoulder, looked at Raina and growled. Outside, snow blew horizontally and two helmeted Silver Eagle soldiers in tactical gear were descending. Behind them, a thin older man in a jumpsuit held his naked head high despite the wind and snow and jogged down the stairs with gusto.

Miky Spike looked at Raina and said, "Don't ever call me 'honey.'"

Chapter Nineteen

Cody Marks sat stewing in the pilot's seat, watching and listening as Tuttle's weird parade of prisoners boarded the jet. His brain raced through scenarios for dealing with his tormentor—shooting Tuttle point blank was a favorite. But before he could make a move, the airstair was up, the door was closing, and Tuttle's hand was on his shoulder, his breath in his right ear, that voice low and filled with sweet doom: "I love you, Mr. Marks. You are special to me because of what you bring to this organization. But if you ever go chickenshit on an operation again, I will snap your neck like one—like a chicken's. Neck."

Cody Marks began to tremble, which sucked because it was the last thing you wanted when facing down a lethal enemy. But the one-two zap of adrenaline from the EpiPen and his glands was too much for even a professionally trained son-of-a-North-Dakota-evangelical-hardass to overcome. He also began to sweat. Like, a lot. He took his hand away from his gun. He felt like throwing up.

"Okay, now," Tuttle said, releasing his shoulder and stepping back. "I have some business to take care of. You need to pull yourself together and prepare for the next leg of the flight."

"So, I'm doing this—flying?" Cody heard these words and hoped they were coming from some other weak-hearted disappointment's voice box. They were not.

"Yes. Wheels up in five minutes." Tuttle said as he reached for door. "To tell the truth, I've never flown a plane before. And I've heard takeoffs are beasts."

Still smiling, Tuttle stepped into the empty galley of the Gulfstream. The exhilaration of his first-ever jet landing had cleared his head. He pulled out his burner phone, found Jasper Joyce's number, and texted: "We are outbound to Tampa. Things are messy. Get to DIA as soon as possible. I have a charter waiting. Bring JN. Tuttle."

He called the Silver Eagle pilot on standby at Denver International, to arrange for him to bring two passengers to Tampa. Then he sent another text to Jasper Joyce: "You have JN, right? Tuttle." After Joyce responded that, yes, he had Jackson Nguyen, Tuttle told his burner phone to "call my Benedict Arnold."

The call was answered in the middle of the second ring by a groggy woman. "Yeah?"

"Is that the way to answer a call from your lover man?"

"What time is it?" the woman said. Her accent was light and Belarusian.

Tuttle thought about this, smiled, and said, "It's show time."

"Who… who is this? Steven?" The woman cleared her throat and dropped her lightly Belarusian-accented voice a half octave. "I told you, we are—I'm not going to do this things anymore. Not on the phone like this."

Her tone seized Tuttle where he was most vulnerable. For several seconds—far too many—he was paralyzed by images of her on the phone with whoever Steven was.

"Tuttle, could you grab me a sparkling water?" Commander Bill was standing at the entrance to the galley. He took a step toward Tuttle. "Who you yakking at?"

Tuttle held up a hand. "Oh. Uh. Hold on…" He turned to the stainless-steel refrigerator, opened it, and grabbed a brightly labeled can of sparkling water. He closed the door and tossed the drink to Commander Bill; it sailed past his right shoulder, bounced off a seat, and rolled down the aisle that ran through the passenger compartment. "Just ahh… just making some arrangements, Commander. Bill. Sir." Tuttle said into the phone.

"Gotcha. Thanks." Commander Bill turned and chased after the can.

"Holy…" The woman on the phone was suddenly alert. "Tuttle?"

"Damnit, Sonia," Tuttle said. He spoke through clenched teeth: "We agreed on no names."

Sonia apologized. In Belarusian. In a way Tuttle found seductive. In a way, Tuttle found everything she did seductive.

"Good god, my little Belarus-nik. Must you break out the full sexy at a moment such as this?" Tuttle said in an accent that was heavily Belarusian.

"Yo. This is cranberry. I was wanting mango-peach, Tut." It was Commander Bill again, standing there in the galley doorway wearing his famous dumbly charismatic smile, offending cranberry-colored can in hand.

Tuttle ripped open the door of the refrigerator, fumbled through the shelf of canned sparkling water, knocking several to the floor, found one that looked mango-hued, read the label, then turned and heaved it at Commander Bill. Commander Bill's left hand was still holding the cranberry-colored can. The mango-colored can, like its predecessor, sailed past its target and into the passenger's cabin. "I got this, bro," Commander Bill said, and pursued the can.

Tuttle closed the door of the refrigerator, stared at his blurred image in the appliance's surface, took a breath, and let it out.

"We are doing this? Today?" Sonia said softly as a Belarusian kitten if a kitten, Belarusian or otherwise, could say things.

"Yes. Yes, we are," Tuttle said, his voice rising and the accent momentarily forgotten. "Today is the day. Everything we've planned. All systems go."

"We are what, Tut?" Commander Bill was walking back up the aisle toward him, the cranberry-colored can no longer in his possession. He popped the top of the mango-peach can, reached the doorway and took a slurp.

Tuttle held up a hand. "Not for your ears, sir."

"Ope. Sorry," Commander Bill said. He stood there, sipping his mango and his peach, for several seconds.

"Is he listening—your commander man?" Sonia said.

"Yes," Tuttle said softly and, he hoped, with equal seductiveness.

"Oh. I gotcha, Tut. I gotcha." A goofy grin illuminated Commander Bill's face. He took another sip and turned, shoulders hunched, and began to tip-toe away. "Plausible deniable-whatever."

"That's right, sir." Tuttle said.

They'd met at a DC bar. She was, she told him, a Belarusian government liaison weary from a week of negotiating butter exports and awaiting a late-afternoon flight to Minsk. He was a weapons-systems buyer and black marketeer wrapping up a back-door score at the Pentagon hoping to get laid before grabbing the red-eye back to South Carolina. He told her he was in farm implements and that many of his clients were Belarusian. During pillow talk in a Best Western near Dulles, he showed her his guns and she'd let him play with the Beretta Nano 9mm she kept in her purse. He let it slip that, in addition to shooting and riding horses bare-chested and archery—things he imagined were popular among virile Belarusians—his interests included training men and, he added pointedly, like-minded women, in military-style skills. He was head of an organization, he said while sipping schnaps from the barrel of the Beretta, that was committed to "keeping America American" and "waging freedom and capitalism around the world." He talked about America's current president, and her ominous turn toward totalitarianism via laws banning the eating of America's beloved beef. "No more quarter pound? No more Happiness Meal?" she said. "No, no, my Pushkin," was his response. During a half hour in their room's shower with its fabulous multi-setting showerhead, she talked about her own affinity for "peoples" in Washington who felt like he did. They giggled, both of them, in a steamy, languorous way, because of how she nakedly emphasized "felt."

As they say in Belarus, one thing led to another. Tuttle helped the enchanting liaison turn her talents for procurement into a mid-level justice department gig that had nothing to do with procurement. She'd moved her meager belongings from Zhdanovichi to Alexandria, Virginia, where Tuttle hooked her up with a sweet two-bedroom condo and the vast network of like-minded peoples who had been seeded in the DC firmament by Commander Bill's late father and, after his becoming late, Tuttle. Soon, Sonia was an invaluable asset, daily pulling the levers of bureaucracy toward the policies and decisions that met Tuttle's, and Silver Eagle's, insatiable needs.

Tuttle hooked up with Sonia whenever he came to Washington, which was often. And when he did, he showered her with Stuckey's Peanut Log Rolls and other valuable and delicious gifts from the American South. He was grooming her for something big, his biggest something ever. But Sonia's enchantingness enveloped him, and Tuttle made a mistake that he'd made more than once in his lifelong pursuit of hedonism: He became so lost in the clouds of lust that he temporarily lost track of his inner control tower.

As luck and irony would have it, it was Sonia who brought him back to earth.

One afternoon, they were on her condo's kitchen table, having crumpled there after several minutes of bath-robed mixed martial arts performed to an extended cut of "Kung Fu Fighting" by Carl Douglas blaring from Tuttle's iPhone. Sonia, a "much-big" fan of Ultimate Cage Fighting, thought the slapping and grabbing were foreplay but, it turned out her aging "American fighter mans" had forgotten to include in his overnight bag certain "medicines" necessary for the final event. Tuttle was hoping an interlude of cuddle time would provide the necessary stimulus. Then, without warning, Sonia brought up the other thing he hadn't.

"What is it you want from me, my baby man? I mean, in the governments?" she said, looking down at him, the side of her face cupped in a hand, her elbow planted next to a freshly opened box of moon pies. A wisp of Sonia's hair fell across her flushed face. She pursed her tiny mouth and puffed at it, her eyes rolling upward with the puff. The hair fell back. She pouted. Tuttle's chest ached. She rested her warm, soft Belarusian hand on his exposed chest.

He could smell moon pies.

Tuttle closed his eyes, tried to conjure a fantasy of their last time together.

Outside, a lawnmower roared to life. He opened his eyes, tasted blood. He'd bitten his lip.

"Just listen to me for once time," she said, her eyes sweet and pleading. Tears balanced on her perfectly mascaraed lashes. "We always do the sexy but I want more. What about my careers?"

Tuttle wanted her to drop the robe and the tears. His heart was stirring in a way he hadn't felt since his last dance with cocaine, but that was where the stirring stopped.

"I... I want you to be, happy," he said. The words felt stupid and disingenuous tumbling out of his mouth because they were. "I mean, I want us to be together." He thought of sitting up but realized his best strategic opportunity was to remain prone. He tried to remember "I love you" in Belarusian but instead blurted, "Ich bin ein Berliner."

She sat up, pulled her robe around her, tightened its belt, and did something no woman he'd bedded or tabled or floored had ever done to him. She got up, clothed.

"Listen," Sonia said. "I am seriously." She looked down at him with a face he didn't recognize.

The lawn mower rattled and wheezed like a black-lunged, gas-powered coal miner. Something yelped in the condo next door. Sonia reached in the box, grabbed a moon pie, and made a grand production of freeing it from its sealed cellophane wrapper. She took a bite. Her cheek stuffed with double-decker marshmallow sandwich was ghastly.

"I... I have something. I've been planning, from the beginning for you and me..." Tuttle reached for her. "If you'd just lay down."

She batted his hand away. Her gaze glazed. She licked a crumb from her upper lip. "It is 'lie.' Lie down," she said. "I know the English.'"

"Well, lie. Lie then." He was pulling on her sleeve, his voice sounding embarrassingly shrill. "Lie with me now."

Sonia pulled away. She stared off. Tuttle thought he heard a distant siren.

Finally, one hand on a hip, her other hand holding the partially eaten moon pie, she tilted her head coyly. "I will do the lying."

It wasn't a siren. It was a train whistle.

"If you will tell me what I can do here, in the capitol city, besides the sexy, and the paperwork. And the meetings with boring peoples," she said. "I know you are man of big plans, big ideas. I want to be part of them. And I won't take no for the answers."

"I want you to help me replace the President." The words were out before he had a chance to choke them back.

The twitch of an eyebrow was all she gave him in response. Sonia ate the last of the moon pie and licked each of her fingers slowly. She folded the cellophane wrapper carefully, tucked it into a pocket, and said, "Tell me how we do this."

So, there, on the kitchen table, he shared his passion with her in hopes she would share hers with him. It came out in a rush: his intense desire to stop the U.S. government's slide toward socialism and authoritarianism and vegetarianism. Soon, Tuttle said, this president would ban more things. Did Sonia want her beloved adopted homeland to become the Belarus of her childhood, in which she'd eaten nothing but spoiled beets?

"It is a superfoods, yes?" Sonia said.

They debated this briefly, Tuttle using every ounce of his remaining self-control to acknowledge that, yes, a good, fresh beet was incredibly healthful before steering her back to his passion plan, a plan concocted with Big Bruddah of the great militia in Michigan she'd heard so much about. There had been months of planning, he said, including the orchestrating of relationships with key people in the militia movement, law enforcement and the Armed Forces. They would launch their operation in the great southern state of Florida, using his connection inside the very big military base there. The President's daughter worked at an elementary school in Bradenton, not far from the base. They would create a fake emergency at the school involving America's much-loved guns and shootings. The President's plane would land at the big Florida military base. The militias and military sympathizers would come together to force her to quit her office, casting her away like the useless cow she was. Their President would be installed, and if a broader, deeper civil insurrection happened—so be it. All he, Tuttle, needed was a willing and brave person to find the ears of people the President trusted. Would Sonia do it? Would she become the nameless hero history would later learn had saved America? Would she be the ear finder, the person who convinced the person that would convince the President to fly to Florida at the ultimate moment?

When he was done telling her, pleading with her, Tuttle was spent.

Sonia looked down at him, her pretty face impassive. She took another moon pie from the box, unwrapped and ate it, letting crumbs fall on her robe and on him. Yes, she said. She would help with removing the socialist, cow-hating president. But, she added, she was lying about the lying. Then she took a shower. Alone.

Over the months that followed, Sonia proved perfectly suited to her role. She took the loose outline of Operation Boogaloo, provided by Tuttle as a bulleted list on a paper towel, and ran with it. Quietly, discreetly, she got cozy. Pulled alongside. Wrapped her arms around. Reached out. In just a few months, she laid the groundwork. Via encrypted texts and emails, she informed Tuttle that certain high-profile senators, congresspeople and even various secretaries of the President's inner circle were aware of their needs and willing to cooperate.

All she needed was for him to say "go."

"I'm saying go," Tuttle said into his burner phone.

"Go?" she said.

"Yes."

"Now?"

"Now."

"Rogers," she said. And the line went dead.

Chapter Twenty

Oklahoma airspace

Tuesday night

With the ride smoothing as they reached stable air, Commander Bill sat in his seat, head tipped back, an Army-regulation cold compress compressed against his bleeding nose, one Navy-regulation cotton ball up each nostril, and an Opioid-Enhanced Silver Eagle brand Combat-Strength Pain Reliever dissolving in his belly.

He stared at the light over his seat, and the throbbing in his skull eased under the warm glow of the medication. He felt, for the first time in a long time, that he had a purpose. He reviewed the events of the past hour: the plane's harrowing landing which had narrowly avoided killing Commander Bill in a hell-like ball of fire when the Gulfstream skidded to a stop just short of the runway's edge; the onboarding of the woman of his worst nightmare, Miky Spike, whom he hadn't seen since forever and who looked fit and tan and was with some camo-wearing, backpacked Black chick who had funky pink hair and an attitude that made him feel funny in a not unpleasant way; and two TSA agents who were all sweaty and duct-taped like informants in a movie who knew too much, one of them bloody and pale and the other tall and pissed off; all of it climaxing with him nearly losing his waning fertility or his manhood at the hands of a device he'd been stupidly curious about after years of devotion to toilet paper—and thought, *Hey, Tuttle wants to make me president.*

Not president of Silver Eagle. President, as in "of the United States." That president.

Commander Bill knew he was "slow on the uptake." He learned that from his father. But it wasn't until he was pulling his pants up while dripping noseblood on the floor of an inclined airplane bathroom that he understood, with clarity, how he found clarity. It was after accidentally hitting himself in the forehead with the claw end of a claw hammer during an ill-fated picture-hanging event that it occurred to him that his wife, who told him to not to get blood in the car when he drove himself to the hospital, really had married him for his money. It was immediately after a lawn dart game in college that had ended with him, in full drunken glory, trying to play "catcher," that he'd understood his gifts did not include athleticism.

Shortly after they'd reached cruising altitude, Commander Bill had thrown caution to the icy wind, caved to the demands of his nervous bowels, and risked a quick visit to the jet's restroom. He was poised over the bidet when the Gulfstream hit what the pilot, Cody Marks, would come to call "a bodaciously awesome pocket of air" in his numerous retellings of the incident.

Now, Commander Bill thanked God for a bloody moment that had once again awakened him. He took the potential name, almost-President Bill, for a mental test-drive and smiled. He imagined his dead father sitting next to him on the plane, seeming to be proud and then telling him how ridiculous it would be to have him, almost-President Bill, leading the country, and then almost-President Bill ordering his father to be escorted away by not-yet-assigned Secret Service agents who saw nothing amusing about a dead man ridiculing the almost-president.

"What are you smiling at?"

Commander Bill opened one eye. Tuttle was leering down at him.

Commander Bill sat up, pulled the compress away from his nose, and tried to look almost presidential.

"Sit," he said to Tuttle, gesturing to the seat facing him with a firmness he thought the almost-president would use.

Tuttle hesitated, looked to the rear of the plane, and frowned. The plane shuddered and lunged; Tuttle grabbed the seatback and swung himself into the proffered seat. "What you need? More pain killer?" He laughed like a man who knew you'd gotten a bloody nose from slamming into a sink while trying to use a bidet during a rough takeoff. Bill ignored the mocking tone.

"Actually, I wanted to confirm what you said earlier."

"About what?"

"About me being, you know, president."

Tuttle squinted at him.

"You still plan on it, right?" Commander Bill said. "Like, not, like Silver Eagle president. I mean, I know I was confused before. You meant, like…"

Tuttle smiled. They said it together.

"President."

"Yeah, like, POTUS," Commander Bill said.

Tuttle seemed relieved. "Yes. Yes," he said. "Now you're on track. Now you smell what we're stepping in. That's our plan. Absolutely."

Commander Bill swallowed a cry of exultation. It tasted like blood.

In the rear of the plane, separated by a curtained doorway from the space occupied by Tuttle and Commander Bill, Miky Spike turned to Raina Richter and growl-whispered: "This is messed up."

Across a small table from them, seated on a plush black leather banquette matching their own, sat the vacant-eyed, sweating and lightly bleeding TSA agent/militia member Steven K. Pettibone and the sweating and wild-eyed TSA agent/militia member Hoots Brady. Hands still tied behind them, both leaned forward uncomfortably. Hoots was fighting his circumstances, spasmodically, futilely struggling to free his hands while trying to use eyes to scream what his mouth was bound not to say. Pettibone seemed lost in his pain and the ugly reality that he couldn't do shit.

On either side of the central aisle, Miky counted seven men seated across from each other at tables matching their own. The men reminded her of every football player and cop who had ever hit on her: big necks and buzzed heads, bodies rippling with memories of hours spent in mirrored gyms, tight black shirts and camo battle dress uniform pants. Her ex, after his running career ended and before he'd become a fat militia bro with a stupid name, had spent a few years swimming in this human-growth-hormone-doctored pool. She'd hated the look then. Hated it more now.

The guys were loud and getting louder. They were playing cards and talking smack. Miky glimpsed coke and rolled dollar bills and a bottle of Jack Daniel's making the rounds. Everyone had a gun on his hip and a war cry in his eye.

Back in Gunnison, Tuttle had bounded up to the two of them in the airport terminal with that goofy-sick grin on his grizzled-weasel face—Miky's first face-to-face with him since his sentencing in the Wisconsin cheese stupidness. Raina gripped her arm in a keep-your-mouth-shut-and-let-me-talk vise and then played Tuttle like the cool co-conspirator she wasn't, telling him Brady and Pettibone were liars and idiots from back home in Michigan, that they needed to be "dealt with" just like "this one," aiming a head jerk and side eye at Miky. Miky figured things would get real, fast—that Tuttle; who looked ridiculously fit for his age but whose eyes rattled around in his naked-egg head in a way that made him seem dangerous and, Miky hoped, stroke-prone; would get in her face and, who knew, pull a knife? But Tuttle listened to Raina's spiel about taking them all with him, and he just gave her a nod, a fist bump, and that was it. Tuttle barely looked at Miky. He was in a hurry; preoccupied with something bigger than two strangers, one bleeding, and the woman he hated enough to make a side trip in a blizzard to pick up from a mountaintop airport.

Tuttle's toy soldiers had hustled them through the snow and onboard the Silver Eagle plane, giving Miky barely a moment to get permission to duck into the ridiculously luxurious bathroom. There, she saw the lipsticked meanderings on the mirror and snapped a hurried picture while one of the muscle-bound morons was knocking on the door telling her to "pinch it off." As she exited, she nearly walked into the lap of the guy the media now called Commander Bill. He'd aged into the perpetually attentive look of the famous and handsome but empty-headed. He stared at her breasts before giving her an ambiguous smile. Miky flipped him off.

Now, Miky turned to Raina and showed her the photo of the mirrored list. She gave Raina a minute to digest it, those eyes of hers growing wide. Raina was about to speak when the curtain that separated their section of the cabin from the forward section flashed open and Tuttle's head appeared. The laughter and talk evaporated. Someone sniffed loudly. Someone else unchambered a round.

Tuttle looked at Raina. He winked.

"Ms. Richter, come with me," Tuttle said. "To the galley. We have to talk."

Raina glanced back at Miky, gave her an "I got this" nod, and disappeared through the curtain.

Tuttle's men let out a collective sigh, then someone said "drink." Bottles and flasks clinked. A combat knife twanged like a javelin into the carpeted middle aisle. The suspended rowdiness resumed.

Across from Miky, Pettibone had fallen asleep, passed out, or died. She studied him, apathetic about which option he'd chosen. Hoots Brady was staring at the tabletop, studying his reflection and, she assumed, his own options. Suddenly, somehow, Hoots struggled to his feet. Avoiding Miky's glare, he plodded like a clumsy penguin through the curtain and into the forward cabin.

Shit, Miky thought. One of the muscle-headed soldiers echoed her sentiment.

Several minutes passed. Miky heard their voices—Raina's, Tuttle's, and Hoots'—rising in intensity and volume, then slacking away. She wanted desperately to rise and drift toward the curtain. But Tuttle's men were watching now. There was no way.

Finally, the curtain parted. In walked Raina Richter, followed by Tuttle and a beaming Hoots. The mouth and hands of Hoots were free. Raina's wrists were bound.

Tuttle seemed furious. Or worse. Miky felt the gut kick of being in his presence again. She could feel his gaze crawling through her skin.

The now-prisoner Raina plopped down in the seat she'd previously occupied as a free flyer.

Hoots, looking triumphant next to Tuttle, said "I told him everything. About her. And you. And, like, her brother." Hoots smiled and drew out the name, "Obama."

The cabin went wary. "He say 'Obama'?" A guy held up the half-empty bottle of Jack Daniel's with the question. All of the Silver Eagle guys looked at Tuttle.

Raina gave Miky a look she couldn't figure out. But it wasn't a bad look.

"He sure did," Raina said. "Barack H. O. He's my bro. And not just in the Black people sense. He's blood, you know. So, whatever happens to me or my friend here, just know you got Barack to deal with. We're tight." She held up her bound hands, twisted fingers on each confirming the tightness of the relationship.

Someone laughed.

"Don't be laughing. She's serious." Hoots said. He spit on the carpet at Raina's feet.

The muscled men murmured. The guy with the Jack said, "What are you going to do with this chick, Tuttle?"

Another guy yelled, "Yeah, want some ideas?"

A third, "I got some ideas right here."

Miky looked at Raina, who smiled. "Oh, I bet you got ideas," Raina said, her voice rising. "But you're too busy right now. Because you're about to overthrow the government or some shit."

The men stopped murmuring.

"Oh I know you're thinking, 'Hey, she's got no reason to be talking this way.' But way I see it, my Black ass has nothing to lose right now. Am I right? Mr. Tuttle here, he's ready to kill me right along with Ms. Spike, so I might as well go down with my lips flappin'."

The consensus was "yes."

"So, let's assess," Raina said. "We got four centuries of oppression up in here, with my brother Barack the only half-White hope my people ever had. But… you guys are going all crazy because the President is maybe taking away your Arby's

Beef'n' Cheddars to save the place we live on? Good lord above. Can't imagine you crackers getting White Wall Street burned down or, heaven help you, someone lynching your daddy for looking too long at a Black lady crossing the street."

A couple of the men were standing. The rest wore serious expressions that could comfortably be called menacing. Miky looked at Raina, who grinned.

"Shut up," Tuttle said.

Miky was beginning to really like Raina.

"So, your man Tuttle hired me to get this Miky Spike woman and bring her to him, because she pissed him off for saving some kids on a school bus and stopping some kind of crazy war between two states?" Raina said. She eyed Tuttle, who frowned. "And what I hear is he's probably got another side hustle going on. He's big on settling old scores and whatnot. All part of whatever his agenda is. See, I know this because I played him good. Made him think I was part of your sorry-ass movement, a militia gal working at Safeway in Gunny, C-O." Raina snorted. "Like a girl with my pedigree would choose to live on the whitest, coldest place this side of your momma's tata and hang with some dudes like these." She looked up at the glowering Hoots and then reached across the table to nudge the semi-comatose Pettibone with her zip-tied hands.

Hoots reached for her. Raina gave him a look that stopped him cold. The two locked eyes. A laugh surfed the cabin.

"Dude, you best leave Barack's little sis be," one of the men said. Another hooted.

Hoots backed off.

Tuttle stepped up. "Okay, okay, I've heard enough. Miss Richter is an ATF agent who is—"

"She's ATF? Holy cow, Tuttle." It was Commander Bill, coming through the curtain, his voice nasal due to the two bloody cotton balls protruding from his nostrils. He scanned

211

the men, most of whom were standing. "You guys drinking back here? On the job?"

Miky couldn't help herself. She laughed.

A man sniffed loudly. Another wiped his nose. One stooped and swiped white powder off a table.

"Just the men releasing some steam, sir," Tuttle said.

"Yeah, steam," Miky said.

"Shut up, Spike," Tuttle said. Miky rolled her eyes.

"This chick's not just ATF. She's Barack Obama's sister. Half-sister, anyway," Hoots said with a sniff. "I'm the one who turned her in, Commander. And may I just say, I'm a big admirer of yours. I didn't get a chance to say it earlier…"

Commander Bill walked toward the knife that was stuck in the floor. Then he spotted Pettibone, and Commander Bill's eyes widened. "Has that man died?"

"My name's Brady, Commander. Hoots Brady," Hoots Brady said. Hoots tried to shake Commander Bill's finger, which was pointed at Pettibone. Bill jerked his hand away.

"Your man Tuttle really has effed this up, Commander," Raina Richter said. "I am, yes, ATF. But, no, I am not President Obama's half-sister."

"She's lying," Hoot said.

The rest of the cabin seemed to frown.

"Lying about which?" Commander Bill said. "You've lost me here, I'm afraid."

Raina laughed. "I just say the thing about Obama because I know it drives White people like Hoots and these men here crazy. I usually talk in my sister from the 'hood voice when I do. That really gets them going. You'll notice now I'm in my educated Black woman voice."

"Bitch," Hoots said softly.

"My point is," Raina said. "I'm sitting here in one of your private jets on the way to what my gut and evidence tell me is an attack on the U.S. government, only Tuttle's all distracted with me and chasing down your old friend, Ms. Spike, plus whatever else he's got going on with someone named Joyce and another one named Nguyen, based on what he wrote on the mirror in the bathroom. This situation is about to go all kinds of sideways. I mean, just look at your team, Commander. Do they really seem ready to take down the most powerful government on earth?"

Tuttle took a step toward Raina. "You need to shut up."

"How did this happen, Tut?" Commander Bill's voice stopped Tuttle. "She's, like, ATF. And she seems to know an awful lot."

"I tell you how it happened," Raina said. "We ladies get Mr. Tuttle distracted. We've heard he's still hung up on some girl he knew back in the 'Nam." She had a thought. To Tuttle, she said, "Let me guess. Her name was Nguyen?"

Tuttle turned a color Miky identified as unhealthy. Commander Bill smiled. A blob of bloodied cotton dropped from his nose to the floor. Commander Bill bent to retrieve it, dropped it, decided to leave it, and wiped his bloody finger on his Silver Eagle jumpsuit. "You do have an eye for the ladies, Tut."

"The mission is still absolutely on, sir," Tuttle said. "We are good to go. These men will be ready." He looked at the men with a sharp frown, who responded with varying degrees of pseudo-readiness. Tuttle glanced at Miky and Raina before adding: "And my eye for the ladies has nothing to do with any of this."

"Tell that to your friend, Sonia," Raina said.

Tuttle's color, which had improved, took a turn.

"I have no doubt your dear, beloved baby from Belarus is even now briefing our president and her advisors on whatever you have planned for today with these men and Miky," she said.

Tuttle, never rattled, was now obviously rattled.

"I never said anything to her about Spike."

"You don't always kiss and tell, honey," Miky said.

Raina laughed. "But you did tell her about all this, didn't you?" She gestured at the men. "About these guys?"

Tuttle's men weren't moving, except the ones standing, who sat. Their faces were stony.

"This Sonia. She one of his girlfriends?" Miky asked Raina, watching Tuttle's face. It flinched. She'd scored.

"Yes, she's also part of our interagency task force. We've been monitoring these military companies and the militia ever since Operation Cheesus. Tuttle's so predictable. Remember Babsy Witt, folks?" Raina said, scanning Tuttle's men. "The woman who died investigating his little cheese deal back in the day? Same thing here. Only this agent didn't get shot."

"Stop talking, Barack Obama's sister," Hoots Brady said.

Raina Richter laughed. "I told you, I'm not…"

Hoots' big hands engulfed her neck. Raina's beautiful eyes bulged. Miky jumped on Hoots' back, bit him in the neck, and thought how stupid it was to bite him and also that he tasted salty. Hoots screamed and let go of Raina, who fell back in her seat, gasping. Miky got off the floor. She punched Hoots five times in the kidneys. Hoots fell, his head hit the table, and he tried to stand but ended up sprawled across Raina Richter's lap, who grabbed Hoots by both ears and screamed something about Jesus. Commander Bill stumbled into the aisle to avoid the melee. All of Tuttle's men scrambled to their feet. Two reached to help Tuttle stand. Three muttered something to each other, pulled Hoots off Raina and helped her to her feet. Pettibone, suddenly obviously not dead, sat upright, saw the assorted threats around him, and instinctively reached for the nearest gun he could find, which was in the holster of one of the guys helping Raina. There was a struggle and a stupidly loud bang. All eyes turned toward Commander Bill, who held a gun in his hand, and then to the long-suffering Pettibone.

One of Tuttle's men snapped off his sunglasses and said, "Now, that dude's definitely dead."

"Sure is," Tuttle said. "But this mission is not." He turned to the two men who had come to his aid. "Follow me, Dirk. You too, Dirk." The three of them pushed past the dazed Commander Bill and disappeared into the forward section of the cabin. Commander Bill tried to holster his gun. He missed the holster and dropped the weapon.

"Shit." Commander Bill said. His face reddened. He looked around. "Sorry about the swear."

Chapter Twenty-one

Arkansas airspace

Tuesday night

Cody Marks was distracted by the meteorological nightmare unfolding to his south and east.

Then he heard the gunshot.

Cody reflexively checked his instruments and listened. A bullet could pierce the plane's skin and leave no damage other than a nerve-jangling whistling wound. The trick was, it had to miss the wiring, electronics, and hydraulics that kept the plane aloft and functioning. When he was assured that it had, Cody double-checked the autopilot and stood, hand on his holstered pistol.

The flight deck's metal door banged open, and Tuttle stepped in, gun in hand, pointed at Cody. Two of Tuttle's men, whom Cody knew only as Dirks, squeezed past Tuttle and managed to take up positions on either side of the pilots' seats in the cramped space, facing Cody, hands folded over their crotches.

"Don't move," Cody said.

Tuttle frowned. "I'm supposed to say that."

"No. Seriously. You don't have time for this."

"You don't even know what this is."

"I know this: You have bigger issues than whatever is going on back there. And if you shoot that thing in here… Well, just back off, sir."

Tuttle thought about this. "Not possible." He said with a headshake. He stepped around Cody.

Miky Spike stepped in. "Stop him," she said to Cody Marks.

Tuttle sat in the pilot's seat, gestured with his gun at the instrument panel. "How do you turn off the auto-whatever?" He reached for a switch.

Cody Marks gasped. "Don't do that. Seriously."

Miky grabbed Tuttle's wrist, the wrong, non-gun-hand wrist. Tuttle swung his weapon around and pointed it at her. The two Dirks drew their weapons.

"Don't shoot. Don't don't don't." Cody Marks said.

Tuttle looked at Cody. Cody looked at Miky. The Dirks looked confused. Miky looked pissed.

"Let go of him," Cody said. "He shoots that thing in here and the bullet hits something, we all could die."

Tuttle snorted and snapped his wrist free. Then he swiveled the gun to point it at Cody. "Now, you. Sit in the co-pilot's chair there. And let me take over this bird. We're heading to Florida."

"What are you going to do when you get there, Tuttle?" Miky said. "They'll be waiting for you. You've been had, once again, by a woman." She laughed.

"Say what?" Cody Marks said.

Miky quickly filled him in on Raina's revelations.

"She's lying. Stop talking. I have a gun." Tuttle said.

"You all have guns," Miky said. She looked at one Dirk, the other Dirk, and then nodded at Cody. "He's got a gun, too. He just hasn't bothered to pull it out. It's how you guys are. Always, with the guns."

"Yes, it sure is how we are," another Dirk said. He stood behind Miky, looking though the doorway of the ridiculously crowded flight deck. Behind him were two other Dirks; all had guns raised. Raina Richter squeezed between the Dirks. "You're gonna need to drop that weapon, Tuttle," Raina said.

"No, he's not," said the Dirks on the flight deck with Tuttle, their guns out and leveled at the Dirks with Raina.

"Oh yes he is," said one of the Dirks with Raina said. "This bitch may be ATF but I believe her. And that bitch may be Miky-the-biggest-traitor-socialist on God's good earth, but you people know Tuttle, too. He'd chase a piece of tail all the way back into prison if she led him on. And apparently someone did. This op is blown, my friends. We need to return to home base."

The Dirks began arguing and waving guns.

"Put your guns down. I'm begging you," Cody said as he drew his gun.

"There you go," Miky said. She looked at Raina Richter.

Cody ignored her. "We need to clear this area."

No one moved.

"I mean, as God as my witness," Cody said, "there's serious trouble ahead, weather-wise. Everyone needs to get belted in. I don't know who shot who back there, but we can't have any more of it. The shooting."

One of the pro-Tuttle Dirks clicked off his gun's safety and racked the slide. Everyone else, Cody included, followed suit.

"Hold on now," Commander Bill said loudly. He was behind the others, just outside the doorway, with the final two Dirks and the surviving prisoner the women had brought onboard. Commander Bill seemed pale, but he put a bit of commander into his voice. "Everyone, listen, listen up." The hubbub faded. "It was a real, uh, tragedy—what just happened. Someone shot that one guy. He pulled a gun, I think, so—"

"It was you, Commander. We all saw it," the Dirk next to Commander Bill said. "You dropped the gun and Dirk here just picked it up."

The other guy held a gun aloft. "See, his gun."

"It's not clear who shot him," Raina Richter said. "I thought it might have been Tuttle," she said with a wicked grin.

"Yes, it all happened so fast," Miky said.

There was renewed waving of guns, murmuring and consternation.

Tuttle struggled to his feet, pointed his pistol at the instrument panel and said loudly, "Everybody stop. Or I'll shoot this plane. Swear to god."

"Sir. Drop it." It was one of the Dirks who supported Raina Richter. His gun was pointed at Tuttle.

"No, you drop it, Dirk," one of the Dirks who'd entered the flight deck with Tuttle said, his gun pointed at the Raina-Richter-supporting Dirk.

There was a lightning round of "you drop it, Dirk"s that ended with a gunshot followed in quick succession by three more. Four Dirks were hit. Raina Richter and Miky Spike rushed Tuttle, disarmed him, and pulled him out of the pilot's seat. Another Dirk raised his gun, yelled, "Stop shooting," and fired a warning shot into the ceiling. The cabin lights went out. The wounded plane began whistling like a whale through its blowhole. Cody Marks yelled "fuck," pushed past the entangled Raina, Tuttle and Miky, and dove butt-first into the pilot's seat. Commander Bill forced his way onto the flight deck, raised a little pink plastic gun that looked like a toy, pointed it at Cody's head, and said, "Tuttle, take over."

"Wrong move, you idiot," Miky said. "He's not on your side anymore."

Commander Bill looked confused.

"He never was on your side," Raina Richter said. "And what kind of girl gun is that?"

Cody grabbed the yoke. The plane keeled to the left. Commander Bill fell into Miky and dropped his little pink gun. There was a scramble, and Raina Richter somehow came up with the tiny weapon.

Cody leveled out the Gulfstream and ran a quick assessment of his instruments. He assumed, correctly, that the round of gunfire had hit men and that the shot to the ceiling had miraculously hit the conduit powering the lights but nothing more. "Good lord we're lucky," he said.

Commander Bill regained his balance and said, "The lord doesn't believe in luck, young ma…" And tripped over one of the bleeding Dirks. The Dirk who'd fired the warning shot grabbed him by the arm and said, "Steady, sir." The bleeding Dirk groaned, grabbed Commander Bill by the ankle, and whisper-growled, "Stop him." Miky grabbed for Warning Shot Dirk's weapon and was rewarded with a wild head punch from Tuttle. She staggered back into Raina Richter, who accidentally fired the plastic pistol, then Raina and Miky fell on top of a bleeding Dirk. The plastic pistol's pellet ricocheted. It hit Cody's right pectoral and the plane plummeted as he ceded control to the pain. Tuttle plopped into the co-pilot's seat, pulled back on the stick, and yelled, "co-pilot has command." Warning Shot Dirk seized the moment, pointed his gun at Cody's head, and said, "Everyone clear the flight deck. Don't let anyone up here. Especially not Commander Bill."

Cody's life didn't flash by his eyes so much as it stumbled in pain.

PART SEVEN

Nunchucks and the Big Bang Theory

Chapter Twenty-two

Southern Georgia

Tuesday night

The snow was light and swirling, the type Michiganders considered a nuisance since it reduced driving speeds. Big Bruddah drove mostly in the left lane, passing the tentative slow birds who were waddling along, apparently worried about the vehicles in the ditch; there were a lot of them, comatose headlights staring into the black Georgia sky, their shadowy drivers and passengers hunched over cell phones behind steamed windows.

"The road is slick, people. But it's not that slick," Zip Pierce said from the left rear seat. "Drive like you have a pair. Like my pal Bruddah here. Just not ninety-miles-an-hour like the idiots. Find a happy median. That's all."

"You made a joke there," Corky Vanderlaan said. He strained to look at Zip across the sleeping mass that was Nunchucks. "You caught that, right?"

"Always had a gift for the jokes, my mom always said. Thought of going into, like, comedy. If I hadn't been drafted into pro ball…"

"You know you've been talking since the Waffle House?" Corky said, turning to look out his window. "It was dark then. Sun will be up soon and you're still going."

"He's been talking since Bruddah yelled at him. About the deal in the Waffle House," said Jerry Plannenberg, who was in the front passenger's seat.

"Oooh, burn," Corky said.

"I'm just picking up the conversational slack from my buddy Nunchucks here. Isn't that right, Nunchucky?" Zip said.

Nunchucky said nothing in his sleep.

"He's been sawing logs since you been talking," Corky said. "You have that effect on people."

Zip let out a long, stuttering belch.

"You guys peck at each other like a bunch of girls," Jerry said.

"Nothing wrong with bunches of girls, am I right, Buddah?" Zip said. "Man, what I would give to be back on the road with a major league team again. Got more action than…"

"It's Bruddah. Give it a rest, Zip," Big Bruddah said.

Jerry picked up a phone from the console that separated the front passenger's seat from the driver's. He turned it on, the screen illuminating his face.

"You remember the PIN?" Big Bruddah said.

"Yeah, man." Jerry entered the pin he and Bruddah had chosen, G-U-N-Z. He studied the phone, and then scrolled up the screen with his right thumb. "Holy shit," Jerry said.

"Yeah, 'holy shit.' I thought we were keeping our phones off," Zip said.

"What's up?" Big Bruddah glanced at Jerry.

Jerry's thumb was still scrolling. "Inbox is packed."

"Jerry's doing the lead on comm, Zip. You know that. We agreed. Someone's got to keep a line open for what's going on," Corky said.

"I never heard that," Zip said.

"Well, you heard it now," Corky said. "Besides that's a burner phone. You'd know that, too, if you'd stop yammering and listen once in a while. It's untraceable. The phone."

"Email inbox?" Big Bruddah said.

"Yeah. Haven't checked texts yet, but I'm betting it's the same." Jerry scrolled some more. "This is unreal. I mean…"

"Where they from?" Big Bruddah said.

"Looks to me like from everywhere," Jerry said. "From Michigan. From, like, Texas. Shit, there's even a group coming from Portland—the one in Oregon. And Florida. Alabama. Cali."

"That's a lot of firepower," Corky said.

"I can't tell you actual numbers. But yeah. A shitload," Jerry said.

"A shitload," Big Bruddah said. "All militia, coming this way." He looked at Jerry. "Right?"

"From what I'm seeing here, yeah, definitely," Jerry said. "There's some, like, chatter or whatever about weather. Guys are running into storms and fires and getting slowed down. But yeah. This is looking sweet."

For a mile maybe two, no one spoke. The radio hid its song under the sound of the wipers, the blower, and Nunchucks' soft snoring.

"Are you guys still pissed at me?" Zip said.

"Shut up, Zip," Big Bruddah, Jerry Plannenberg, and Corky Vanderlaan said.

"Hey, look. Snow's letting up," Zip said.

"Shit," Big Bruddah said. "You're right." He straightened in his seat, leaned forward, and pressed slowly on the accelerator.

Zip sniffed. "I had it figured we'd be driving out of this stuff the farther we got into the ol' peach state. All those years traveling during a 162-game season; you see a lot. There's no way this time of year you're gonna see snow in Georgia. I saw snow in Tennessee once during, like, April, back when I played minor league ball…"

"You make no sense at all," Corky said. "This is Georgia. And this is May."

Zip thought about this. "All's I know is…"

Corky cut him off. He leaned toward Big Bruddah. "Hey, Bruddah, given all the guys that are coming, we're definitely gonna need more ammo or, like, a bigger plan or all three. We don't want to show up to this party empty-handed."

"I hear you, man. I know," Big Bruddah said. He punched the steering wheel. "My f-ing basement. Who'd have figured we get like a thousand-year rain or whatever? I mean, we just had one last year. Doesn't make any sense."

"We just passed like the millionth billboard for a strip club," Zip said.

"No strip club's open at this hour, Zipster," Corky said.

"That last one said 'Open twenty-four hours,'" Zip said. "'Couples welcome.' What's up with that?" He snickered.

"No one wants to see your fat butt this time of night," Corky said. "Or any time, for that matter."

"It's practically morning," Zip said. "Besides, you're just saying that because you're Mr. Church Whatever."

"My dad was a tool and die guy who cheated on my mom and drank the food money," Corky said. "We've been over this. You guys carry on and strip club all you want. I've seen what that kind of behavior can lead to."

"You never went to, like, pornos or anything—even in college," Zip said with a snort.

"Nope. Nose to the grindstone. I was a swimmer."

"Any good?"

"Junior year, I was all set to go to the Olympic trials."

"No shit."

"Yeah. They picked some Black kid to go instead of me. Always figured it was an affirmative action sort of deal. I mean, whoever's seen a Black guy who could swim?"

"You can't make this stuff up," Zip said.

"Actually, you can," said Big Bruddah. "You can make it up. People make up shit like that all the time. In books, movies. Hell, you could be making it up. It's all make-up-able. Everything."

"Easy, bruh. Dude's just talking," Jerry said. He lightly punched Big Bruddah's right shoulder. "Like he does."

Big Bruddah glanced at Zip in the rearview and then at Jerry. He shook his head.

"The government stepping in with their affirmative action deal pretty much wrecked all the sports," Zip said. "These days, pro ball is, you know, overrun with Mexicans and so on. Everybody's, like, 'Carlos' or 'Juan' or whatever."

"Which is sort of the point of our thing here," Corky said. "Right, bruddah? Government running amok. Regular people losing their rights and whatever."

The truck hit the rumble strip on the highway's shoulder. "Whoa," Big Bruddah said. He jerked the wheel back into the right lane. "Sorry, dudes. Thinking too hard for my own good."

"My opinion, we're being overrun, basically. By non-Christians and such," Corky said. "And the trans-whatevers. All the morals declining. Disrespect for life. Disrespect for institutions, defunding cops. And it's the regular, everyday Americans who lose out."

"Yeah," Zip said, "People who built this country came here for freedom, for the right to live the way they wanted to live. They wanted a place where people were, like, free to manifest their destiny or whatever. Laws and orders allowed them to do that. Laws. And orders."

"It wasn't free, though," Corky said. "They earned it for us."

"Oh yeah, of course. They had to defend against all the threats—the Indians trying to steal the land. Always had people trying to, you know, mess with a good thing, trying to wreck the static quo."

"Gotta admit, the Zip-ster's right," Jerry said. "Which is why guys back then put all that emphasis on guns. The fore-whatevers."

"Sun's coming up," Big Bruddah said.

"Yeah, and you're up to cruising speed, dude. Let's make some time," Corky said.

"Definitely," Big Bruddah said. He inched the cruise up a little more.

"Back in the day, they knew what stood between them and all this danger and shit was guns," Jerry said.

"Yeah," Zip said. "I read—I forget where—the Second Amendment would've been the First Amendment but Hamilton or someone got in a tizzy about it. So, they gave him the free speech thing first and then jumped to what was most important, which was your God-given right to your arms, to bear them, you know?"

"People always twist it around, saying 'America is overrun with guns," Corky said. "I'm like, 'hey, ever think maybe God knows we're specially equipped to, like, keep the peace on earth?' Maybe guns are our responsibility."

"Fo' shizzle." Jerry said.

Zip snorted. "Imagine Thomas Jefferson or whoever being told by some gal president—let's not even get started on she being a woman with all the hormones and periods and whatnot—imagine her telling George F-ing Washington he couldn't raise a cow, let alone buy an AK-47. The minute that happened, he'd have taken that gal over his knee. That's in the Bible, right big guy?" He looked at Corky. "Man has authority. Over the women. Not enough of that going on. The authority deal."

"This nation was founded on Christian values, Zip. Yes," Corky said.

"Oh, I give you that. I may not be all religious, but I have, you know, good Christian whatever. Values," Zip said.

"Same here," Jerry said.

"The Founders wanted a Christian nation. That was clear. You can talk all you want about the Muslims and Jews and whatever. These were White Christian men," Corky said. "And they'd be…"

"Emphasis on 'men.' Not a homo in the bunch, am I right?" Zip said.

"You talk a lot about homos," Jerry said.

"What's that supposed to mean?" Zip said.

"Whatever it means, my man." Jerry said.

Corky pressed on. "Jefferson, Washington—they weren't perfect. None of us are. There's certainly some evidence that, say, Jefferson had children with that slave. But he wasn't out there killing the babies."

"Sally whatever. I heard that, too," Jerry said. "

"Nothing wrong with a guy getting some action. Am I right?" Zip said.

"Lemmings," Jerry said.

"Hemmings," Big Bruddah said. "Sally Hemmings."

"The landowners had needs and rights and there's no evidence certainly that any of what is reported about Jefferson and others is necessarily true," Corky said.

"Or that it wasn't, you know, contextual," Zip said. "She might have led him on—the slave gal."

"Yes, Corky said. "These were men of faith, so who are we to judge? They certainly weren't taking drugs and allowing abortions is my point. That all started happening during the 1960s. Up until then, I'd say this country lived by an agreed-on social order that was very Christian in nature. But suddenly, the liberals started burning bras and draft cards and the cities—"

"The so-called 'civil rights' movement. Don't forget that," Jerry said.

"Led by the good Reverend Doctor Martin Luther King, a proven womanizer," Corky said.

"I never got how he could be both a doctor and a reverend. Something fishy there," Zip said.

"I hear you," Jerry said.

"Detroit went up in flames. And I was there, baby," Zip Pierce said. "Right in the middle of the action. The natives were out of control, I'm telling you."

From his position wedged between Zip and Corky, Nunchucks snorted. "You guys are idiots." His volcanic voice rattled with phlegm. He cleared his throat. "We're all going to need our rest and you guys keep yammering on and on about who you are and what you believe in or don't believe in."

"Says the guy we know absolutely nothing about," Jerry said.

"I got nothing to hide," Nunchucks said.

"Well, you hide nothing pretty well," Jerry said.

Nunchucks sat up, pressing his girth against Zip's. "So, what you wanna know? Want me to tell you about my family?" There was a smile in his voice.

Zip coughed. Corky flicked at the power lock switch on his door. Jerry said, softly, "Dude."

"Well, we know your family situation is private," Big Bruddah said with a glance into the rearview mirror.

"It is?" Jerry said.

"Shut up, Jerry," Big Bruddah said.

"You guys kill me," Nunchucks said. He sat up as best he could, forcing groans from Corky and Zip, who struggled to make room in the backseat—there wasn't any. "We are, like, one more cow law away from total government control. You're halfway to a war or civil uprising or whatever you call it, you got no plan of what you're going to do when you get there and all you can do is talk talk talk about stuff you been arguing about your whole lives." Nunchucks hunched forward into the space between the front seats. "Am I right?" He directed the question at Big Bruddah.

"Yeah, sure, man. I hear you," Big Bruddah said, his eyes fixed on the road ahead. "We get caught up in this shit."

Nunchucks leaned back, eliciting a new round of groans. He glanced to his left, at Zip, and then to his right, at Corky. "We all know our main dude here got flooded out and lost a lot of our ordnance and other shit through no real fault of his own but all you seem to care about is who thinks what about… You want to know something about me? I got raised on a farm in Frankenmuth, Michigan by a skinny old mom and a big, fat father who scared the shit out of me and my sisters every damn day but who taught us to work our asses off, to shoot like soldiers, to protect our neighbors, ourselves, and the government of our founding fathers, and to respect the flag and the Constitution. I got off that farm by serving four tours in Iraq and seeing enough hell on earth to realize there's a lot more where that came from and that I'm pretty damn good at fighting in it."

"Wow," Zip said. "I just ripped one. Silent but deadly, men. Be warned."

"Zip. Shit," Jerry said, trying to hold his breath as he spoke. He leaned over and flicked up the blower setting on the truck's heater. "Let the man talk. None of us has heard that many words in a row from Nunchucks. Ever. And I gotta say, they're good words."

"Yeah," Corky said. He lowered his window an inch or so, letting in a whistling stream of fresh air. "Keep talking, Nunman."

Nunchucks glanced at Zip, then continued. "We should be thinking ahead. Guys are all gonna be down there trying to get Hoeksma in and replace this crazy woman, but we can't just be, like, part of the mob. Because, if that happens, we'll head back to Michigan with, like, these bullshit beef laws repealed, the Constitution defended, and a good guy in charge, but all these other clowns and militias and shit will have a say in things and we won't. I mean, I ain't doing this for no Happy Meal."

"Wow," Jerry turned to look at Nunchucks. "I don't even know who you are right now."

"Yeah," Big Bruddah said to the rearview mirror. "Where did that even come from?"

Zip laughed. "I can't believe this guy can even string that many, you know, thoughts together," he said. He cocked his head to look at Nunchucks. "Seriously, I had you figured for some kind of, like, retarded guy or whatever. Impaired. I mean, knowing your reputation and all."

"Zip," Jerry and Big Bruddah said.

Nunchucks made a sound that could have been a growl, could have been a laugh. He stared at the ceiling for a moment, then took a deep breath and let it out. "Listen, I've been on some pretty serious meds, man. Let's just leave it at that. Some prescribed. Some my own, you know, recipe. Besides, you guys talk too much. Couldn't get a word in."

Corky pressed the button to close his window, cutting off the whistling wind. "To your point, Nunchucks," he said, "someone on 4chan the other night was talking about how, in the original revolution, a lot of guys were out there protesting British oppression, but most of them had no plan to do anything about it. Then, boom, men in Boston went for it. They dressed up like Indians and dumped the tea in the harbor. And America happened. I mean, we can sit here and talk all we want, but when this is over, seems like we need to be, like, sharing the spoils or whatever, right?"

The other men nodded and murmured and chewed on this.

"So, you're on, like, parole?" Zip said.

"Shut up, Zip," everyone except Zip said.

Jerry turned to get a better look into the backseat, "Seriously, Nunchucks. I mean, dude, you're a vet. First off, thanks for your service…"

The rest of the men grunted variations of the service appreciation mantra.

"… and second," Jerry said, "Tactically speaking, we could use any wisdom you got about our situation. I mean, what do you think we need, short of robbing some ammo dump somewhere."

"That is, if you have any ideas. I've known a lot of guys who are just talk," Zip said. He was staring out the window. "Never bring anything but words to the ol' table."

"Shut up, Zip," Nunchucks said.

Zip gurgled—a laugh, swallowed.

"I been thinking on it, to be honest," Nunchucks said.

"And?" Big Bruddah said.

"Well, you know they got all these fireworks stores around here? I mean, we passed one a ways back. Used to stop at one of them when I was driving down to Florida with the family. They're, like, everywhere along the highway. And a lot of them are open, like twenty-four hours."

Zip snorted. He looked at Jerry. "Guy barely speaks and then starts yammering about fighting the government with bottle rockets. You can't make this stuff…"

"Gunpowder." Big Bruddah and Jerry said it together.

Big Bruddah caught Nunchucks' eye in the mirror. "That what you thinking?"

"You got it," Nunchucks said. "What else you think the Chinese put in fireworks? It ain't baby powder. We get as much of that shit as we can. That's a lot of black powder, am I right? We could make a big big big bang out of that."

Corky laughed. "That's kind of genius—you ask me."

"I like it," Big Bruddah said with a quick look at Jerry.

Jerry grunted what sounded like approval.

"If you think there's a store ahead, Nun, then I'll keep going," Big Bruddah said, his eyes back on the road. "Otherwise, I'll do a U-turn and find one we already passed."

"Nope. Swear there's one or two coming up," Nunchucks said.

Big Bruddah accelerated.

Chapter Twenty-three

Tarrytown, Georgia

Wednesday morning

A massive billboard beckoned like a sign from boogaloo heaven: "Fireworks Warehouse 911 Ahead Biggest Inventory East of the Mississippi Open 24 Hours Free Gas With Purchase of $50 or More Next Exit."

Big Bruddah exited the highway, drove into the deserted Fireworks Warehouse 911 parking lot, circled around the gas pumps, and stopped near the entrance. The stores in an adjacent strip mall were dark, but Fireworks Warehouse 911 was garishly illuminated. Through plate-glass windows, the big-box store displayed row after row of brightly packaged munitions. There was a six-lane checkout area. Above it, a banner read "Make America Boom Again." One guy, wearing a red, white, and blue shirt, was sitting on a stool at the middle checkout counter and flipping through a magazine.

As Big Bruddah shifted into park and killed the engine, the truck cab exploded in red, white and blue flashing lights.

"Cop."

"Jerry said, stating the obvious," Corky said.

A police car, LED light bar frantically announcing its arrival, slid to a stop next to the truck. The white vehicle's sides were emblazoned with "Tarrytown City Police" in block black letters, slanted forward. The front doors opened and two men in uniform got out. Both were dark-skinned. The driver, tall and a few pounds past heavy, wore a turban and a neatly trimmed beard. The other cop was short and slim, clean-shaven. He wore a white kufi.

"What is this, the United Fucking Nations?" Jerry said.

"My sweet lord. Sharia law come to life," Nunchucks said.

The passenger cop circled the rear of the truck, pausing to look in the back. The driver cop walked around his vehicle and one-knuckle knocked on Big Bruddah's window. "Open, sir, please," he said.

"Yo," Jerry said softly, glancing at Nunchucks. "Be cool. Nothing crazy. Keep your weapons in your pants."

Zip snorted. "Oh I'll keep my weapon—"

Another tap from the turbaned cop. The other cop stood at Jerry's window. "Please, sir, keep your hands where I can see them," he said, his voice muffled by the window.

Zip cocked his head to look out at the guy in the turban. "Wow. Just wow. Both of them. Like something straight out of Baghdad. Can you believe this?" Tarrytown must be one of those places they all come to. You know, one family member following the other. Like up in Michigan. Southfield."

"Zip. Not a word."

"Be careful here, big guy," Zip said. "You can't trust these people."

"Zip, stating the obvious," Corky said.

Big Bruddah pressed the power window button. "What can I do for you officer?" he said.

"Sir, as my partner said, please, we ask that you keep your hands where we can see them."

238

"Of course," Big Bruddah said, not moving his hands from where they were trembling in his lap. "I'll do that when you tell me what this is all about. We've done nothing wrong here."

The other cop knocked on Jerry's window. Jerry powered it down and looked at the officer with the practiced subservience of an ex-convict who'd killed a man but didn't want a cop to feel threatened by his resume.

"Sir, put your hands on the dashboard." The cop looked toward the backseat. "You men in the back. Please, your hands; put your hands up on the seatbacks in front of you."

"How about you show us some identification," Zip said.

"They're wearing uniforms with badges, Zip," Jerry said. "They're in a fucking police car."

"Well, they don't look like any cops I know," Zip said.

"Your hands, guys. On the seatback and the dashboard," the cop at Jerry's window said.

Slowly, Jerry, Corky, and Nunchucks—growling softly—complied with the cop's request. Big Bruddah remained frozen.

"Sir, I said 'put your hands where I can see them,'" the first cop said. "Now."

"Sir, please," the other cop said, "don't make a deal out of this."

"Who's making a deal?" Zip said. "Would you like me to pull my gun? Would that be a deal?"

"Zip." Jerry was facing forward, hands on the dash. He spoke out of the side of his mouth: "Bruddah, dude, do it before things get weird."

"Yeah, man," Nunchucks said, his voice sounding like a whispering wolf, if wolves could talk and then, also, whisper. "These mudheads got the tactical advantage. Show him your hands. Nothing you can do."

Slowly, Big Bruddah raised his hands, willing them to stay steady. He gripped the top of the steering, turned his head to stare at the cop.

"Driver's license and registration," the lead cop said.

Big Bruddah reached for the glove compartment.

"Whoa whoa whoa, there." The second cop said. He held up a hand.

"Sir, please. Think about what you're doing," the first cop said.

Big Bruddah felt an icicle of panic dribble down his back. He grabbed the steering wheel and then looked at the cop.

"We just need your license and registration," the second cop said.

Big Bruddah again reached for the glove compartment.

"Stop." The second cop said. "Stop. Please."

Big Bruddah jerked his hands back to the steering wheel.

From the backseat, Zip said, "Jihadi Arab Assholes."

"Don't even have the balls to pull your weapons. What kind of candyass cops are you?" Nunchucks said. "Draw down on us and let us see what you got."

The turbaned cop stepped closer. "Watch your tone back there," he said to Nunchucks and then turned to Big Bruddah. "We can't just let you reach for something like that. Very often, people have things hidden with which they intend to do us harm." He withdrew from the window, thought for a moment, then stepped forward again, looked at Zip, and said, "For the record, I'm a Sikh. It's a whole different deal."

"And, yeah, I'm Muslim. But African-American, you know. A convert," the cop in the kufi said. "Originally from Memphis. Elvis forever, my brother." He grinned and held up a two-fingered peace sign.

Big Bruddah faced forward, avoiding eye contact with the cops. "I'm not sure what you officers want from us," he said.

"We're just out here, buying some fireworks, and you're all up in our faces. I can't very well show you my license and registration without reaching into the glove compartment."

"I can't. Breathe," Corky said, sounding very much like a man who couldn't breathe.

Big Bruddah, hands gripping the wheel, looked over his shoulder. Corky's face was pale.

"Seriously," Corky said, his voice as tiny as a two year old's. "I can't. Breathe. It's, like, a panic attack. Heart attack? I've never had a heart attack. I just can't… I can't breathe. And my chest—"

"Okay, okay," the turbaned cop said. "We need to help your buddy but we'd love to just see some ID here. Is there a license in your pocket?"

Corky began praying. "Dear sweet baby Jesus…"

"Oh don't mention Jesus," Zip said. "They don't care about him; that's for sure. I have half a mind to jump in the back of this beast and show both of you cops or whatever you really are where the real firepower is."

"Zip." At least two of the other men said it.

"That's it. Everybody out of the vehicle," the second cop said.

The cops popped open the truck's doors. At first none of the men moved.

"Let's go," the first cop said. "Now."

Slowly, they stepped out. The cop in the turban ordered them to sit in a line on the curbed sidewalk, their backs to the building, hands up. Corky's face was gray. Before he could sit, his knees buckled. The second cop grabbed him by the arm, steadied him, and helped him to a sitting position on the curb. He looked at his partner. "I'm going to get him some help." He triggered the microphone clipped to his shirt. The radio squawked. "Dispatch, request an ambulance to our location. Possible heart or panic attack."

"Roger that, Jimmy," the dispatcher said.

"That's Officer Jimmy to you, Sarah," the cop now doing business as Officer Jimmy said to the invisible but helpful Sarah.

"Gotcha, Jim-bo," Sarah said. "Hey to Maresh." The radio squawked and went dead.

Officer Jimmy looked at the big cop. "Sarah says—"

"I heard," the cop said.

Jimmy knelt on one knee, looked Corky in the eye. "How are you feeling here, bud?"

"It's my chest. Like someone is kneeling on it." Corky was struggling to talk. He eased back on the sidewalk, "Oh, Momma."

The cop named Maresh looked toward his partner. "Dude gonna be okay, Jimmy?"

"I think so. Nobody's dying on our watch; that's for sure," Jimmy said. He looked at Corky and smiled. "We're hired to protect and serve. This would be the serve part." He patted Corky's shoulder.

"Okay, listen up," Maresh said to the assembled men. "We have an issue from earlier in the evening to address. But first, I note an unusually high number of weapons on your hips. I'm going to guess that these are legally carried. My fellow officer here will be walking down the line. He will take your weapon, place it on the sidewalk behind you, and then you will slowly— and I mean slowly—find your license to carry and present it to him. While you're doing that, I'm going to step around your vehicle, and check for the license and registration in the glove compartment." He began walking to the passenger's side of the truck.

The men grumbled as Jimmy took their sidearms. Then each retrieved his carry permit. When Jimmy had confirmed their right to bear these particular arms, he said, "We're solid here, Maresh."

Maresh shut the door of the truck. "Jackpot. Got a license, a registration, and, yes, a 9 mil Glock."

"That's also permitted," Big Bruddah said.

Jimmy retrieved a bottle of water from the patrol car and returned to where Corky was lying on the sidewalk.

"We've got to get you in a sitting position, my man, in case it's your heart." Jimmy the Cop helped Corky sit up. "Sorry, I know it hurts." He supported Corky with a hand on his back and helped him take a sip from the bottled water. "Help is on the way, man. We got you."

In the distance, a siren howled.

"I can't. Breathe," Corky said. "My chest—"

"Hey, Jimmy. Hey, Maresh. What's going on out here?" It was the guy from the store. He was holding the door open, seemingly cautious about exiting to find out what, in fact, was going on.

"That's what we'd all like to know," Zip said. "We just wanted some fireworks is all."

The siren grew louder.

"They're almost here, man," Jimmy said to Corky. "Wish we could help you more. But they'll have stuff for the pain and all."

"So, here's the deal," Officer Maresh said. "Earlier this evening, some men answering your description physically assaulted a waitress at a Waffle House in—"

The ambulance whooped whooped its arrival. Jimmy the Cop waved it over to where he knelt next to Corky.

"We ain't paying for no ambulance," the guy from the store said. He was still holding the door open, one foot outside, the other one lagging, as though he had a store-full of customers he couldn't ignore.

"Relax, Dansby," Maresh said. "No liability here for you. I'll tell your old man you were doing your job. He's got you working the graveyard. It's the least."

Dansby grinned. "You're not a bad guy for a towelhead." He cackled and stepped out of the store.

Two uniformed EMTs—one man, one woman—jumped out of the ambulance, walked to the rear, and opened the rear doors. They pulled out a gurney and various medical-looking stuff, the gurney's legs opening with a metallic click.

"Well, Dans my man, you're not a bad guy for a thirty-year-old cracker selling cherry bombs for his daddy," Jimmy said. Dansby scowled at Jimmy.

The EMTs moved quickly. In seconds they had an EKG hooked to Corky and he was breathing through an oxygen mask. With Jimmy's help, they helped him onto the gurney.

"What's up with these guys?" Dansby said, nodding at the line of men with their backs to him.

"Never mind, Dansby. I'd just go back inside and mind the store if I were you," Maresh said.

Dansby retreated into the store.

The woman EMT held an IV bag in the air as her partner inserted a needle in Corky's arm and Jimmy offered soft words of comfort. "You're good, buddy. You're good. These two are the best. Our hospital's a heart center, so no worries, okay?"

Corky had closed his eyes, but he nodded, his body relaxed as he took in the oxygen.

"It's definitely a heart attack. Not a big one," the EMT said to Corky with a reassuring smile.

"Hold on there, amigo or whatever you call a girl amigo," Zip said. "You and Jose there, your partner, both of you look like you're from south of the border, like Mexico or whatever. Am I right?" Zip looked at Big Bruddah. "Maybe we ought to check their papers before they haul away our friend Jerry here."

"It's Corky. I'm Jerry, you moron," Jerry said.

The EMTs ignored Zip. They finished loading their stuff into the ambulance, and then followed with Corky on the gurney.

The woman got in with Corky, holding the IV and talking softly to him.

"Hey, Corky, you okay with these two taking you away?" Jerry said.

Corky managed to raise his non-IV'd arm and gave the OK sign.

"Cork, are you signaling OK?" Zip said.

"Yes. He's saying it's OK," Big Bruddah said.

"I read it as the White power sign," Zip said. "Or maybe the grip for the old circle change—a great pitch I used to throw until the ol' arm gave out."

"C'mon Zip, let it go. Cork's in serious pain here," Jerry said.

The male EMT shut the rear doors and slapped the butt of the ambulance. He nodded at Maresh. "We're gonna break our record on this one."

"Record?" Jimmy said.

"Yeah, we start the clock when we depart with a heart patient. Time is critical. Our best is eight forty-six. Saving lives, you know."

"Same here. Always the goal. Good luck with that, my man," Maresh said. "Take care of him."

"We'll keep you posted, amigo," the EMT said. He got into the ambulance, dropped it into gear, and the ambulance accelerated away.

"Those two are going to have hell to pay if anything bad happens here," Zip said. "I swear. Glad Corky's carrying."

Jimmy activated the mic on his shoulder. After a squawk, the now-somewhat-familiar voice of Sarah said, "What's up there, Officer Jim-bo?"

"Dispatch," Jimmy said, "please advise Luis and Maria that their patient is armed. They'll need to secure that weapon."

"Gotcha." The radio squawked and Sarah was gone.

"Zip, you're just a complete idiot," Big Bruddah said.

Chapter Twenty-four

Big Bruddah had had enough curb sitting. He stood.

"Look. We got a deal in Florida we need to be at," he said. "You don't have cause to keep us here. So, we're gonna be on our way. And we'll be checking in on Corky."

Jerry and Nunchucks took his cue and stood.

Jerry eyed Maresh. "You're the reason our buddy's in that ambulance. Woulda been no heart attack except for you guys getting him riled up. Got to think we'll be suing your asses at some point."

"I can assure you; your friend is in the best of hands," Jimmy said. He put his hand on Bruddah's right shoulder, and said, "Please. Sit." He repeated this with Jerry and Nunchucks.

They remained standing.

"Zip," Jerry said. "Stand. We're leaving."

"Guys, sorry," Zip said, "it's my gimp knee. It's the one I tore up sliding into home, May of '74. Two game series with the Brewers in Milwaukee. Runner on first and third. Tried the old double steal—"

Jerry grunted and grabbed Zip's hand. "Shut up and get up." Zip groaned, farted loudly, and stood. Jerry let go of his hand and Zip stumbled backwards into Jimmy.

"You need me to call for backup, Maresh?" It was Dansby. He'd returned to the door and opened it ever so much.

"We're good here," Jimmy said, pushing Zip away. "Get back inside, man."

Dansby retreated.

"As I was saying, a waitress up north had a hot pot of coffee dumped on her," Maresh said. "They put out an all-points-bulletin on the guys that did it, in particular the one guy, whose description fits your hairy friend here."

"An ABP. Sweet," Zip said.

"APB, dumbass," Jerry said.

"To tell the truth, it wasn't actually an APB," Jimmy said. "More like a personal request to all departments. From the sheriff up in Montgomery. Seems the woman with the coffee pot was his sister-in-law. She said you were coming this way. Gave us the partial on your plate and a description. One of the guys on our local force here; Herk, Herk Swenson; he saw you guys exit the highway out here. Herk was coming off his shift. Heading home to Esther—that's his wife—and the kids."

"They've got two," Maresh said. "One each. Eliza and Kai. Cutest things. Norwegian dad, Zimbabwe mom equals beautiful babies. Who knew?"

"Anyways, Herk saw you guys and called it in," Jimmy said.

Nunchucks moved surprisingly quickly for a large man. He whirled, grabbed Jimmy's wrist, unsnapped his holster, and grabbed his service weapon. Before Maresh could react, Jerry and Big Bruddah also had the big cop on the ground and disarmed.

"Holy shit. What's going on?" Dansby said from the open doorway.

Nunchucks fired Jimmy's gun. The window to Dansby's right exploded and behind him chunks of the store's ceiling showered onto the fireworks displays. Dansby jerked back inside and ran toward the checkout area.

"Damn. Overreacted a little there," Nunchucks said.

"You think?" Zip said from where he was crouched behind Big Bruddah's pickup.

"We're working on my impulse control," Nunchucks said.

"I guess. Holy shit, man," Jerry said.

"What are you thinking, dude?" Big Bruddah said.

"At least I didn't shoot him."

"You're gonna wish you did," Dansby said. He was standing in the man-sized hole in the window holding what looked like a camo-painted AR-15 semi-automatic.

Nunchucks fired again. Dansby looked down, seemingly in awe of the camo semi-auto, which was now in the glass at his feet. There was blood in the glass. Dansby looked at Nunchucks for an explanation. Then he slowly fell to his knees. And Dansby died.

"Now I shot him," Nunchucks said.

Minutes later, the two cops were sitting, their backs against the rear wall of Fireworks Warehouse 911. The store manager and heir to the Fireworks Warehouse 911 fortune was sitting there, too, but he was slouching forward, his head near his legs due to his recent death. Big Bruddah was trying to think, to plan next steps, as he paced back and forth in front of the prisoners and the dead Dansby.

Zip, his face haggard and pale in the early morning light, hadn't stopped talking since the shooting. Nunchucks was in full-on militia mode; at attention, he held Dansby's weapon as though he was ready to use it again, because he most definitely was.

Jerry knelt and looked each of the cops in the eye. "So, we need to deal with you two before anyone else arrives," he said.

"Just get it over with," Nunchucks said, taking a step toward the prisoners.

"Nunchucks, one damn thing at a time." Big Bruddah said. "You already gave us one dead body to deal with. And some kind of ABP or whatever…"

"APB," Jerry said.

"It's not an APB," Jimmy said softly.

"I don't care what it is. We got people looking for us now. And a dead body. And we need to be in Florida," Big Bruddah swallowed the rising anxiety in his throat. "We got to focus, stick to the mission."

"Damn, Bruddah. Chill," Jerry said.

"I am chill."

"No, really. I'm serious," Jerry stood. "Bruh, listen. We're all good here. So what, Nunchucks shot some random dude. Today's the day for that. Am I right? I mean, chaos is cool. Mayhem—whatever. We're about to make that big statement we all been talking about. Maybe this is part of it. God's will and all. Now that blood's been shed or whatever, why not light the match on the whole damn boogie?" Jerry said. "I'm just saying."

Big Bruddah looked down. He stared at the shoes of the seated men and forced himself to breathe slowly. He began kicking a shoe softly, but he stopped when he realized it was on a dead man's foot.

"Bruh, listen. You know I'm right. Nun just gave us a gift, not a problem. I mean, we got an opportunity to make examples of the types of people who are ruining everything in this country. Just look. Look," Jerry said. "We got the BLM crazies and the Muslim assholes represented right here." He stopped himself. "Either of you queer?"

Jimmy shook his head. "You are one seriously messed-up dude."

"Transgender?" Jerry said. He squinted at Maresh. "You a tranny with that pretty hat?"

"I told you I'm Sikh," Maresh said, sitting taller.

"Whatever," Jerry said. "What I'm saying is we make it look like these two shot Dansby…"

"Danny, I think his name is—was." Zip Pierce said, "Danny."

"And we make it look like Dansby shot these two," Jerry said. "Boom, we got your big-ass, full-on boogaloo flashpoint right there."

Jerry had a point.

"You have a point," Big Bruddah said. He stared at Maresh and sighed. "For the love of God I got no idea why you didn't just shoot me back in the car when I reached for the glove compartment."

"Exactly what I was thinking," Jerry said. He nudged Maresh's foot with the toe of his steel-toed boot. "If I was a cop, I woulda shot us for not cooperating. Or for standing up when you said, 'sit down.'"

"We don't shoot people for no reason," Maresh said.

"Wasn't 'no reason,'" Jerry said. "Guys act up, you got authority to deal with them."

There was a loud click: Nunchucks preparing the AR-15.

"No way," Jimmy said. "C'mon, guys. You're not going to shoot us like this. That kind of thing only happens in bad movies."

"Well, maybe you fell into one, did you think of that, young man?" Zip said, laughing and looking at Big Brudda. "Am I right, Bruddah?" He looked at Jerry. "Am I right, Jer?"

Big Bruddah stared at the pale, graying face of the dead fireworks seller. He looked at Nunchucks, who was slipping into a wild-eyed mode that had him cocked and waiting for the signal to pull his own unstable trigger. He heard Zip's voice and wished he could strangle it. There was a fan and the shit had most definitely hit it. Zip and Nunchucks had moved from headaches to mind-numbing problems. With them in the way, how could they ever get to Tampa? Then there was the dead guy and the two cops. Adding more bodies to the mix, well, that seemed like a sure way to bring every Georgia cop down on them. Cops were weird. Didn't matter your color or turban or whatever—you bled blue. You kill a cop or two; cops are coming for you. He glanced at Maresh and Jimmy. They were stupidly calm. Ridiculously nice. Usable. He thought hard for several seconds, a plan forming in his head, the years of militia training taking over, an old confidence surging. Finally he said, "Look. We need to get on the road, like now," he said. Without looking him in the eye he said, "Nunchucks, go uh… go up front. To the store. Grab some shit. Look for some big stuff—but not a lot of it. Just enough to make a good bang."

Nunchucks wavered for a moment, the AR15 pointed at the turbaned head of Maresh.

"Nun. Go," Big Bruddah said.

Nun frowned.

"You're the guy for fireworks. It was your idea. Go get some. Hurry."

Nun went.

"Now it's time to teach these two a lesson," Zip said. He hitched his pants and sniffed.

"Actually," Big Bruddah said, "I think there's another play here." He looked at the two cops. "We're not gonna kill you."

"Wow. You've got to be kidding me," Zip said.

"Shit," Jerry said.

"No. Listen up," Big Bruddah said, trying to ignore them. "We're gonna do a, like, a reciprocal thing. You hear me? You scratch our backs, we scratch yours." He scanned the faces of the others. A smile flickered on Maresh's face.

"An eye for an eye. Or, in this case, a no-eye for a no-eye," Maresh said.

"Exactly."

"Hold on a minute," Jerry said.

Big Bruddah held up a hand to Jerry, his eyes still locked on their prisoners. Big Bruddah turned to Zip. "Ummmm… go get me the spare gas can from the truck."

Zip hesitated.

Jerry sighed. "Zip. Do it."

Zip trundled off.

Big Bruddah turned to Jerry and said, "You're right about this being the start. We can light the match. Right here. But once we do, we gotta haul ass to Florida for the rest of it. We can't afford anything or anyone to hold you and me back on that mission from here on out. That means no shooting cops. No more busted coffee pots. No more bullshit from anyone else. Understand?"

Jerry thought about this. "Okay, dude. Your call."

"Damn right it's my call," Big Bruddah said.

Big Bruddah, grunting under the weight of the dead store clerk, whom he'd slung over his shoulder in militia-approved fireman's carry, followed Jerry and the cops into the fireworks store, their feet crunching on broken and bloody glass.

Nunchucks was frantically unloading a shopping cart full of fireworks onto a waist-high pile near the front entrance. In place of his battle dress uniform shirt, he wore one with a wild tropical pattern. Dansby's camo AK leaned against a now-empty display of 50% off! Cherry Bombs.

Big Bruddah lowered his burden to the floor. When he'd found his breath, he looked at Nunchucks and said, "Whoa, dude. That's plenty. We got no more room in the truck."

Nunchucks looked up. His eyes were just the wrong side of wild. His hair was sweat-stuck to his forehead.

"You OK, man?" Big Bruddah said.

"Yeah," Jerry said. "You're looking a little rough. And what's with the shirt?"

The door opened. Zip. Lugging a red gas can.

Nunchucks' face twisted. "What's with the gas?"

"Holy moly, big man," Zip said, wheezing from his task, "Where'd you get the Hawaiian shirt? Been kicking myself for not wearing one. Boogaloo boys wear them all the time." Zip dropped the gas container to the floor. It tipped over, and gasoline began seeping around the cap.

"Whoa, Zip," Jerry said, righting the can.

"Got the shirt off the rack at the back of the store," Nunchucks said, his eyes narrowing. "They sell 'em here."

"No shit." Zip shuffled toward the promised shirt display before Big Bruddah could stop him.

"Hurry up, Zip, we ain't waiting," Jerry said.

"Guy was one of us. Dansby was," Nunchucks said. "I shot a boogaloo boy. Damn, man. I didn't know. It's why they sell the shirts, I think. Found a bunch of militia shit in the back room, too, in the office. Posters and, you know, books."

"No shit." Jerry said.

"Yeah," Nunchucks said. He looked at Big Bruddah. "Got a picture of your ex as their screensaver—her eyes got little hamburgers over them." Nunchucks smiled grimly. "Kinda funny—the burgers."

Zip returned with a pile of shirts he could barely see over. He'd ditched his battle dress uniform top and was wearing a bright-blue one with a yellow floral theme.

"That's some kind of crazy." Big Bruddah said. "But we really can't stick around and worry about that stuff. We got things to do. People to take care of. That starts with stabilizing this whole situation." He picked up the AK-15, took a deep breath and smelled the gasoline and the fireworks. He looked at the wild-eyed Nunchucks and the pile of explosives, at Dansby's forlorn corpse, and at the jubilantly stupid Zip Pierce. He decided his plan made more sense now, not less.

Nunchucks met his gaze. Nunchucks was crazy. But he wasn't stupid.

"What are you guys gonna do now?" Zip said. "Gonna blow this place or something? Gonna make, like a statement here? I mean that'd be cool but now that we know he was one of our guys, maybe, I don't know…"

Nunchucks' move toward the door was expected and predictably slow. Big Bruddah shot him, and he fell into the shattered glass previously occupied by Dansby.

The first of the fireworks broke open the morning like a kick in the head from a constipated mule. The rosy sky screamed. Gunpowder thunder echoed through the mountain hollows and shattered glass in the neighboring storefronts. Big Bruddah gunned the big truck, took the turn onto the service drive, and accelerated toward the freeway on-ramp.

"Whoo-hooo," Zip Pierce said from the backseat. "The big man took out the big hairy man. Wow. Just wow. I don't believe what I just saw."

"You popped your cherry, man," Jerry said from his seat next to Zip. "Congrats." He leaned forward and punched Big Bruddah in the shoulder.

"I said all along that that Nunchucks dude was a problem," Zip said. "Had to go. Am I right? Had to. I mean, it's like you said, those two Jihadi brothers are gonna say that Dansby guy shot Nun and Nun shot Dansby over Nun wanting to blow up the store."

"They're gonna say it because we told them to," Big Bruddah said.

"I know. I know. But it's a brilliant ally-whatever. Alibi."

"Actually, just more of an explanation," Jerry said.

"Yeah, it will look like two crazy militia dudes got caught in some kind of fight those cops just stumbled into."

Jerry shook his head. "Just hope those cops tell it better than you do."

"They will," Big Bruddah said, hoping he was right. "Calculated risk to leave those two. But the Sikhs, they got some kind of honor code they live by; Maresh dude will stick to his word. Black guy will follow along."

They were rolling now, the expressway mostly empty at this hour, the sun peeking across the rolling fields and hills to the east. Big. Bruddah glanced in the mirror. The fireworks were punching the sky. He could hear the detonations—artillery in a new war.

"You're right, man," Jerry said. "Those guys are a different breed when it comes to shit like this. Honor codes can get in the way, you ask me."

"Yeah," Big Bruddah said. "Codes are good and all, except when they make you do weak things."

"That's right out of Rub Spike's mouth, isn't it?" Jerry said. "Your ex-father-in-law?"

"Uh-huh," Big Bruddah said. He felt a pang of sentimentality that wasn't appropriate for the moment. He swallowed it, looked in his mirrors. They were alone—no traffic, northbound or southbound. There was a steep drop off on the right side of the roadway. He glanced back at Jerry. "Looks like now is another one of those times, my man. When a soldier's got to be strong."

"Soldier's creed," Zip said. "'Follow orders.' Am I right? I mean, I never served but I could've if my talents weren't, you know, on the ballfield…"

"That's right, Zip," Big Brudda said, checking his mirrors again, looking in the northbound lane. Still clear.

"You made exactly the call I would've made." Zip said. "You got rid of the wink link, Nunchucks. Now, it's move forward, locked and loaded and ready for…"

Big Bruddah swerved onto the shoulder. Jerry unsnapped Zip's seatbelt and reached across Zip's belly. Ca-chick. Whoosh. He released and shoved open Zip's door, groaning as he held it against the battering wind. The dramatic shift in air pressure pounded the men's eardrums and scoured the cab, sending loose trash into the truck's slipstream. Before Zip could yelp, he was gone too, sent tumbling down the roadside embankment as easily as a human Subway wrapper, Hawaiian shirt promotional version.

PART EIGHT

Boogie till the Cows
Come Home

Chapter Twenty-five

Washington, DC

Wednesday morning

As hurricanes go, BeeBee was a baby—a relatively weak category one with maximum sustained winds of 75 mph. She was significant due to her premature birth, which was the earliest in Florida history. She'd spent the first days of her life suckling unusually warm Gulf moisture. Now she was crawling toward Tampa Bay even as the previous tropical worry, Avalon, was throwing a category four tantrum over Silver Eagle's headquarters in South Carolina.

In saturated Michigan and the Ohio Valley, it had begun to rain again. Out west, the blizzard was abating in the Rockies. Avalon had blown out the Carolina blazes but the wildfire season had arrived early in California, Utah, and New Mexico. Record cold was bringing ice, snow, power failures and traffic nightmares through Tennessee and Georgia. Texas and Arizona were baking in a heat dome, which had fried the grid in the Lone Star State; there, rolling blackouts and roiling urban areas were the order of the day. To top it off, the President had just hung up the phone, ending a conference call with the governors of three Atlantic states; all were begging for federal help to battle coastal erosion from early-season storms.

She looked across the Resolute desk at her chief of staff. "So," the President said with a sigh, "where are we with the thing?"

"Well, the Silver Eagle jet will be on the ground in Tampa within the hour."

"They're going to land. In a hurricane."

"Actually, they'll get there as the leading edge comes onshore. There's some kind of top gun Silver Eagle pilot onboard, ma'am. We see no reason that he won't go ahead and bring it in—especially with Wilbur Tuttle calling the shots."

"Landing at the airport, right?"

"Yes. Our people tell us Tuttle considered landing at MacDill, under the guise of a Silver Eagle training flight cleared by CENTCOM base brass, but he never got that clearance."

"Old man is slipping."

"Or he ran into issues onboard his flight. Remember, we have our asset on the plane; we just can't contact her at this point. In any case, their flight plan is for Tampa Executive Airport, and then we believe they'll try to grab ground transport to MacDill-CENTCOM."

"But we're ready."

"Oh yes, ma'am. Our people are locked—"

"Don't say 'locked and loaded'. It's a no-bullshit day.'"

"Sorry, ma'am. We're ready."

"Now," the President said with a sigh, "about the boogie boys and girls? What are you hearing from the director—from our people inside these groups?"

"That's the best part. As you know, the numbers inbound to Tampa were significant. From all over the country."

"See previous remark re: bullshit."

"Well, it's turning into a train wreck. Some have encountered road closures due to flooding. Others have been involved in multi-vehicle accidents in the snow—no serious injuries, fortunately. The wildfires have held up several groups coming in from the West. Also, one militia in the deep south," the chief of staff swiped at her phone and began to read, "had an internal altercation that appears to have resulted in a shooting."

"Fatalities?"

"Apparently. But if it's any consolation, those killed were militia members."

"It's not."

"What?"

"A consolation." The President sighed. "What else?"

"Well, the Texas incident and the weather issues, especially this new hurricane, are all over the news. It's all getting big play online. The Texas folks were arrested with a lot of weapons in their vehicles, so there's a great deal of media speculation about what they were up to. We have kept a lid on what we know but among the rank-and-file militia guys, the fear is that law enforcement is going to set up roadblocks."

"Are we?"

"What?"

"Setting up roadblocks."

"Well, ma'am, as I've said, we have conspiracy charges prepared for some of these people, but there's no real grounds for stopping them."

"Until they do something."

"Right. But that may be moot."

The President raised an eyebrow.

"A lot of the groups are already delayed, so their timeline is screwed. It's fed a general reluctance to proceed."

"Seriously."

"Yeah, they appear to be backing off."

"Backing off. As in, going home?"

"Yes, to boogie another day, ma'am. That's the word."

"Almost too good to be true."

"Well, it is, ma'am. True. At least all signs point to that."

"Any word on our old friend Mr. Watts? Is he okay with the backing off?"

"Big Bruddah, you mean," the chief of staff said.

"Yes, Michigan's finest militia hero."

"Well, that's the catch."

The President closed her eyes and shook her head. "Hit me."

"One of his guys, Corky Vanderlaan, was hospitalized in Georgia, a mild heart attack. Local police say he was part of a group of men involved in a double murder and fire at a fireworks store, plus an incident with a waitress at a restaurant. This Vanderlaan is actually cooperating, trying to save his skin."

"They killed a guy and blew up a fireworks store."

"Killed two guys."

"You were saving this news for me?"

"It's just come in, Madam President." The chief of staff checked her notes. "It was a spectacular fire, as you can imagine. Local media are now on it. The cable people are right behind. Security footage shows Watts shot one of the guys who, we think, was with him—a truly bad dude they call "Nunchucks" but whose real name is Lionel Morrison. Mr. Nunchucks appears to have shot the clerk at the store who, wait for it, was a dyed-in-the-wool militia member. Then Watts shot Nunchucks. And set the fire."

"More militia guys shooting militia guys. Good lord, people."

"Yes, Watts appears to have fled the scene with Jerry Plannenberg, who's a convicted murderer and big-time White supremacist, and, get this, Zip Pierce, a former major league baseball player and retired high school athletic director from suburban Detroit."

"The name is familiar."

"He played a few seasons with the Cubs and Royals. Pitcher. And his high school program won a few soccer regional titles. He is, as they say, "beloved in the community." That's what our people tell us."

"The chase. Cut to it."

"Apparently, he's been sniffing around the militia movement for years," the chief of staff said. "It was Pierce who bragged about how Watts and his crew were driving to some deal in Florida with guns. Stroke of luck that two local officers in Georgia rolled up on them at the fireworks store. They were briefly detained, the cops were. But apparently Watts made a deal with them, then lit out for Florida with Pierce and Plannenberg."

"Cops reneged on the deal, obviously."

"Yes, Madam President. They've been a big help."

"And now they're in the wind?"

"In the wind? Is that not a tad bullshitty?"

The President allowed herself a wry smile, "Big Bruddah and his gang are missing?"

"We are locking down their corridor, ma'am. We will wrap them up, very soon. Mr. Vanderlaan told us they are bound for MacDill-CENTCOM. The two police officers in Georgia confirmed they were heading that way."

"Under the assumption I would be at MacDill due to their fake incident at my daughter's school. The bastards."

"Yes ma'am."

"Tell me again. She and everyone down there are good?"

"Yes, her detail say she's hunkered in at home. The school is closed for the day. An electrical issue was going to be the reason, but the hurricane gave us a better excuse."

"I need to talk to her."

"When this is over, ma'am."

"I know. I know." The President shook her head, sighed. "Did I mention these guys are sons of bitches? When they mess with your kids…"

"Yes, ma'am."

"Okay. Okay." The President let her mind and gaze drift around the room and briefly thought for what felt like the zillionth time, "An office that's actually oval, how weird." Then she looked at the chief of staff. "Sorry, long day."

They both smiled. "Understandable, Madam President."

"Other than Bruddah and his buddies, how do we wrap this mess up?"

"Our plan is to arrest the big fish, Tuttle and Hoeksma, when they land at Tampa, along with their personnel."

"Without bloodshed?"

"We're hoping, ma'am. But no guarantees. Our people need to defend themselves. We do have the asset on that Silver Eagle plane, and she should help."

"God be with her."

"She's a good one, ma'am. The best."

"I hope so," the President said. "And the rest of them?"

"MacDill is on high alert. Local law enforcement, the FBI, the state police. We're getting collaboration between the agencies."

"And our favorite crazy governor in Florida? Out of the loop?"

"Yes. Out of an abundance of caution, we've fed his office intel about hurricanes and convection ovens. He's chasing that today."

"Convection ovens."

"Yes, ma'am. Big ones. In Cuba."

"Now," the President said, "about the conspiracy—the traitors."

"Well, I know this is a sensitive subject."

"The fact that we have people working in this building, along with members of our legislative branch and military, who meant this nation harm, yes. Sensitive."

Her chief of staff proceeded with caution. "We have warrants for the four staffers…"

"…whose names will never be uttered in my presence again."

"Yes. And we also have warrants for Senator Wooly and Representative Hazelton, as well as the five servicemen and servicewomen we know were collaborating from inside the base in Tampa. Those warrants will be executed, as we discussed, simultaneously with the arrests of those onboard the plane. When that happens, and when we have word from Florida that the others are in custody, you'll talk to the media, as we agreed."

The president rolled her chair back to take a rare look out the window. She shook her head, laughed, and said, "Well, I guess that means we're locked and loaded."

Chapter Twenty-six

Northern Florida

Wednesday morning

Just south of the state line, they'd stopped to pee and to switch spots. Now, Jerry was driving and Big Bruddah was texting.

By the time Big Bruddah ended his digital discussion, Hurricane BeeBee was making forward progress challenging.

"Stupid weather. Way early for one hurricane. Now there's two," Jerry said. "Where are the damn wipers on this truck?"

"Out there. On the windshield," Big Bruddah said.

"Funny man."

Big Bruddah reached over and turned the wipers to high speed.

Jerry grumbled his thanks.

"It's happened before. The hurricanes. I'm sure," Big Bruddah said. "We've driven through worse. And the guys I hired to fly our little surprise to Tampa, well, they seem cool with it."

"Yeah, damn rough weather to fly in, let alone you got two guys flying an old cargo plane that served in Viet-fucking-nam."

"It's a C-130. Plane is up to the job. These guys say 'no problem,' they are good to go. Took a bit of discussion. Some of the logistics got weird. Not surprising, given the cargo. Shifty. Lot of unstable weight. But they're on their way."

Jerry glanced at Big Bruddah. "Gonna be a helluva statement when they get there.

"Oh yes, my man. Swear to God. No one's gonna forget this," Big Bruddah said, his attention back on the phone, his thumb scrolling. "But… holy shit. No. No way. No. Fucking. Way." Big Bruddah scrolled some more. "Guys are turning back," he said, his eyes on the screen.

"What guys?"

"Our guys. Militia guys. I don't believe this. I do not. Believe… No. Nooo." He yelled at the phone, at the faceless texts and emails. "Dudes from Texas got in a fight over a bag of pork rinds from a vending machine. Got in a shootout. With each other. One dead. Two wounded. The others scattered to the wind, worried about getting arrested."

Jerry glanced at him. "Okay, that's just one group."

"Yeah, but it's making big news. There's lots of talk. People are freaking."

"Dude, we just blew up a fireworks store. Making news. That's what today's about. Like I said. It's the deal."

"I hear you man. But it's…" Big Bruddah scrolled and read, scrolled and read. "Other guys are bailing too. Snow stopping some. Fires and rain. And they're freaking about the hurricane. Afraid of getting stopped by, you know, weather or cops or whatever before this thing even gets started."

A gust of wind slammed the big pickup. For several minutes, they rode in tense silence, the truck buffeted by waves of rain, the wipers valiantly trying to keep up.

Both said it together. "Those pussies."

"Do a little dance. Make a little love. Get down tonight." Tuttle sang to the rocking motion of the Gulfstream, his shaved head moving to the beat, his hands gripping the controls as confidently as a drunk surfer riding a killer wave. From the seat next to his, Cody Marks glowered at the gun held by Warning Shot Dirk.

Tuttle clicked the microphone. "Attention, passengers. We are beginning our descent. Weather conditions in the Tampa Bay area are hurricane with a chance of boogaloo." He clicked off the mic.

In the passenger cabin, the shot Dirks sat up and buckled in. They were not seriously injured by their standards. Two had bullets in one shoulder, one was missing an ear and a non-essential fragment of his skull, and the fourth had an embarrassingly superficial flesh wound to his right side. All bled confidently.

From adjacent seats, Commander Bill and Hoots Brady avoided the death stare of Pettibone by watching Raina Richter and Miky Spike, who were talking, their heads close together.

Not far behind Tuttle's plane, the Gulfstream carrying Donovan Reed and Jackson Nguyen plunged, rose, and plunged again. The pilot, who'd identified himself as Dirk, yelled through the open cockpit doorway: "Strap in, boys. We're in for a ride."

The pilot seemed thrilled at the prospect of taking on the weather in Florida. Jackson figured that was why the guy hadn't questioned him or Donovan when they'd rolled up to the hangar in Denver. At Jackson's insistence, Donovan Reed had introduced himself as Jasper Joyce and Jackson as Jackson Nguyen. The pilot hadn't even asked for identification. "Let's rock 'n roll," he'd said.

Now, Donovan Reed was greenish. Jackson, who'd been pacing and swaying along the aisle, dropped into the seat across from Donovan. "Funny thing, motion never bothered me," he said. "Boats, planes—whatever—I'm fine."

"So, you're fine and dandy landing in a hurricane." Donovan said.

"These guys know what they're doing," he said.

As if to underscore the point, Dirk let out what sounded like a war whoop. Then the speaker in the passenger cabin squawked, and the two men heard Dirk's voice from both places, "Ladies and gentlemen, prepare for landing in Tampa, where the current air temperature is seventy-two degrees, and the conditions are hell on earth."

As Tuttle confirmed landing details with the tower, Cody Marks turned to Warning Shot Dirk. "He can't do this," he said. "He's out of his mind."

Warning Shot Dirk said, "Oh, I hear you, man." The muscular soldier turned the gun toward Tuttle. "Sir, yield the controls." He looked at Cody. "You handle the landing. I'm in no mood to die this way."

Eleven wobbling, bucking, heart-threatening minutes later, they were on the tarmac. Cody Marks was soaked with sweat and relief. Tuttle and Warning Shot Dirk glared at each other. Commander Bill and Hoots clenched each other's hand on their shared armrest. The remaining Dirks, Raina Richter and Miky Spike eyed each other. And the late Steven K. Pettibone slumped sideways against his armrest.

The Dirk piloting Jackson's plane shouted "hallelujah momma jomba," a phrase he had never previously uttered, as his wheels hit pavement minutes behind Cody Marks, Tuttle, and company. In the cabin, Donovan leaned over a full air sickness bag, and Jackson massaged what certainly would be a colorful bruise in the spot where his head had hit the bulkhead.

"Stay buckled, friends," Dirk the pilot shouted. "Gonna be a fun taxi to the hangar. Sit back. Relax. And enjoy the lovely scent of vomit."

Donovan moaned.

Chapter Twenty-seven

Tampa Executive Airport

Wednesday

Inside a large private hangar, the passengers on Tuttle's flight shook off the effects of the landing and replaced them with wary anxiety. The two shoulder-wound Dirks, Raina loyalists, stood and walked slowly toward the exit. Raina and Miky followed closely behind. Flesh Wound Dirk, also Raina-loyal, got up, turned around, and backed toward the door, gun raised, his eyes darting back and forth. Amputated Ear Dirk, the last of the Raina believers, followed suit, although unsteadily, his sense of balance clearly out of kilter. One of the Tuttle-loyal Dirks nodded to Commander Bill, who wasn't making eye contact with Hoots after their brief handholding incident. The Tuttle-loyal Dirk mumbled "I've got you, sir," and started toward the exit, motioning for Commander Bill to follow. Hoots followed. Commander Bill just sat, his nose caked with dried blood, puffy eyes glazed and haunted, his gaze drifting from where Pettibone's blood had stained the bulkhead to Pettibone's dead face, then to another Tuttle-loyal Dirk, who'd also risen, drawn his gun, and was nodding toward the aisle. "Let's go, sir," the Tuttle-loyal Dirks said. Finally, slowly, Commander Bill stood. The four men—one gun-wielding Tuttle-loyal Dirk in front of Commander Bill and Hoots, the other behind—moved to within a few feet of Miky, Raina, and the others. They clustered at the closed door, like anxious business passengers with somewhere bad to go, guns and mistrust in the air.

The door to the flight deck opened. Warning Shot Dirk walked into the cabin; gun drawn. Tuttle was right behind him, head down, thumbing a message on his phone. He walked into the back of Warning Shot Dirk. Warning Shot Dirk staggered forward. One of the pro-Raina Dirks flinched. The other pro-Raina Dirk racked the slide on his weapon. Everyone else with a slide to rack racked it.

"Relax, people," Tuttle said, and no one obeyed.

The plane's exit door opened, and a heavy wet sheet of humid air blew in from the open hangar door, pushing the anxious-to-depart passengers a group-step back. The stairs slowly descended to the floor of the brightly lit hangar, inviting them to disembark.

"Look," Tuttle continued. "It's time for us to come together. Our belief is the President is en route and that Operation Boogaloo is still, uh, operational. You need to remember; Ms. Richter here is a proven liar. She infiltrated our organization dishonestly. What she said earlier, about me being supposedly compromised by some female spy, well. Who among us hasn't gotten a little side action that another woman got angry over?"

One of the Tuttle-loyal Dirks giggled softly. Another one chuckled, not as softly.

"If Ms. Richter wanted me so badly, she should have mentioned it when we first met. She didn't have to tell about my whole 'other woman' thing."

Hoots released a strangled hoot.

"We all know Ms. Richter has made up various stories about herself—even admits one is a lie just to agitate those of us who despise Barack Hussein Alabama or whatever we call him. And now, she's what? Claiming to be ATF or CIA or DEA or NAACP? Give me a break."

"You actually said she was ATF earlier," a pro-Raina Richter Dirk said.

"Actually, no. I didn't. Someone said I said that but I didn't. Say that."

"If she's not ATF, why does she know all the shit about the boogaloo, dude?" The pro-Raina Richter Dirk said.

"What time is it?" Amputated Ear Dirks said, wavering slightly.

"She made all that up. She couldn't possibly know any of it," Warning Shot Dirk said.

"Exactly," Hoots said. "She can't know it. There's no way."

"But she said it," Miky said. "You heard her. She knows it."

"But it doesn't mean she really *knows* knows," a suddenly uncertain pro-Raina Dirk said.

"Oh, good lord," Miky said.

"Right. I mean, she said Tuttle's been nailing some, like, undercover government spy?" Hoots looked around at the others.

Amputated Ear Dirk snorted, reached to scratch his missing ear, and screamed.

"Guys, Tuttle was sleeping with a spy. He just admitted it," Miky said.

"You're putting words in his mouth," Hoots said.

"They just came out of his mouth a second…"

"How do you know he was telling the truth?" A pro-Tuttle Dirk said.

"Right," Commander Bill said, sniffing. Blood oozed from one nostril. "And, yes, we are here to make me president. That's a fact. Tuttle told me. But that doesn't mean this woman here knows it. She can say anything."

Miky looked at Raina. "Yes, actually it does mean that." Miky said.

"What she said she knows is fake," one no-longer-pro-Raina Dirk said.

"Fake. Yeah," the now-clearly-shifting-sides-other-pro-Raina-Dirk said.

Other Dirks nodded. Mutterings of "fake" filled the damp air.

"Besides. Doesn't matter," a Tuttle-loyal Dirk said. "This is about what our government did. Not about us."

"That's right. The beef," Warning Shot Dirk said. "That's the point here. Right, sir?"

Commander Bill nodded. "Roger, Dirk. And it's about her shooting that man over there," he added softly, nodding to the man he'd killed.

"Exactly, sir," Warning Shot Dirk said.

"She's the problem. I knew it the moment I saw her," Commander Bill said.

Amputated Ear Dirk, his loyalty now clearly shifted, looked at Raina. He steadied himself on a seatback. "You know what you do," he said, his speech slurry. "You and your people. You sit here and you spin your little webs and you think the whole world revolves around you. Well, it doesn't, Rai:... Rhianna..."

"Raina," another Dirk said.

"...Reba. In the whole vast configuration of things, I'd say you were nothing but a scurvy little spider."

The group frowned.

"That's from *It's a Wonderful Life*," Commander Bill said.

"However, point well taken," said Hoots, smiling.

"Okay then," Tuttle said. "Okay. Well, let's boogaloo then. Dirk here is on point." He looked at Raina and Miky and drew his gun. "I'll be handling the ladies, of course."

Hoots cackled.

"Let's move, people."

A gust of wind buffeted the airplane. Nobody moved, except the dead Pettibone, who slowly leaned forward until he was face down on the table in front of him.

Three anxious Dirks shot Pettibone.

"Hold your fire," Warning Shot Dirk said. "Already dead. Hold. Your. Fire."

Raina took the stairs two at a time. Miky was one step behind. Miky reached the bottom just as a matching jet, its engine whining, rolled into the hangar. Raina froze, washed by rain and wind.

"Stop." It was Tuttle. "Stop, you miserable, wretched bitch."

"Run," Miky said. Raina ran. Tuttle raised his gun.

He fired.

Chapter Twenty-eight

Tampa, Florida

Wednesday

Big Bruddah and Jerry made their final stop for breakfast burgers at a fast-food joint and topped off the tank of the truck. Jerry was back to riding shotgun, scrolling through the messages and emails they'd received on the burner phone. Big Bruddah was gripping the wheel of the pickup truck, fighting for control against a relentless headwind. They'd driven out of the rain for the moment, but the sky was greenish gray. Across the grassy median strip, a dense pack of vehicles crawled north, headlights on, like the driving dead fleeing a highway-borne plague. Big Bruddah glanced in his mirrors. "Looks like we're the only dudes driving into this town. Everyone else is leaving."

"People can't stomach a little rain; they should move to the desert."

"I hear you." Big Bruddah studied the evacuation jam. "Tuttle's already down here. I know he is. President will be here too. Might be here now. Anything on there about the school—her kid's school?"

Jerry tapped and swiped for several seconds. "Nothing so far."

They pondered this.

"They probably got a blackout on the story," Jerry said. "On account of it's POTUS."

"Yeah, what I was thinking too. Covering it up. The way they do."

"Exactly," Jerry said, eyes locked on the phone. "No way Tuttle didn't get word to her, get her moving down here. Man has ways to get shit done. I give him that."

The truck hit a wall of rain Big Bruddah hadn't seen coming. He tapped the brakes and the front tires ran off the concrete lip of the lane. He jerked the wheel back to the left, steadied up. "This is crazy. I had those guys in the airplane take off in this shit, man." Big Bruddah said, face forward, shoulders hunched, knuckles white on the wheel. "But hey, they been doing this for a long time."

Lightning ripped the sky dead ahead, followed almost immediately by a salvo of thunder. The truck lurched.

"Steady, big man," Jerry said.

"I'm good. I'm good." Big Bruddah said.

"Yeah. Category one is nothing, am I right?" Jerry said.

"Guess so."

"You're not going pussy on me, are you?" Jerry said, laughing.

"Bite me. Shit is what it is."

Jerry shook his head. He picked up the phone. "So, Tampa International?"

"Actually, the Executive Airport there. Private hangars."

Jerry entered the information on the phone. "It's only a twenty-six-minute drive up Bayshore from Tampa Executive to MacDill."

"Yep. That's the plan. Go there first. See what kind of damage our guys in the C-130 can do, hopefully get Tuttle's attention—"

"More like the damn world's attention."

"Yeah, then head up to MacDill for the grand finale."

"This is a big-ass moment, man," Jerry said. "I mean, Tuttle pissed on us. Then everyone else bailed."

"Yeah. And now look at us. Someday, we'll buy our grandkids some fucking hamburger Happy Meals and tell them all about it, am I right? How we're the dudes that ended up launching the whole deal."

"Yeah," Jerry snorted a laugh.

The rain was pounding the truck again. The wipers were flailing. Above the din, a muted siren rose and wailed.

"Hear that?" Jerry said.

"Yeah."

"Tornado siren is my guess. They get tornadoes all the time with these damn things."

"Had a few of those in our time, back home. Tornadoes."

"Just like we had blizzards."

"Big bad rainstorms."

"You name it."

Both men laughed. Big Bruddah fumbled for the wiper speed control. "High as it goes, I guess."

"Can't see for shit," Jerry said.

"Yeah, blower isn't clearing the windshield either. Steamin' up here."

Big Bruddah wiped at the glass with his hand just as the truck hit standing water. For several sphincter-clenching seconds, the truck was waterborne, its giant tires looking for concrete to bite and not finding it.

Both men saw the hazard lights of the other truck just before they slammed into it.

Jackson Nguyen unclasped his seat belt and stood as Dirk, the Silver Eagle Security pilot, brought the luxury jet to a stop inside the hangar at Tampa Executive Airport. Jackson's knees buckled slightly and he steadied himself on a seatback, looked at Donovan Reed, who was huddled in a nauseous funk, and said, "You stay here."

Donovan raised a hand weakly and let it fall.

Jackson ducked to look out the windows as he made his way to the exit door. Across the hangar, an identical Silver Eagle jet sat, door open. At the top of its airstair stood a cluster of men, some with guns, two holding their shoulders. One appeared to be bleeding from the head. A tall-ish one was familiar—Bill Hoeksma. At the bottom of the stairs, a woman was on her back on the concrete floor. A woman with a messy pink mohawk knelt next to her. A slight, bald man stood over them with a gun.

Jackson was about to yell for Dirk to keep the door closed when Dirk opened the door.

Seconds later he stood two steps down his plane's stairway, no longer insulated from the elements or the moment. The metal walls of the hangar moaned. Rain blew through the open door. The woman on the floor held one hand hard against a bloody thigh and was yelling at the man. The other woman helped her sit up. The man looked toward Jackson.

Sheesh. It was him. Wilbur Tuttle.

The wounded woman slapped at Tuttle's gun. It skittered across the floor. Tuttle reared back as if to punch her, paused, and then lurched toward the gun. The woman with the mohawk got to it first. Tuttle jerked the gun from the woman's grasp, punched her in the jaw, and ran out into the rain and wind. The mohawked woman was on all fours, momentarily stunned. The wounded woman looked wildly around the hangar. Her eyes found Jackson. "He's getting away!" she yelled.

Jackson looked back at the open door of his plane—the warm, comfortable, safe cabin beckoned—then back at the women, who were trying to rise. "Shit," he said, and ran after Tuttle.

From the top of his Gulfstream's stairs, Commander Bill also weighed his options, and then stumbled down, past the two women and into the hurricane. Ten steps onto the tarmac, the wind slapped him so hard it reminded him of his father. Commander Bill could barely see, barely breathe. His clotting nose dripped bloody water.

Tuttle, hunched against the elements, was a few hundred feet away from the hangar trying to open the pilot's door of a small, single-engine airplane. The Asian guy jumped on Tuttle's back. He shouted something Commander Bill couldn't hear, but he thought sounded like "bastard."

Tuttle broke free.

Sirens, near and distant, rose above the mad melody of wind and rain. Commander Bill glanced to his left as the first of what sounded like a parade of vehicles roared up to the hangar.

"Yo, Billy." A voice from behind him.

Miky Spike.

Her fist.

His world went scarlet.

The ancient C-130 Hercules waddled down the runway and somehow found its way to cruising altitude. The pilot, known to Big Bruddah only by his militia name, which was Narco, banked toward the northwest and settled in for the brief trip to Tampa.

"Smells like shit in here," his co-pilot, Redbone, said.

"You think?" Narco said. "Might be the 12 Black Angus behind you. Could be they're nervous."

As if to underscore the point, a chorus of ugly moos erupted from the cargo compartment.

Redbone laughed. "Who'd have thought when we rehabbed this beast that we'd be turning it into a cattle hauler?"

"Oh, I hear you. But man does not live by running weed alone," Narco said. "That game is dying, given legalization and all. Cows aren't illegal. Not yet anyway."

"Which is the point."

"Yeah, who'd have thought the President of the United States would throw out the Constitution?"

"I saw it coming. To be honest," Redbone said. "Just wish we could be down on the ground, you know. Be in on the fight. Not up here with the cows in the sky."

"Dude, everyone's got a role to play. We're, like, the boogaloo air force, way I see it. No shame in that."

The moos grew louder.

Commander Bill stared up at Miky Spike and Raina Richter. He was cold and soaked. Shards of pain sliced through his skull, but he couldn't feel his face. Miky Spike was doubled over, shaking her hand as though she'd hurt it. She held the other hand against her bleeding thigh.

The punch to the head had given him remarkable clarity: Tuttle's plan was blowing up; he, Commander Bill, had killed a man (again); and now, the police were here. Clearly, he wasn't going to be president of anything. He needed to get somewhere other than here. Now. He struggled to stand.

Raina Richter raised something into his field of view. A little pink gun. She aimed it at his left eye and pulled the trigger. Scarlet returned. Then it all faded to black.

Chapter Twenty-nine

Tuttle ran across a grassy area toward the service drive that bordered the deserted airfield, moving ridiculously well for an old man. The wind and rain had ebbed briefly, however, and Jackson quickly closed the gap. "Stop, man. Just give it up," he said, the words coming out ragged.

Tuttle stopped. Turned. Wheezed. Pointed a pistol.

"Whoa. Whoa. No." Jackson raised his hands and cringed. "Don't… don't shoot."

"Damn it. It's you," Tuttle said and lowered the gun. "You just need to go. Now is not the time. For this." He was trying to catch his breath.

"Go? Go?" Jackson wiped the rain from his face and managed a laugh. "That's priceless." He squinted. "You're looking for me, remember? You've, like, destroyed my life. You tried to kidnap me?"

"Harsh. Not. Not a kidnap plan. Never was," Tuttle said. He closed his eyes and shook his head. "This. Not now. Just. Go." He waved him away.

From the hangar came the pop-pop of small arms fire; from above, in the distance, the low rumble of an approaching airplane. Jackson turned toward the hangar, which was alive with running people and flashing lights. Beyond it, a stream of muscular vehicles, lights flashing, approached. He flopped his arms and turned back to Tuttle. "What the hell?"

"Actually, I've been looking for your sister," Tuttle said.

"My sister."

"Lalani. I knew her back in the day. In your old country."

"This. Is about that?"

"No no no. This," he said, gesturing toward the hangar, "is about something else." He squeegeed his head and face with his free hand. "Look. Your sister and I had a thing. I've had a helluva time tracking her down. You were my only option."

"Option? You're talking fucking options. This is, like, nothing to you? People got—they got killed. Donovan Reed…"

The noise from the hangar seemed to be fading. The rain began again. The airplane was a persistent anomaly in the leaden sky—the only flight incoming or outgoing. Both men searched for it, futilely, in the dense cloud cover.

"Dude, you could have just called," Jackson said.

Tuttle shrugged. "I'm not a big phone call guy. Besides, you have some very very committed security people. Annnnd, let's just say I have a taste for the dramatic."

An amplified male voice said, "Colonel Tuttle, put down the gun and step away from that man." Jackson turned. The two women, one limping and holding her thigh, the other assisting her, were making their way toward them.

The plane, some distance off, was apparently descending, its engines heavy and ominous.

Tuttle glanced toward the approaching women and then at Jackson. "Look, I got another thing. So, hey. I'm going to need to circle back on this."

With that, Tuttle was off, flailing across the water-soaked sod.

The plane appeared, tearing free of the clouds like a silvery apparition—massive, with four propellers across its wings, similar to the planes from the war Jackson's family had fled in a chopper piloted by a fevered lover from Ann Arbor. The lumbering ancient behemoth was descending, as if drawn by history toward them. Jackson, rooted in place, watched as the first dark object tumbled out of it, then another. The women, soaked and gasping, reached Jackson.

"What the actual fuck?" the woman with the pink mohawk said.

Fifty yards away, Tuttle stopped. He turned toward the oncoming C130.

"Run. Cows," Jackson said softly as the animals, some mooing and bleating, plummeted from the monster airplane. He obeyed his own words; he and the two women stumbled away, running clear of the plane's path.

Cows began to hit the earth, sending up geysers of gore, the plane coming onward, dropping cow after cow, Tuttle's expression going from amazement to confusion to fear.

He raised his gun.

The heavens opened in an avalanche of rain. Tuttle, his face a mask of fury and what seemed like fiendish joy, clenched his eyes against the torrent of water and Black Angus and fired again and again.

Jackson turned away briefly, just to look at the women and flick rain from his eyes. He heard the moo and the grisly sound a falling bovine makes when it crushes a man. He saw the horror on the women's rain-streaked faces.

Then the plane was gone.

And it was over.

PART NINE

What Became of Them

Chapter Thirty

One year later

Donovan Reed closed his laptop, waved away a pestering seagull, glanced at the woman in the neighboring lounge chair and said, "What do you think?"

"Tough to hear above the waves, but your friend sounds pretty smart," she said. She slid her sunglasses down over her eyes from their perch on her head. "Although I can't say Ted Talks are my favorite thing to watch on the beach. Very sexy of you for the idea, however."

"Well, I can't say he's exactly a friend anymore, either."

"You two will find your way back. You were almost there, as I recall. Until the infamous Colonel Wilbur Tuttle intervened. Fortunately for you, I came running with my law degree."

"My agent called you and hooked us up."

"It was a Brit expat thing. She saw you in trouble and figured I could lend a hand, I suppose. And she was right. I got you off, so to speak."

He ignored the joke. "Not all that difficult, since I was defending myself from a horrible, horrible man."

She turned, put her feet in the sand, and looked over her sunglasses. "Self-defense is not always easy to prove, especially when the witnesses are dead." She adjusted her swimsuit and took a long sip from the drink on the tiny table between them. From under her chair, she pulled a thick stack of paper bound by a rubber band. "Besides, we've been over this a few million times. Better to talk about it with your therapist. I'll handle your other issues."

Donovan smiled. "Care for an afternoon nap?

"Not now, love. You, sir, have a script to read."

Jackson stood on the front porch and eyed the sky with suspicion.

"Sit," his mother said.

"Getting dark in the southwest. Storms over the lake, the radar says."

"Sit."

"Let him be," said his father from the white wicker chair next to hers.

"Jackie and the weather," his mom said.

He turned to look at them. Their accents were the same. But they'd grown smaller. So had the house. His room was a dried up ten-by-twelve museum of his high school years. "No one's called me Jackie for a long time."

"A man recording video talks from my kitchen table for half the world to see needs a little 'Jackie' from his momma," his mom said. "Keeps you humble."

"Humble me all you want, Mom."

From the garage, there was a banging. A feminine laugh.

"Lalani, what on earth are you looking for out there?" his father yelled.

"Whatever I can find," Lalani said.

Jackson laughed. It was good to be home.

The brutal physical therapy, prescribed and performed by a friend who worked with other runners at nearby Western

State College, was complete. She could muster five miles pain-free.

Miky, thank God, was beginning to feel like Miky again.

She finished stretching on her front porch, stood, and looked out past her Subaru and the rental car in front of her barn, past the weed-filled garden that desperately needed attention, and took in the mountains, purple-gray in the morning light.

She called for Nothing. The dog trotted up, sniffed her sweat, and turned away.

From inside the house came the voice that had helped her get through it, the voice she was beginning to understand she couldn't live without. "He hates when you stink. Just like I do."

She looked to the sky with a smile and then went inside to take a shower.

Graham Parker, long-time conservative radio talk show, took the cue from his director, and leaned into the microphone. "And we're back with our special guest today, via telephone, from his new home in our president's penal system, former Michigan governor, the commander of the number one private military force in the world, Silver Eagle Security, Bill Hoeksma."

"Graham? Graham?" Commander Bill said.

"We're here, Commander."

"Sorry, it is very noisy here."

"Sir, as you were saying before the break, what this president has done to you and your team is unconscionable. And unprecedented. Every single person, yourself included, who tried to stop this horrible attack on America—this so-called Operation Boogaloo, which was driven by a few very bad seeds in the militia movement and, yes, inside your Silver Eagle organization—is now in jail."

"That's right, Graham. It's insane. I was trying to stop the crazy thing, the boog— Whatever. That's why I'm, you know, appealing my conviction."

"Yes, yes," Parker said. "It was Colonel Tuttle, a few bad folks from inside the militia movement, and some rogue agents, as you testified—who obviously went over a metaphorical cliff here."

"Actually, there's wasn't, like, a cliff—"

"No, sir, I meant… Tuttle and these rogue agents lost their way, quite obviously."

"Yeah. Between you and me, Tuttle had been, well, frankly, ill for some time. Yes. And some rogues. Many, several rogue guys, were involved."

"So, in truth, you saw the nature of what they were doing and—"

"We were trying very very hard to stop it, Graham. And if we weren't, we were obviously, at the very least, not doing anything, you know, wrong."

"Exactly. And the push for change, for the boogaloo, was really something precipitated by this administration," Parker said.

"Oh, right. Absolutely. The President knew she was provoking them. It's like she wanted it."

"She could've stopped the boogaloo, then?"

"Of course. But she led them on and got them to a point when there was no turning back. She made her bed, so to speak," Commander Bill said. "What she caused them to do to Colonel Tuttle—"

"Yes, sir, horrible."

"I mean, it's awful what a cow can do to a man. And the animals themselves. My goodness. What are we coming to when people raise these creatures and then just slaughter them like that?"

"Yes. Yes," Parker said. "Let me ask you this. Do you think that your trial, in any way was influenced unfairly by the very big public outcry over the death of Zip Pearce? He was a minor celebrity, a former major leaguer and athletic director at a high school here, and well known in certain circles in your native state. Think that impacted your situation?"

"How could it not? They threw the man from a car. People wanted blood for that. I can understand why. And I had nothing to do with it. Nothing."

"People say the connection to you was the environment you created; the culture your company fosters. Fair?"

"Absolutely not. Our organization is not about violence, Graham. It's about freedom and security and..." Commander Bill paused. "It's about a lot of things. I can get you some literature if you want. Or people can go to our website. But let's just say we're good people. Good good people."

"Right. Yes. Now, the men convicted in his murder are Big Bruddah Watts, formerly Bo Watts, and Jerry Plannenberg."

"Oh, two real gems there."

"Yes, sir. Both were nearly killed in an auto accident, as our listeners know."

"Yes, they're soon to be imprisoned for their horrible crimes and for being the masterminds of the boogaloo, along with Colonel Tuttle."

"Yes, sir. Of course. If they survive their injuries, prosecutors are confident they'll be convicted."

"I lost an eye, Graham. An eye."

"Sir, to clear the air on one point: You and Mr. Watts have a history. You know each other from another moment in Michigan history..."

"Yes. I honestly barely remember him or any of that. As you know, I was cleared in that mess, which I really had very little understanding of at the time. And I have really been focused on building my business ever since."

"Sir, tell us about the person you supposedly murdered."

"Oh, as I said, I don't remember that at all. The FBI agent, Babsy Witt. The gal with the purple hair. And I didn't… It was Tuttle. He shot her, as the courts proved."

"No. Sir, I meant the most-recent murder, uh, alleged victim."

"Ope. Sorry. Can't keep things straight," Commander Bill thought for a moment. "It's so sad, Graham. That whole thing. I feel so awful for him and his family, Petco was the name, I believe—"

"Pettibone, sir. A TSA man in Colorado."

"Yes, yes. Well, he was working with this other guy…"

"Brady. Hoots Brady, both originally from Michigan, governor, and members of a local militia group."

"Yes," Commander Bill said. "I hate to speak poorly of the dead but obviously they are, were, both, as you said, bad seeds."

"Yes, Mr. Brady is currently awaiting sentencing on multiple charges."

A recorded voice broke in. "You have one more minute."

"Oh, good lord. My time is almost up here," Commander Bill said.

"Clearly, gulag-type stuff, sir."

"Thanks, Graham. It's hard. Very very hard. I can't sleep. I… there's… I have to use the toilet in front of others…"

"Governor, about Mr. Pettibone."

"Who?"

"The man you—quote unquote—murdered."

"I honestly never met the man."

"Unreal."

"Yes, kind of hard to shoot someone you never met."

"And you stand by your testimony, Commander, that our old friend, that libtard nightmare turncoat b-word I can't say on a family show, Miss Miky Spike, had something to do with the killing."

"Yes."

"And you testified it was Miss Spike who shot you in the eye, leaving you blind in that eye?"

"Yes, I wear a patch. It's very uncomfortable. I hate it, really."

"All the fault of Miss Spike?"

"Yes, I'm pretty sure it was her. But she was with that Black gal—"

"This mysterious special agent, Raina Richter?"

"Yes."

"Is it true they are maybe lovers? I mean, these are two women who testified so vociferously against you. And one of them, Miss Spike, the ex-wife of Mr. Watts with whom you have this history from that other militia operation, no doubt has an agenda against you. So, if she and this Raina Richter are lesbos, wouldn't that matter?"

"I wouldn't know if they were like, lovers, Graham. But if I did, I would say yes. Very likely. From what I've heard. They were."

"Our time is almost up, Commander. I mean, they've taken away your freedom for up to ten years. There are very strong rumors that your marriage is ending. You're living under these terrible conditions. Your business was ravaged by a hurricane—to the tune of perhaps $100 million. There is still considerable talk about you getting your name and record cleared and running for your party's nomination for higher office. Any word to this awful president, to your supporters, to the many countries and people around the world who admire you and your company and want to see you back on your feet again?"

"Well, let me just reassure everyone out there that they shouldn't believe all the negative stuff they hear. My marriage, well, frankly it's never been better. The wife and kids are just taking some time back in Michigan. As soon as my name is cleared and I'm released from this godforsaken place, I'll join them there. I have several good people working on the financing to rebuild the Silver Eagle compound, probably in Michigan."

"Oh, that's good to hear, Commander."

"Yes, yes. As far as the financing goes, let's just say it's good to know people in powerful positions around the globe who see the value of what Silver Eagle offers."

"And returning to Michigan?"

"Well," Commander Bill said, "that just makes sense. The climate is much more stable there. I mean, it rains and snows. So what? Everywhere else in this beautiful country of ours, hurricanes and fires and stuff keep getting worse. So, I think it's a safe bet to return to our home state, frankly."

"So, you're worried about the climate," Parker said.

"Well, no. No. Not all. It's just all of these crazy storms and such."

The phone line hissed.

"Commander Bill?"

The line was dead.

Also available

THE GREAT AMERICAN CHEESE WAR

PAUL FLOWER

Cheese has never been this serious — or this deadly...

Governor Bill Hoeksma of Michigan is a simple, gun-loving son of a billionaire who idolizes George W. Bush.

When a mysterious illness afflicts members of his inner circle, his conspiring advisors point to a rumored viral weapons attack – via monkeypox-carrying prairie dogs – launched by the Wisconsin government. Governor Bill decides the Michigan militia should lead the military response, chaos ensues, and he falls unwittingly into a scheme of his powerful father's making.

That scheme begins with cheese research and a Hollywood movie star. How it will end all depends on two unlikely heroes: an aging lesbian state senator, and a high-school teacher starting to question her life choices.

When the conspiracy runs out of road, will anyone emerge victorious from the Great American Cheese War?

Acknowledgements

Thanks to my kids, their kids, and their significant others for grounding me in an amazingly wonderful real world so I can play safely in a fictional one. Thanks to Brent Nichols for telling me how to land a plane in Gunnison, CO during a snowstorm. Thanks to Dave Kagan for his insight and support despite the deal with the coffee mug. Thanks to my editor, Abbie Headon, for the magic she performs, the therapy she provides, and for believing in my work. Thanks to everyone at Farrago, especially Pete Duncan, for saying "yes" even after my first book of fiction for them turned out to be, well, true. And thanks, most of all, to my wife, Lori, for enduring a pandemic summer spent watching me write.

About the Author

Paul Flower was born and raised in Michigan and still resides there. He has been writing professionally for 40 years. While much of his career has been spent in advertising and marketing, he worked in broadcasting for a short time. Paul's previous novels include *The Great American Cheese War* and *The Redeeming Power of Brain Surgery*, and his writing has appeared in national and regional magazines. He and his wife have four grown children and a rapidly evolving number of incredibly beautiful and intelligent grandchildren.

Note from the Publisher

To receive updates on special offers and news of other humorous fiction titles to make you smile – sign up now to the Farrago mailing list at farragobooks.com/sign-up.